Broken Brotherhood

Rasheem Rooke

ISBN: 978-1-7363974-0-4

Dedicated to my three Aces
Aisha, Ari, and Alexis

Prologue

Tuesday, September 10th

The small, farm style home in Waldorf, Maryland was littered with empty beer bottles, overflowing ashtrays, and discarded potato chip bags. Five men were seated in the back room at a round table. Four were poker players and the last was a card dealer.

The sound of betting chips clanking together at the middle of the table was the only music filling the room. Each player had contributed two gray chips, an initial bet of ten thousand dollars each. That meant the prize started at forty thousand dollars.

Each of the players received a pair of cards. Three of the four players felt good enough about their cards, so they each contributed four additional gray chips to the pot, adding twenty thousand dollars apiece. The total winning prize grew to one hundred thousand dollars.

The fourth man looked at his cards and groaned when it was his turn to make a bet. Instead of surrendering more chips, he slid his cards back to the dealer. "I'm not messing with y'all," he said. "I'm out."

This particular gambling house only used five-thousand-dollar gray chips. The other Ribisi houses assigned different chip denominations. One house used one-hundred-dollar chips for the cheapskates. Another used one-thousand-dollar chips for those who didn't mind a little more risk. But for those who wanted more of a roller coaster ride, they came here to Waldorf.

One hundred thousand dollars now sat at the center of the table. The money, supporting the chip value that had been collected at the beginning of the night, was ready to be paid out to the winners at the end.

The dealer's name was Clay. He was a transplant from the west coast who made his way east after exhausting all his options in the Vegas casinos. Apparently, they don't look too kindly on dealers lying about misdemeanor convictions.

Clay laid out three cards, face up, on the table. His hand movements were swift and steady. Even though they sat in a small, unassuming house in southern Maryland, Clay dressed the part of a big time dealer. He was decked out in a white dress shirt, black tie, and black vest.

The exposed cards were a king, jack, and a ten of diamonds. Clay's eyes widened because of the improbable potential that was before him. Someone could have a royal flush.

A royal flush is a poker hand that consists of the top five cards within a suit. With a king, jack, and ten of diamonds showing as community cards on the table that anyone could use, all a player needed in their hand was an ace and a queen of diamonds. Those five cards together, ten through ace, and all the same suit, would be unbeatable.

As a professional poker dealer, Clay knew the odds of that happening were almost impossible. The chances were one in thirty-one thousand. Impossible.

Of the three players left in the game, one of them immediately threw his cards back to Clay in an amateur move. "I fold."

Two players were left.

They eyed each other from across the table and then looked back at their cards.

Clay motioned to the man on his left. "You gonna bet, check, or fold?"

Before the man could answer the question, two shotgun blasts tore the hinges off the front door. It was kicked down by what could only be described as a giant. He had a grisly mustache and an untamed beard. His head would've been bald were it not for the strip of spiked hair down the center.

Everyone at the table dove for cover behind furniture. Clay flipped the table over, sending gray chips flying throughout the room.

By the sound of the boots running in the house, Clay thought they were being invaded by a small army.

Men screamed and begged for their lives as a prelude to multiple gunshots. Clay listened to it like a soundtrack. He trembled as he was pinned between the flipped table and a wall.

He could only watch as the mohawked Goliath snatched the table propped in front of him and tossed it like a pillow being thrown from a bed. Goliath grabbed Clay by the neck and lifted him out of his hiding place. He dangled him in the air.

Goliath then yelled in his grisly voice, "Priest!"

The men were frozen until Priest walked in. He was nearly as large as Goliath. His uniform was identical to the giant's—dirty denim jeans and a white t-shirt.

Over their shirts they wore black leather motorcycle biker vests with different patches and insignias on them. A rectangular white patch with black letters was sewn into

Priest's right breast. It read, "PRESIDENT." Goliath had one on his too. His read, "ENFORCER."

Clay made out Priest's name on the opposite breast. There was a Christian cross embroidered underneath it. As if the night's event hadn't done it already, the image Clay saw stitched into the bottom left-hand corner of the vest sent a chill down his spine. It was a diamond. And at the center of the diamond was symbol "1%er."

Having grown up in California, Clay saw several motorcycle clubs during his youth and knew exactly what the symbol meant. It represented the small percentage of motorcycle clubs that consider themselves outlaws. They engaged in anything from drugs and violence to other forms of organized crime.

Clay didn't know what was more terrifying. The often-violent actions of one-percenters or the fact that they proudly promoted their allegiance to a life of violent crime.

Priest walked over to Clay just as Goliath let him go. Clay dropped to the floor like a bag of sand. Priest squatted to get closer to Clay, who was still on the floor.

"What do you want?" Clay cried out.

"Steak. And a set of double D tits in my face."

Priest's men laughed.

"But what I want doesn't matter. There's something I need." Priest scowled as he talked.

"The money! Take it!" Clay said, pointing to a duffle bag a few feet away. It was full of the cash that was collected at the start of the night.

Priest looked at the bag and then back to Clay. He shook his head. "The money's nice, but that's not why I'm here. I'm looking for someone. Where is Anthony Ribisi?"

Clay had a dumbfounded look on his face. "What?" he said. "I haven't seen Anthony in over a year. I don't know where he is."

"What a shame. I keep hearing that."

Goliath pulled out his gun and stepped closer to Clay.

Clay lost it and cried uncontrollably. "Please!"

Priest held a hand up toward Goliath. "Not this time." Then he looked back at Clay. "From what I understand, this is a Ribisi gambling house, yes?"

Clay ferociously nodded his head.

"Then someone should be able to find Anthony. Tell whoever is running this joint that we're going to tear every gambling house down, brick by brick, until we find him. Until we find Anthony.

"Tell them that the Broken Brotherhood is coming."

Chapter 1

Anthony

I returned to the bedroom to find Coco getting dressed. Leaning against the portal, I watched her layer on clothing, one piece at a time. It was like listening to Miles Davis conduct a blues ballad. First percussion, then horns, then piano. Her movements looked like an arrangement of choreographed harmony.

In her preferred style of dress, the goal was comfort. A gray v-neck t-shirt draped her torso. For a moment, it betrayed the absence of a bra. The peak of her nipples stretched out beyond the fabric of her shirt. But only for a second. Once she put on and zipped her powder-blue hoodie, they were hidden.

"You just gonna stand there and watch?" she prodded. She struggled to pull her black leggings over the curve of her behind, and then said, "Never mind. You'd be no help."

She turned around, sat on the bed, and put on her running shoes. Complete and ready to go, she stood up again and walked over to me. The way her clothes caressed and moved with her body made me jealous of each article of clothing, especially since she was leaving me.

"My car will be here soon," she said.

I already knew that. "Do you have to leave?"

"Do you have to stay?" Coco leaned in for a hug. "Besides, don't you have to get to work?"

I wrapped my arms around her, knowing the answer to both questions. I knew there was no way I'd be able to go with her. I was out of everyone's life and because of that, they had peace. They were all safe, including Coco.

"Mmm. Silence. That's what I thought," she said. "Well, at least I got to spend time with you and didn't have to worry about sharing the infamous 'Anthony Ribisi'.

"God," Coco said with the roll of her eyes. "Who picked that stupid name for you anyway?"

"You do remember that my middle name is Anthony, right?"

"I do. Middle name, as in, between your first and your last name. I like your real name much better, I might add. You are Jelani Jones. A caring, loving, and compassionate man. They can use *your* middle name and *their* last name all they want. But it doesn't matter. You're not the monster that mob tried to make you."

I think this was first time Coco mentioned my other name since she had started visiting me months ago. I was careful never to bring it up, for fear that it would trigger some trauma related to the night she was held hostage and almost died.

And no matter how hard she tried to separate the two names, the unfortunate truth is that Anthony Ribisi was created to be a violent caricature of Jelani Jones. The two names represent different sides of the same scratched and scuffed up coin. The mob hadn't tried to turn me into a monster. It had succeeded.

She leaned in even closer and kissed me on my lips. It was a soft kiss, almost as if she was careful to hold some of it back to keep me wanting more. We kissed until the honk of a horn could be heard from outside.

"I've gotta go," she said.

"Yeah," I replied. I let go of Coco and turned to grab my shoes.

"Don't bother. It's easier this way when I go down by myself. Just walk me to the door and kiss me goodbye."

And that's what I did. We held hands all the way to the door. We kissed each other one last time.

I watched her out of the window as she slid into the backseat of the waiting car. I watched as the car drove away.

It's easier this way, she told me. She was wrong. Nothing was easy about it.

Chapter 2

Coco

In the back seat of the car, Coco reflected on her recurring love experience. She smiled at the thought of his smooth brown skin. His broad shoulders and strong back. Coco loved the man's bright smile and intense eyes. There was nothing about Jelani that she didn't love.

She'd spent a four-day weekend with a man she never thought she'd have feelings for, especially after dealing with his secret life that almost cost her her own. Funny how things change over time.

Just keep using your God given name, Coco thought to herself. A life without aliases, pseudonyms, and nicknames would make her beyond happy.

As long as Jelani Jones stayed away from DC, and far away from ever becoming Anthony Ribisi again, then he had a chance at building a new life. And just maybe Coco could share that new life with him.

Even though he hadn't asked her, the near weekly trips brought Coco closer to the idea of relocating. It could be a permanent way to keep Jelani out of DC, she thought to herself. If Jelani returned to DC, the life of Anthony Ribisi would be waiting for him.

Relocating might have been the only option. And Coco was happy to contemplate it. Lost and happy in her thoughts, she didn't hear the driver talking to her. She was focused on the clouds outside her window and the daydreams in her head.

"This your first time in town?" the driver asked for the second time.

"I'm sorry. No ma'am." Coco replied. "I actually love it here. Thinking about moving," she said with a smile.

The idea excited the driver. "Ohhh! Ain't no place like it!"

"Well... I'm just thinking about it," she bashfully said. Just then, they pulled up to the airport.

"Aww, that's okay, baby. New Orleans ain't going anywhere no time soon. Take your time. Just come back every chance you get."

"That's what I'm working on, ma'am," Coco said before exiting the car. She walked toward the airport doors while searching for her driver's license and plane ticket.

"That's exactly what I'm working on."

Chapter 3

Anthony

I ran away to New Orleans, but little did I know that while I was running, I'd also be chased by fate. The problem is that my plan wasn't a plan. But for me, and considering my state of mind, it all made sense.

The pain of losing Marco was unbearable. He had accepted me, an outsider, into the Ribisi fold. And he was the only father figure I had ever known. So, the pain of his loss grew day after day.

I faked contentedness for those around me. But in truth, I was an exposed nerve. Contact with everything caused shock-waves of grief that I couldn't control. It was unavoidable, immeasurable, and a constant pain.

And it wasn't just Marco's death, it was the betrayal that it represented. I grappled with the idea that he was murdered by his best friend and closest confidant, Dominic Nicholas. Otherwise known as *Nick Nick*.

While me and Marco's son Johnnie, was able to avenge his death by murdering Nick Nick, that didn't bring me satisfaction.

Nick Nick and Marco built an empire together. And if Marco couldn't trust the man who had become his brother over time, what did that mean for any of us? It was a paradox I couldn't mentally process.

As a therapist, maybe Coco sensed it. Maybe she allowed me to get closer to her to keep my mind preoccupied. Maybe it was her way of sacrificing her own healing from the trauma my life brought into hers to help me become a better man.

All I know is that while I was in my deepest and darkest hell, Coco was there to keep me balanced, make sense of the madness, and find happiness. And it worked. I was happy. Until one day I wasn't and there was nothing she could do to change that.

She could no longer rescue me from my darkness. I needed to breathe and felt like separation would give me time to think and clear my head. So, I planned a non-plan.

I packed a bag for the weekend, grabbed the emergency money I kept in a lockbox hidden in the duct of my central air conditioning unit, hopped in the car, and drove. That was the best I could come up with. I didn't have a city in mind, I just headed south on I-95.

At first, I thought I'd stop in Richmond, which was less than two hours from DC, but I kept going. I continued driving south, but changed the scenery on the road. Instead of continuing on I-95, I exited to I-85. Approximately four hours later, I passed a sign for Charlotte. Four hours after that, Atlanta.

I stopped for gas and bathroom breaks. That was it. Atlanta was the destination my mind had ultimately settled on. Maybe I'd find a place to sleep, enjoy a few days' rest, and then head back home. But that didn't happen. I had filled my gas tank just as I entered Georgia and still had a good amount of fuel. I pressed on.

Before I knew it, I-85 had come to an end and I-65 was

taking me farther south. I had never driven through Alabama before, but from what I heard of the state, there was no way I wanted to stop there.

And then I saw it. A sign that spoke to my spirit. I-10, heading west. New Orleans. What would become my new city was waiting for me.

It was supposed to be a long weekend away from home to clear my head. But after two weeks, I knew I wasn't returning. I tried my best to keep in touch with everyone, but didn't tell them where I was. Their attempts to pry information from me were unsuccessful. Then one at a time, I slowly began rolling back phone calls and text messages. First Coco, then Johnnie, then Smitty. And finally, the hardest of all, Johnnie's twin sister, Jena.

Like Johnnie, me and Jena practically grew up together. While we weren't officially siblings, we treated each other as such. It wasn't until after puberty hit all of us, I could see that the annoying little girl was developing into a woman. A beautiful one, at that. But it wasn't until our twenties that the harmless flirting began.

Then came the night her father was shot. She had been by his bedside at the hospital and before we knew Nick Nick's role in everything, we listened to him when he commanded me to keep Jena safe and not let her out of my sight. So that's what I did. She packed a bag, and I took her to my place.

In retrospect, I should have known that the combination of our continued flirting over the years and the heightened emotions of that night made coming back to my place a bad idea. But retrospect can always see clearly when looking backwards.

We were at my apartment. We were both emotional. Both became too comfortable with each other. And before we knew it, we were sharing the same bed. As a result, the best and worst thing that could've happened, happened. Jena became pregnant with my child. And here I was, over one-thousand miles away.

My cowardly mission was complete. I ran away from home. I ran from everyone and everything that needed me.

And even though I was ashamed of it, I didn't look back.

Chapter 4

Johnnie

Johnnie Ribisi and Squid walked through the door to see the mayhem that was left behind. By the time they got there, Axel and Blake had rolled up the two remaining corpses in an oversized carpet. There was a white box truck out front to transport the dead bodies.

Looking at the destruction and blood, Squid's eyes bulged more than normal. "Not again," he said.

"What's that saying about lightning striking in the same place twice?" Johnnie said.

"Glad these guys don't believe in overkill," Squid said sarcastically.

With a narrow face and long head, his name was more than fitting. His body was long and stringy. His eyes didn't fit into his pale eye sockets. Squid looked just like the creature from which he got his name.

"Who did this?" Johnnie asked.

"You know who," Squid said. "It's the same guys. Same place... meet lightning."

"That's it," Johnnie said. "This was the last gambling house we owned." The weight of defeat was felt with each word.

"You're right. You know where they're coming next, right? We need to find them before they find us," Squid said. "Makes no sense for us to wait for them to bust down the doors to our homes. We need to take the war to them."

"Really? How? There's no money. All the houses are in pieces. The gamblers are dead. And we don't even know who the hell we're taking the war to!"

Axel and Blake walked past Johnnie with the rolled up the carpet hoisted on their shoulders.

Walking out the door, Axel said, "But unlike the other times, they left one alive."

Axel gave a head nod toward the kitchen and then looked at Blake, "Come on man! Hold up your end! This is like four hundred pounds here!"

Johnnie and Squid looked at each other and then raced to the kitchen. On their way, they heard the carpet drop as it was being hauled out the front door.

"Sorry!" Blake said, off in the distance.

"What a screw up," Squid murmured to himself.

Clay sat at a small yellow kitchen table. The matching chair he sat in was missing an arm rest. His black tie was undone, and the top of his shirt was unbuttoned. From the looks of the ashtray on the table, the trembling cigarette between his lips may have been the last of the pack.

When he saw Johnnie and Squid, he jumped up to meet them. The sound of broken glass could be heard crunching under his shoe as he walked.

"Ok, I waited," Clay said. "Now I'm getting the hell out of here!"

"In a minute," Squid said.

"Kiss my ass!" he shot back. "I didn't sign up for a goddamn blood bath."

Johnnie wanted to be patient. He understood what Clay just witnessed was probably the most violence he had seen in his entire life. It made sense that he would want to leave as soon as possible. But Clay was the only person to see these guys and live. Johnnie needed answers and Clay was the only one who could provide them.

"Take a few breaths," Johnnie said in a hushed tone. "Talk to me."

Clay closed his eyes, clasped his hands together and held them in front of his mouth. Following Johnnie's instructions, he took three deep breaths and did his best to relax.

"Johnnie... Your father was always good to me. My Vegas background messed up any chance of me working in the Maryland casinos. Since you're his kid, I'll do my best."

Even though Clay was trying to be helpful, his comments made Johnnie wince. The dealer saw it as a compliment, but Johnnie didn't see it that way. He wanted to be his own man. His own boss. And not live in the shadow of his dead father.

Johnnie rolled his eyes. "Ok. Great. Just tell me... who are these guys and what do they want?"

"They're an MC."

Johnnie looked at Squid and shook his head, as to indicate he wasn't familiar with the term.

"Motorcycle Club," Squid said in a matter of fact tone.

Clay continued, "Clearly a crazy bunch. They call themselves the Broken Brotherhood."

"Broken Brotherhood?" Squid repeated.

"And they're one-percenters, man," he said, providing another term that meant nothing to Johnnie.

Johnnie shrugged again.

"These guys are killers," Clay said.

Squid waved it off as overdramatic. "One-percenters... doesn't sound too threatening. You don't think you're just being soft?"

"You can kiss my ass, Squid."

"Ok, fine. They're bad. But why are they targeting us?" Squid asked.

Clay laughed to himself. "Us? You think this is about you?! They don't even know who you guys are. They're looking for Anthony."

Chapter 5

Remo

Tastee Diner on Cameron Street in Silver Spring managed to remain a staple of the downtown scene. The development that overtook all of the District stretched northward and found itself encroaching on the closest city to the north. Mom and pop shops were bought up, redeveloped, and flipped at a lightning-fast pace, but Tastee Diner was still Tastee Diner. It seemed it would always remain the same.

When Remo walked in, he grabbed the closest menu, scanned the room for an empty section, and sat down. It was deserted compared to other areas of the diner, making it just right for him.

Noticing the ketchup drippings on the tabletop, he grabbed a napkin and wiped them away. He grabbed another napkin and cleaned the chair too.

"Did he get any on the hotdog?" he said.

The olive-skinned man undid the top button of his Brunello Cucinelli blazer. It was navy blue with pinstripes, the same color of the short gray hairs sprinkled throughout his stubble and head. Were it not for the close cut hairstyle that wrapped from the sides of his head to the back, Remo would have been completely bald.

In one motion, Remo slipped out of the jacket and placed it on the back of the chair. He groaned as he sat down, as if his exhaling provided relief for his aging joints. Even though he worked out to keep his body as finely tuned as possible, he was still in his mid-sixties. And a man that age came with rattles and squeaks. Remo removed his black round horn rimmed glasses, carefully dropped them in the inner pocket of his blazer, and reviewed his menu options.

A waitress walked over to him, holding a clear pot of coffee and a mug.

"Care for any?" she asked.

Remo nodded. She placed the mug on the table and extended her arm to pour the coffee.

Her name tag read, "METTY." Attempting to properly pronounce it, Remo said the name aloud.

"Good," Metty said.

"Short for anything?"

"Metasebia," the waitress said.

Only her face, hands, and neck were visible. Rich brown tones peaked out of her white button-down dress shirt. Her skin was the color of espresso, mixed with chocolate and steamed milk. Her eyes were a smoldering brown.

Metty's slender torso was complimented by mesmerizing hips. As the frame of her body moved, it was like every part of the woman performed its own hypnotic dance.

"Has anyone been over to help you, hun? There's a staff switch at midnight, so I just got here."

"I just sat down," Remo said. "But if you give me a couple minutes, I'll know what I want."

"Ok. But fair warning," she sung out, "this isn't a bruschetta, carbonara, and red wine kind of place."

The smile on her face let Remo know that this was her attempt at a joke. He laughed.

"What makes you say that?" he asked.

"I used to work at Neiman Marcus, so I know a five-thousand-dollar Italian suit when I see it. If you want fancy, head south on Georgia Ave until you hit Gallery Place. You might find something there."

She gave Remo a wink and flashed another smile. "I'll be right back for your order."

Metty walked away with her coffee pot.

No sooner than she walked away, a couple in their early thirties stumbled into the section Remo was sitting. Remo sneered in their direction as the solitude he briefly enjoyed was disturbed. The man and woman talked so loud Remo thought their volume button had to be broken.

From the sound of it, they were Eastern European. Remo spent some time traveling through that part of the world and could easily recognize those dark, deep set, almond shaped eyes anywhere. Both had a mane of dark brown hair and their faces were perfect circles. The only distinction being the clef in the man's chin.

The dining tables barely had a foot between them, so their boisterous entrance only made a tight space even tighter. The couple sat together on the same side of their table, with their backs to Remo. And with every move, they bumped Remo's table to the point where it shifted an inch each time.

Remo's first thought was to leave. He looked around the room for another table, but only saw spaces with even more people. He also enjoyed Metty's pleasant nature and didn't want to risk getting a less pleasant waitress.

"How bad can it be?" he muttered to himself.

Remo decided to stay. And it was a decision he would come to regret.

* * *

"How's that burger? Cooked just right?" Metty asked.

Remo looked down and laughed to himself. There were more ketchup stains on the table than when he first sat down.

"Other than my neighbors," Remo said, loud enough to be heard, "everything was swell."

With a nervous glance, Metty acknowledged the back of the couple's head and said, "You're not from around here, are you?"

"I am. But it's been a while." He motioned for Metty to move in closer. "I'm only in town for a bit and I'm looking for someone. Anthony Ribisi. You hear of him?"

"Oh yeah!" Metty exclaimed.

"You got a little excited there, I see. How well do you know him?"

"Jeez," Metty said. She covered her face in embarrassment. "It's not like I know him for real."

"It's ok. Beautiful women are his type. It wouldn't have shocked me if you knew each other."

"Beautiful, huh?"

"Absolutely. If don't mind me asking, where's your family from? No, don't tell me... Somalia?" Remo said with the snap of his finger.

"Close," Metty said. "Ethiopia. But I'm sure you didn't come here to flatter me. Like I said, I know who he is. He used to work at Marco's Restaurant. You hear of it?"

"I have."

"It burned down some time ago. Haven't seen Anthony since. I don't think anyone has. He's been a ghost."

"Only dead people have ghosts."

Metty thought about those words. The idea of it made her

sad. "Well," she said. "It's been well over a year. Maybe he's dead then."

The solemn look on her face was interrupted by a forceful knock against the table. The woman across from Remo had bumped it when she stood up. She turned around and looked directly at Remo when she did it. Remo didn't doubt that it was intentional.

Remo looked at the woman and then her date. "Hey guys, do you mind?"

The man turned toward Remo and said, "Sorry. It's tight in here. My wife's just going to the bathroom."

His indignant spouse said, "Don't apologize to him! Did you hear what he said about us?"

"You two have been bumping my table all night. How about a little consideration?" Remo said.

Leaning toward Remo, the woman said, "The only thing I need to consider is if I'm going to have my husband beat your ass or have my uncle do it. In Romania, you would be dead for talking to me like that."

The woman brought her rudeness a little too close for Remo's liking. Since her face was within inches of Remo's, he covered it with the palm of his hand and pushed her back with all his might.

"But this is Maryland," Remo said. “Not Romania.”

The woman flew backwards and crashed into the table where she was once sitting. How did her husband react? He jumped up to defend his lady. That was a bad idea.

The man threw a wild punch. Remo leapt up from his seat, evaded the punch with a slight lean backwards, and then sprung forward with a tight fist of his own. He connected.

Remo grabbed the dazed man by the back of his head and crashed his face on the table. Once. Twice. Three times. Blood poured out of the man's nostrils.

The few patrons who were in the restaurant jetted for the door.

Metty looked on in horror at the violence. She bolted to the phone at the cash register. It was near the front door.

She trembled with the receiver in hand. Metty's fingers fumbled across the keypad. She couldn't dial 911. When she thought she had finally punched the correct keys, a busy signal blared in her ear. She hadn't dialed the right number at all.

Slamming the phone down after a third try, Remo stepped in front of her. He had put his blazer back on. He showed no sense of urgency. Almost as if he hadn't pulverized a couple just moments ago. Save for the blood droplets of different sizes dotting his white shirt, you wouldn't have known he was in a violent altercation.

Remo reached into his pants pocket and pulled out a roll of bills. He peeled off a twenty.

"This is for the burger," he said, placing the money on the counter.

He threw down five additional twenty-dollar bills and said, "This is for the damage."

Then one last time, he shuffled through the wad of cash and found three one-hundred-dollar bills. He grabbed Metty by her wrist and placed it in her hand, along with a sheet of paper with his number and name on it.

"And this is for messing up your night."

Remo let go of Metty's wrist and pointed at the phone number.

"If you hear anything about Anthony, call me. And if you see him... tell him I'm looking for him."

Chapter 6

Anthony

Metairie, Louisiana is approximately eight miles outside New Orleans. Since the city was outside the main tourist attraction of the Big Easy, it was the perfect place to maintain a low profile and make a little money. The chance that I would bump into someone I knew was slim.

Cafe Roma was a salad, pasta, and pizza joint on North Causeway Boulevard. It was like a traditional Italian restaurant, but at the same time, it wasn't quite at match. Sometimes I found myself comparing the menu to Marco's. I knew it was unfair, but I couldn't help it. The dining room was small and intimate. And the best part was that Cafe Roma didn't get a lot of new faces, and that was exactly what I was looking for.

When I first moved to town, I had lunch at Cafe Roma every day for three weeks. I figured giving the restaurant my money on a consistent basis was a good way to get on the owner's radar. And sure enough, it worked.

After three weeks of small talk, I told the owner that I was new in town and looking for a part-time job to help me get back on my feet. I told him I wasn't looking for a lot of hours, just something to keep a few dollars in my pocket.

The owner liked me and told me I could start working immediately, so I did. Turnover was high at Cafe Roma, so it was almost like I was doing him a favor. I quickly noticed that there were only two employees the owner could count on, me and Gabe.

Gabriel St. Cyr was born and raised in the city of New Orleans. His lineage traced back to the original French settlers. The St. Cyr bloodline survived the transition to Spanish control, back to French, and then finally the American acquisition of the land through the Louisiana Purchase.

During that time, his family had mixed with Native American, enslaved Africans, free Africans, and Haitians. His family's extraordinary history, from past to present, was something Gabe was extremely proud of. He was also willing to share it at a moment's notice to anyone willing to listen.

At first look, Gabe seemed like just a regular white guy. But the roots of his family tree kept his family secret throughout generations. His family was diverse with color and culture.

On occasion, he would pull out his phone and scroll through pictures and videos of family gatherings. It was a mixture of baby showers, gumbo nights, birthday parties, crawfish boils, and weddings. My favorite images were the ones of his entire family dancing in a second line behind brass bands and waving handkerchiefs in the air. And in the middle of the hype was the white boy. Gabe danced along with family members as dark as me. That's the magic of Creole genetics.

Gabe and I bussed tables together every weekend. Fridays and Saturdays were busier than other nights, so the boss preferred to have his best, scheduled to work together.

"Jelani!" Gabe said, attempting to get my attention. "Grab

table six for me real quick! I need to take this phone call." He held his phone in the air.

Covering each other's tables wasn't a big deal. We looked out for each other at work. Maybe that's why the boss could rely on us. Maybe it's because we consistently relied on each other.

"Publisher's Clearinghouse?" I shouted back.

"HA! Something like that!" he said, running out the back door.

I made my way over to table six. There were three men with empties all around them.

"Pardon me," I said. "Do you mind if I get these out of your way?"

"Nah. We good," one of the men said. I noticed him before. He was a regular who came in the restaurant every other week with his younger brothers.

I nodded my head and went about my way.

After ten minutes, Gabe came back into the restaurant. I couldn't tell if the sweat on his forehead was from worry or the heat. He didn't know I was looking, but I spied him pacing at the back before he decided to approach me.

"I need to talk with you," he said.

Gabe didn't wait for me to respond. He just spun on his heals and walked to the area he paced earlier.

"Here's the deal," Gabe said. "I need to ask you for a favor. If this isn't your speed, let me know and we can act like this conversation never happened. But I'd like for you to hear me out first."

"You've got my attention."

"I do jobs... on the side," he whispered. "To cut to the chase, they're not always legal and occasionally, I need an extra person to help me out.

"I just got a call about a last-minute job and my regular man is out of town this weekend. I have to replace him."

"And you want to know if I'd be that replacement?" I asked.

"In a nutshell... yeah."

The first thing I thought was that I didn't leave a life of crime only to come down to Louisiana and find a new life of crime. My hesitation was apparent.

"Listen," Gabe said, "it's an escort job that we've done a bunch of times. A drop off and pick. It's really a cakewalk. He's just some middle-aged guy with money who likes to feel more important than he really is."

"Before I could respond, a shout came from behind me. "Aye busboy!"

We both snapped our heads toward table six. "Not you Gabe! The *black* guy! Didn't they teach you how to clean to tables in the Lower Ninth?"

It was clear that the reference to my skin color and the Lower Ninth Ward was an obvious effort at insulting me. The Lower Ninth is the poorest ward in New Orleans. So in an unimaginative way, lacking all creativity, he was making a poorly veiled comment about my race and connecting it to a perception of socio-economic status. In a word, it was complete bullshit.

Both Gabe and I started walking toward table six. Gabe was moving as fast as he could to keep up with me. He probably thought that I was ready to smack the white boy, but being reactionary wasn't my style. I just wanted to *talk*.

The three guys were on their feet by the time I reached them.

"Try to stay calm," Gabe quietly said to me.

Now face-to-face with the asshole at table six, I said, "Why don't you say what you mean?"

"I don't know what you're talking about. I just want these dirty ass dishes out of the way."

Gabe stepped between us. "Not a problem. I'll make sure this is taken care of."

"I appreciate it Gabe," the guy said. He then looked at his brothers. "Listen guys and listen well. Rule number one... anytime you want a job done right, make sure it's done by one of your own."

His brothers let out a laugh and table six guy continued to press his luck.

"One of your own, I say," the man continued. "And never by someone who looks like he just ran away from the plantation."

The slavery reference was a bridge too far and Gabe knew it. Gabe closed his eyes and tightened his face in frustration. He turned to face me, "Ok, now we gotta kick their ass."

The anticipation of a rumble hung in the air. At that very moment, the jingle from the front door interrupted the ass whipping that was about to occur. Four Jefferson Parish sheriffs walked in.

One of them yelled, "Where can a cop get a good pizza around here?!"

Chapter 7

Anthony

The sheriffs showed up right on time. There was no telling where a clash with these guys would've gone. Fights turn into unintentional homicide quickly. I left Washington, DC to stay out of trouble. Not to end up in the middle of it. No fights. No deaths. No guns. And absolutely no illegal jobs from Gabe. New Orleans served as my chance to fade into the background. And that's what I intended on doing.

The sheriffs had dinner and remained at the restaurant for the majority of the night. Table six got tired of waiting around for a potential scrap and left sometime before the cops did. Gabe headed out as well. I stayed behind to finish cleaning the dining room. I wanted to make sure the morning staff was ready to go when they arrived.

After leaving the restaurant, I locked the door, and walked to my car in the abandoned parking lot. It stood alone, like a solitary palm tree on a deserted island.

My car keys were in hand, but the restaurant keys were clipped to my belt loop and jingled with every step.

My eyelids had already started hanging. I struggled against the fatigue to keep them open. I couldn't wait to get home.

Then off in the distance, I heard a car racing in my direction. It snapped me back awake. The pair of headlights grew brighter as the car came closer. It spun out to a stop in front of my car. I recognized the people inside before they got out of the car.

"Great," I said aloud. It was table number six.

Chapter 8

Johnnie

The guys went back to Johnnie's hangout. It sat at the entrance of the city. It was close to where the Baltimore Washington Parkway merged with Route 50 and emptied out onto New York Avenue. The dilapidated warehouse sat on Queens Chapel Road NE, just off Bladensburg Road NE.

There were a few gas stations, fast food restaurants, low budget hotels, and other warehouses around the spot. One or two mega night clubs found their way to the area as well.

The area was perfect for Johnnie and his crew. It provided both the seclusion they needed and easy access to and from the city. Not to mention, Taco Tuesdays were a big hit at the strip club.

"Broken Brotherhood?" Axel said. "I never heard of them.

"I'm pretty sure there are a lot of things you haven't heard of," Squid quipped back.

Axel wasn't fazed by Squid's condescension. He knew him long enough to not be bothered.

Blake was at a utility sink in the corner. He was running

water over a few rags. As he wrung out the tattered sheets, crimson colored water flowed from the rags into the sink. The headphones in his ears kept him deaf to the conversation that was happening.

"Blake," Axel said.

There was no response.

"Blake!" Axel yelled.

This time, Axel grabbed the closest thing to him, which was an old dusty running shoe that had been lingering around for weeks. Axel cocked back his arm and launched it toward Blake. His accuracy was scary. The sneaker hit Blake in the back of the head.

The look on his face was the same look someone would give if he had been awaked by a siren blasted through a megaphone. He was startled and snatched the headphones out of his ears.

"What?!" Blake said.

"Broken Brotherhood? What do you know about them?"

"No more than you, asshole!"

"Stop playing around," Johnnie said. "This is serious."

"I say we find these guys and let them know who they've messed with," Axel said.

"I agree," Johnnie said. "But we can't just go knocking on doors now, can we? We need money and we need guns. I don't want to go searching for something we're unprepared to find."

""Then what are we going to do?" Axel said.

"I think I have figured something out," Johnnie said.

Just then three loud knocks boomed from the front door. The sound echoed throughout the half empty warehouse. No one moved. Blake shut off the water, crept to the door, and looked through a small rectangular window.

"Uh, Johnnie?" Blake said.

Johnnie nodded his head. "I've been expecting him. Like I said. I have a plan."

Blake opened the door and in walked a Lawrence Taylor doppelgänger. The New York Giants defensive back terrorized the offensive line of opposing football teams, long before Johnnie and his crew ever watched football. They had no idea how uncanny the resemblance was.

His name was Smitty. He was a former Metropolitan Police Department detective, turned night club bouncer, and was the confidant of Johnnie's deceased father, Marco Ribisi.

Getting straight to the point, Smitty said, "I think I found him."

"Are you sure?" said Johnnie.

Smitty glanced around the room at the assembly of young men Johnnie had recruited to be in his crew. Unimpressed, he took a deep breath and said, "I said, I *think* I found him."

Chapter 9

Johnnie

Squid shouted at Johnnie from across the room, "Why do we even need this guy? We can take care of the bikers on our own. Who needs Anthony Ribisi?!"

Before Johnnie could reply, Smitty answered, "If you could've handled them, you would've by now."

"He's right," Johnnie said.

"I've looked into the Broken Brotherhood. These guys are real," Smitty said.

Squid was still skeptical. "Well, how come we've never heard of them?"

Visibly annoyed by Squid's general disposition, Smitty looked at Johnnie and continued talking.

"They have been wreaking havoc all over southern Maryland. The closest they've been to DC is Waldorf. And when was the last time any of you all spent any real time in Waldorf? Your house was an easy job for them. You don't know the area and you clearly don't know the local players. Setting up shop there was an amateur move, Johnnie.

"My professional opinion is that you need Anthony if you

want to keep the operation going and if you want to fight the bikers. They won't stop until they find him. So, it makes sense that you find him first."

"We don't need him!" Squid exploded in frustration. "We can handle it!"

Everyone looked at Squid as the air stood still. The silence was broken a few seconds later as Smitty was the first to speak.

"Johnnie," Smitty said. "Does your friend know about Operation Uber Ride?"

"Ah... Operation Uber Ride," Johnnie repeated. "That's what we called it afterwards because Anthony didn't share details about his plans beforehand. I almost forgot all about it.

"About four years ago, my father drove up to Atlantic City for an extended weekend. He wanted to get away from the restaurant and the gambling houses to blow off some steam. He might have even been doing some homework. To see if there was something new he could bring back from the casinos to our operation.

"I never asked him how the trip was. All I know is that when it was time for him to return, his car had been wrecked and he was exhausted. Maybe he blew off too much steam.

"My father hopped the Amtrak train to come home. Once he got to Union Station, he made his way outside to an arriving Uber car. A black Nissan Sentra with DC license plates. After riding in the car for a few minutes, the exhaustion had to have set in, because he dozed off.

"Maybe it was the look of an old man with luggage at a train station or maybe it was just the sheer stupidity of the Uber driver, but he mistook my father for a sleeping tourist and decided to take him for a ride. When my father woke up, he wasn't at home. Instead, he was on a dead-end street. The driver was still at the wheel but there was a second masked man in the back seat pointing a gun at my father.

"He did what he was told without putting up a fight. He turned over his wallet and cell phone. The guy in the back lifted the driver's license out of the wallet and said, 'Now we know where you live.' I guess that was their way of scaring other people into not going to the police. But they didn't have to worry about that. Not with Marco. My father went to someone much worse than the police. He went to Anthony. So, what did Anthony do?

"It took him about three weeks, but every single day, Anthony showed up to Union Station with luggage, and ordered an Uber. For three weeks, he carved time out of his schedule at approximately the same time my father had been picked up. He rolled the dice, hoping the same Uber driver would pick him up. And after three weeks, it finally did. A black Nissan Sentra showed up, with the same DC license plates.

"Anthony jumped in the back seat, took a good look at the driver, and was confident he matched my father's description of the man. Before faking a nap, he texted me and Smitty a simple message. *Track cell phone location. Bring cuffs. Two pair.* So that's what we did.

"We couldn't have been more than ten minutes behind, but by the time we reached him, he had already disarmed the gunman sitting in the back. He was pointing the man's own gun at him. The driver was unconscious behind the wheel.

"After cuffing both men to the steering wheel, Anthony popped the trunk and grabbed his luggage. He opened the suitcase and pulled out a metal canister. It was gasoline. I don't need to tell you what happened next, do I?"

The men in the room listened to Johnnie's story as he relived it. Johnnie could smell the accelerant as he reminisced. The heat from the fire still provided warmth to his memory. The three men, Johnnie, Smitty, and Anthony, drove away.

Listening to the duo in the car scream in agony, as flames engulfed the Uber vehicle.

"Gentlemen," Smitty said. "This is why you need Anthony. He's thoughtful enough to anticipate moves. He's patient enough to wait for the right time to act. And he's merciless enough to destroy anything and anyone in his way. Can you say any of you are the same?"

The room fell silent again. Breaking the silence, Blake was the first to speak.

"It sounds like Anthony had everything covered. Why did he even text y'all?"

Smitty flashed a grin. "Even the best gets a little lazy, every once and awhile. I asked him the same thing. His response was that in his rush out the door that day, he forgot to bring cuffs of his own."

"We were just a backup plan," Johnnie said.

"And that's why we need to bring him home," Smitty said.

"Bring him home? Where exactly is he?" Johnnie said.

"New Orleans."

"Nola!" Blake said. "I love New Orleans! Jazz, beignets, and shrimp po' boys. Nothing beats the Big Easy."

"Shut up, Blake," Squid said out of nowhere.

"At least, I think that's where he is. I need to go down to make sure."

"What makes you a hundred percent sure he's there?" Squid challenged.

Smitty huffed. "Johnnie, put a muzzle on that puppy before I take him for a walk."

Never one to back down from a fight, Squid began walking toward Smitty. Smitty knew a fight would be unfair but was hoping Squid would come just a little too close.

Johnnie stood in Squid's path to prevent him from reaching Smitty. "Squid, you're my boy. And I like you. But if you don't sit your ass in that chair," Johnnie said, pointing to the table on the other side of the room, "Smitty will knock you into next month. And he'll enjoy it."

Squid stared at Smitty as reality set in. This was a fight he couldn't win. Squid turned around and retreated.

"Like I said... I'm not completely sure. But you remember his girlfriend, Coco, right? I've been tracking her credit card."

Amazed, Johnnie interrupted Smitty. "How?!"

Smitty held up a hand. "Those are trade secrets, my good man. I take this private eye thing seriously. So, I've been tracking her and I noticed multiple trips to New Orleans. At first, I didn't think much of it. But over time, I could see it was happening damn near every week.

"It's not like she has family down there, so I asked myself, 'why?'"

"Anthony..." Johnnie said.

"Exactly. She'll probably head back down in the next week or so."

"And you?"

"I'll book a flight ahead of her. When she lands, I'll be a step behind her the whole time. If I'm right, she'll lead me to Anthony."

"Good work, Smitty. You really do have a knack for this private eye thing."

"Don't congratulate me yet. First let's wait for the next trip. Then we'll see how right I am."

Chapter 10

Anthony

The oldest brother was the first person out of the car. It didn't take long for his younger brothers to follow behind.

For the first time, I was able to see the identical Confederate flag tattoos on their biceps. The three men surrounded me. The oldest brother stood between me and Cafe Roma while the two younger brothers blocked me from reaching my car. I was trapped.

I shifted my stance so I could keep an eye on everyone. It was only for a moment. The men didn't wait long before making their move.

The two younger brothers lunged at me and grabbed me by the shoulders. They wrapped their arms around mine. I bucked against their bodies but was turned around, facing my car.

"Spin him around!" The older brother shouted.

He tried to put himself in position to throw a punch at me. But I didn't make it easy. All the struggling between me and his brothers made it just as likely that he would hit one of them.

I noticed the tussling was wearing one of the brothers out.

His grip on me grew weaker. *No endurance,* I thought to myself.

I threw my hip in his direction. The jolt was hard enough to knock him off balance. I pushed him off with an arm that had become free. He flew against the car. His head and the metal came together with a loud thud.

That's when the older brother charged at me. Before he reached me, I crashed the other brothers' head down on my knee. I felt the bridge of his nose buckle and flatten. Blood spurted everywhere.

Before I could hit him again, the older brother was able to get to me. He grabbed me from behind with a choke hold around the back of my neck. I heard the unmistakable "*CLICK*" of a switchblade.

"Alright!" he said. "You wanna spill blood? Let's spill some blood."

His brothers gathered themselves to their feet, ready to savor the win. But instead of smug excitement on their pained faces, all I saw was fear. It didn't make sense to me. They had me right where they wanted me.

But then we heard another "*CLICK*" come from behind us. And this time, it wasn't a switchblade. Instead, it was the click of a Smith and Wesson being cocked. And it was in the hand of Gabriel St. Cyr.

Gabe pressed the barrel of the gun against the back of the older brothers' head.

"So..." he said, "how committed are you to spilling blood?"

Chapter 11

Anthony

Gabe held up a shot glass filled to the brim with bourbon.

"Here's to saving your ass," he said.

I held up my shot as well, trying not to spill the brown liquid as the two glasses collided together.

"I don't know what you're talking about," I said while signaling the bartender for two more. "I had them right where I wanted them."

Gabe laughed out loud. "Yeah. Right."

We sat at the small bar in a music club that was the size of a walk-in closet. Negril Cafe was a well-known venue in New Orleans on Frenchmen Street. Patrons regularly gathered for strong drinks and live music.

Bob Marley's portrait gazed down on us from the wall. A hummingbird hovered over a martini glass. The wall art was a thing of beauty, yet Gabe and I still focused on the most important part... consuming drinks.

Gabe shouted over the music and gestured toward the jazz band. "Not bad!" he said.

From the corner of the bar, I surveyed the rest of the club and shrugged my shoulders.

"I don't get you, Jelani!" he shouted again.

The band stopped playing and the lead singer announced, "Alright y'all. We'll be back in fifteen. Feel free to approach any one of us to pick up a CD."

I thought it funny that musicians still sold CDs.

Light clapping echoed between the nearly fifteen people in the crowd. The music break was right on time. It gave us a chance to hear each other without shouting over the band.

"I've been trying to figure you out," Gabe continued. "I thought you'd like this place, but you look so damn uncomfortable. Nervous almost."

"I'm good... just still learning the lay of the land. I don't fully know this city yet."

Gabe leaned back on his bar stool. The look on his face said it all. "You're lying. I don't know why but I know you're lying."

Gabe put consideration into what he said next. "Look... you show up in town, out of the blue. You never talk about family. Don't share memories. It's like you've never even had friends. It doesn't make sense. I know there's a lot more to your story.

"For example, from the little I've observed, I have no doubt you could've handled the brothers back at the restaurant. If you had the right tools, of course."

"What's your point?"

"Okay. We're going to keep playing these games. My point is... I get the feeling that you're rarely without the right tools. My point is... walking around with that level of vulnerability is probably new for you. My point is... while you're good at the Cafe Roma job, you're not a damn busboy. That's my point."

"You haven't really made a point yet," I sarcastically interrupted.

Gabe continued as if I hadn't spoken a word. "That's why I

approached you about the job earlier. When I get a hunch, it's usually right. And I got a hunch about you. So what's up? You wanna tell me what I think I already know?"

"All you need to know is that I'm just trying to keep a low profile, make a little money, and enjoy this wonderful swamp air y'all got down here. Nothing more."

"Well, I still need an extra man and this job can check all of those boxes. You won't need to do anything but ride in a car. Your profile will stay low and you'll make more money than what you'd get after a month of work at the restaurant. And you can take in all the swamp air you want."

Gabe had lobbied hard for my involvement. And just as he had hunches about me, I had hunches about him. He was trustworthy, diligent, and thoughtful. I didn't doubt his assessment of the job. And the one thing that Gabe didn't pick up on was that the action from earlier stirred a sense of nostalgia that I didn't know I had for my previous life.

"Just ride in a car, you say?" I asked Gabe before I downed my third shot.

"You won't even need tools," he said. "It's just a ride. He's the paranoid type and contracts transportation from his home to the casino every time he gets the urge to gamble. He isn't in the life and doesn't have enemies. Like I said earlier, he's just a guy with money who likes to feel special."

After giving it some thought, Gabe convinced me that the job would be simple.

"Point A to point B, back home, and no guns. I think I can do that." I said, nodding my head.

“Great! It's settled,” Gabe said. “You can meet the rest of the team tomorrow night. But for now, let's drink!"

He looked down the short bar to the bartender. "Another round!"

The bartender made his way back with two more shots of

bourbon. We clinked our glasses as if we were signing a contract. It felt like a ritualistic commemoration of a covenant.

The self-congratulatory look on Gabe's face was amusing. He swallowed the shot in one gulp, turned to me and said, "Like I said... it's a hunch. But you ain't no damn busboy."

Gabe was right. He had no idea about the monster I used to be, or how hard I worked to let the past be the past.

He had no idea. And it was better that way.

Chapter 12

The Broken

Wednesday, September 11th

Owned by the oldest member in the motorcycle club, Harvey's Hangout sat on a lonely northbound strip of Route 301 in Maryland. It was located just south of the District in Charles County.

There were gas stations every two miles or so, which contributed to the occasionally sparse traffic. But for the most part, it was an underused route.

Harvey's was the quintessential setting for an outlaw motorcycle club. It was isolated. Being at Harvey's was like being in limbo. Lost in purgatory. And as a result, there was no reason for anyone to be anywhere in the area, other than the bikers.

All sixty-seven members of the club were assembled for their weekly meeting. It was referred to as church because the meetings were sacred. If a member wasn't in a hospital or jail, his presence was obligatory.

Club members were littered throughout the bar that seemed to be holding itself together by duct tape. Every piece of wooden furniture had something missing. An arm rest.

Planks of wood from chair backs. In some cases, entire chair legs were missing and had been replaced with wood of a completely different color.

Even the bar, which was an oblong circular island in the middle of the room, suffered from physical neglect. Faded patches of bar top couldn't be ignored.

Harvey was at the cash register. He had a stack of one-dollar bills in his leathery hand. A lifetime of sun exposure left his skin wrinkled, freckled, and tough. The yellow stained gray of his beard and mustache matched the hair on his head.

"Ninety-six. Ninety-seven. Ninety-eight. Ninety-nine..."

"One hundred!" The wide-eyed biker said, rubbing his pudgy sausage fingers together in Harvey's face.

He reached into the pocket of his black biker jacket and pulled out a pair of teardrop diamond earrings. Harvey handed him the money and the biker slammed the earrings down on the bar.

After the biker snatched the cash, he turned on his heals, and yelled out, "Thanks!" Then he ran to the other side of the room.

He moved so fast that he nearly knocked Liza to the floor. She walked up to the bar in enough time to overhear Harvey whisper to himself, "What a sucker."

Harvey slid the jewels next to the cash register.

"Who? Jimmy?" Liza said, looking in the direction of the sausage fingered biker.

Her raven-colored hair was contrasted by her piercing ocean blue eyes. She leaned against the bar to get a good look at the earrings and her unrestrained cleavage spilled out of her unbuttoned top. Harvey's eyes followed the frame of her body down to the black miniskirt that had become even shorter as she stretched over the bar.

"Yeah," he said. "Jimmy."

"Those are pretty!" she squealed out.

"Almost as pretty as you... and far less valuable."

"You better stop it, old man. What would happen if Priest heard you talking like that to me?"

Harvey flashed a frown of consideration. "You're right. I am old. Old enough to be your grandfather. But that ain't nothing a little blue pill can't fix. As for Priest, I'm not scared of him. I could beat both his father and his grandfather in a fair fight. I'm sure my old ass can take Priest too."

"Funny you should say that. Priest is waiting for you in your office. Maybe I'll come back there to watch that fair hand to hand combat."

Harvey swung his motorcycle jacket on over his body and prepared to head to his office. The front of the jacket detailed his name and his title. The patch read, "HISTORIAN."

"Harvey," Liza said before he could get away. She nodded toward the earrings. "How much are they worth?"

"The earrings?" he chuckled. Harvey then held up both hands and extended all ten fingers.

"A thousand dollars!" Liza exclaimed as quietly as she could.

Harvey reached over and grabbed the earrings that were still sitting near the register.

"Now multiply that by three."

Liza's surprise quickly turned to disdain. She put her hand on her hip and scolded the old man, "Harvey! You gave that man one hundred dollars. How could you do that to him?!"

Harvey had already begun walking toward his office. He stopped at the question, turned around and stared at Liza.

"He's a grown man," Harvey said. "He knew what he was doing."

At that, Harvey tossed the earrings. Liza, startled by the flying jewels, caught them.

Then Harvey said, "Since you care so much... you can either give them back or shut up and put 'em on."

Liza was hypnotized by the sparkle of the diamonds. The stones twinkled like stars in a darkened sky. She looked at Harvey.

"Keep 'em," he said. "Whatever I've done to him, now we've done it together."

Chapter 13

Priest

Harvey entered the room and walked past the Enforcer. As soon as he cleared the threshold, Priest looked at the Enforcer and gave him a signal to leave the room. That left Harvey alone in his office with Priest and Priest's younger brother, Maddox.

Maddox wore a black leather biker vest and had a long brown shag of hair. Other than that, when compared to every other member of Broken Brotherhood, Maddox was an anomaly. His clear skin, clean face, piercing blue eyes, and strong bone structure made him better suited for a modeling career than a road warrior.

There was also another glaring difference. Maddox had a conscience.

"Fellas," Harvey said. "What's the hold up? Church was supposed to start twenty minutes ago."

Priest threw his arms up in desperation. He pointed at Maddox and said, "I don't know! Ask him!"

"Maddie. What seems to be the problem?" Harvey said.

"This is stupid. This whole thing is stupid." Maddox said.

He paced the floor and then stopped in front of Harvey. "I mean... don't you think everything we've been doing is too much?"

"It doesn't matter what I think, Maddie. I'm not the president. And last I checked, your patch said... Oh, wait. You don't have a position. Your opinion doesn't matter either.

"If this is what Priest wants to do, then we hit the houses. You don't need to understand. Hell, you don't even need to know the whole plan. Just do what you're told. That's how this works."

"But it's not just me. The Brothers have been talking and a number of us think the houses were a bad idea."

"Once again. We only have one president," Harvey said. "That's the way it's always been. When your father was president, no one questioned his leadership. The same for your grandfather. Especially for your grandfather. When he said, 'run through the wall,' the brothers said, 'which one?' and did it. No one questions the leader."

"When will it stop?" Maddox asked.

Harvey was taken aback by the forwardness of Maddox's question.

"Priest," Harvey said. "Do you want me to answer that question, or will you?"

Priest stepped between Harvey and Maddox. His patience had run thin.

"You heard that brothers were concerned about our present course of action. I understand. But I've heard some things too. I've heard that brothers are concerned about your standing in the Broken. I heard that brothers question how you've been patched in, even though most can't remember you ever being a prospect.

"So don't come to me, talking about all the things you've heard. Because I've heard things too, from men who have earned their way into this family and trust their leader. If you don't trust your leader, then leave. Take off those colors and hang them on the bar on your way out. And maybe the Broken will let you walk away in one piece."

Maddox knew the truth. He knew that his membership was owed to motorcycle club magic. He hadn't gained admission by the traditional route. He had been insecure about it, ever since he joined.

Despite his name, he kept a low profile and stayed out of his brother's way. He intentionally didn't ride to any of the gambling houses to avoid the inevitable violence. But the writing was on the wall. Maddox knew he couldn't run from it forever. And now, he chose to speak out, even though speaking out could come at a cost. But was it a cost he was willing to pay?

Maddox didn't respond to his brother. He stood there in uncomfortable silence.

After a few seconds, Harvey broke the tension. "We need to start the meeting."

"That's right," Priest said. He turned his attention back to Maddox. "If that's all, go let the Broken know I'll be out shortly."

Maddox didn't move.

"Go!" Priest demanded.

With that, Maddox left the room with his defeated spirit. At that moment, the Enforcer stepped back in.

"Keep an eye on him," Priest said to the Enforcer.

He nodded his head and left Harvey and Priest in the room without saying a word.

Harvey approached Priest, who still stood by the door. "People are talking, huh? I thought you and I were the only ones who knew about how your brother skated."

"We are," Priest said with a straight face. "But Maddie... he doesn't know that."

Chapter 14

Priest

The room buzzed with camaraderie, conversation, and alcohol. The Broken Brotherhood was assembled, but the meeting hadn't started. Instead, shots were being devoured and prospects were being hazed. Several women in black vests and colorful make-up accentuated the crowd of men like adornments on a Christmas tree.

Everyone was in their own world, until Priest walked out of Harvey's office.

Priest approached the bar at the middle of the room. With every step, the room grew quieter. Once he reached the platform at the middle of the bar, the room fell completely silent. The surrounding men walked closer and inhaled with anticipation.

Maddox had sunk into a corner of the room. He was present but wasn't excited to be there. Harvey, on the other hand, enjoyed the moment. He stood in the back, observing the room. He knew what was about to happen.

Priest held sway over the club unlike any past leader Harvey had ever seen. Certainly, unlike his father or grandfather. The type of charismatic influence Priest intentionally wielded left Harvey equally intrigued, impressed, and amused. The manipulator in Harvey loved every minute of it.

Priest cleared his throat as he looked over the silent crowd. "Brothers!" he began.

"Yeah!" The chant came roaring back at him from the men in the room.

"This month, we set out on a course that will forever change our family. An opportunity was presented to us to develop and grow in a way that hasn't happened in generations. It's not necessarily growth in human numbers. But in power!"

The men yelled out "Yeah!"

"Influence!" Priest said.

"Yeah!"

"And control!" Priest continued. "Beloved family... we have been invited to roll through the nation's capital and make it ours!"

Cheers erupted from all over Harvey's Hangout.

"Now from what has been shared with me, many are asking 'why?' Why DC? Why did we disassemble those ratty gambling houses the way we did?"

Priest paused for a moment as his brothers cheered. Then he continued.

"Weren't we perfectly fine riding our hogs throughout Charles County? If that's our backyard, why would we leave it for a big city? Why go into a city with giant-sized challenges and insurmountable opposition?

"Some of you might question the motives behind moving to this city, thinking there's nothing for us in DC. But I disagree! The Broken has a big future in that big city.

"Now I know you all aren't as religious as I am, but allow me to use my favorite book to answer some of your questions.

"Our current experience is very similar to what's in the

Hebrew Testament. Moses and the Israelites had come out of Egypt, in search of the promise land. This was the land that God said that He would deliver to them. A land flowing with milk and honey.

"After wandering around in the wilderness, they had finally reached their destination. But did they rush in and claim it? No! Instead, Moses sent twelve spies into the land. They came back and reported that the land was wonderful! But along with the spacious land, food, and beauty, there were also giants!

"Fear swept over the people. They thought they wouldn't be able to settle in the promise land without a deadly confrontation. And so, the people, believing that they couldn't defeat the giants, defied Moses and defied God. They abandoned the hope of a promise land!"

Priest now had the cadence of a preacher.

"The people must've forgotten that God brought them out of Egyptian bondage. They must've forgotten that God destroyed Pharaoh in the process. They must've forgotten that God protected them as they traveled with a cloud by day, and a pillar of fire by night. It slipped their minds that when they were thirsty, He provided water and when they were hungry, He provided food! Those ungrateful bastards forgot that God was with them every step of the way.

"It's safe to assume that if God carried them to their promise land, that God would also provide the strength they needed to overtake the giants! But they doubted, faltered, and God sent them back into the wilderness. Because of their lack of faith in God, everyone in that generation had to die before God would allow the Israelites to see the promise land. Even Moses had to go!

"They all had to die! Well... except two. Among the twelve spies, two stood up to the others who came with that fearful report. Since they had the right faith, God rewarded them, and allowed them to enter the promise land with a new generation of Israelites.

"And that's where we are today. The Broken has an opportunity to roll into the promise land, like thunder, and take it! We can make it ours! But brothers, I'm going to be honest... there are some giants in town. Giants who have been there for a mighty long time. Giants who have their own businesses and weapons to protect those business.

"But I stand before you with the same spirit that Joshua and Caleb stood before Israel. They were two of the twelve spies and they reminded the people that God was on their side. Brothers... that's what I'm telling you. God is on your side! He has made a way for you! He has prepared each and every one of you for this fight!

"We have been physically broken and emotionally broken. We come from broken homes, broken families, and broken relationships. However, in spite of our brokenness, we have found an unbeatable strength in each other. We have taken our broken pieces and have made them whole. And now, we are so much stronger than any God-damned giant in that city!

"So if you're asking 'why?' My answer is a simple one," Priest said.

The rhythm of his words became slower and more measured.

"God has placed us together, at this point and time, and with this opportunity in front of us. He wants to see if we have the spirit of Joshua and Caleb or are we faithless, like the rest of Israel.

"This moment will never come again. This is our test, brothers. The test is all that lies between us and glory. The test is our why. And we will strike down any giant that stands in our way."

The crowd erupted. Priest looked at his brothers. There

was a wave of energy that he could've surfed if he had a board. There was only one thing left to do. Get confirmation that the Broken Brotherhood was all on the same page.

"I hope that answers all of your questions," Priest said, calming his brothers at the sound of his voice. "But I have one question for you. Who's ready to do this work? Who's ready to hunt, catch, and kill? Who's ready to become a giant-slayer?! Who's ready to take over DC?!"

And just like that, Priest had once again worked up the crowd in a matter of a few sentences. Grown men were howling like they were reliving their high school days, during a pregame speech in the locker room. Men were lifting drinks in the air, slapping high fives, and jeering loudly.

A chorus of 'Yeah!' bellowed throughout the room. The sounds were transformed into the men shouting in unison, 'Hunt! Catch! Kill! – Hunt! Catch! Kill! – Hunt! Catch! Kill!' The room was on fire and Priest glanced over at his brother Maddox. Everyone was on the same page, except his baby brother.

With each chant of 'Hunt! Catch! Kill!' Priest knew that the Broken Brotherhood was on his side. If there were any reservations, they had been put to rest. The club was ready to hunt, catch, and kill.

Priest had the MC Club right where he wanted them. Like a vicious dog being trained by its master. He had them eating out of the palm of his hand.

Chapter 15

Anthony

We sat around the living room of the two-bedroom house Gabe rented in the Gentilly neighborhood of New Orleans.

The house was old. But not to the point that Gabe would consider moving. Rent was dirt cheap. There was a faded water line, etched approximately nine feet above the floor. It created a trail around the perimeter of the room. Gabe caught me staring at it.

Gabe got up from his seat, walked over to the wall, placed his palm on the discolored line. He traced it for a few feet.

"This is where the flood waters stopped. The house soaked in the waters of Lake Ponchartrain for weeks before it receded. The landlord asked if I wanted him to paint over it, but I don't.

"He replaced the drywall up to the stain. But I wanted this intact. It's my daily reminder of how our own government screwed us over."

As a northerner, I didn't have a frame of reference to help me comprehend the impact the flooding had on the city. Gabe constantly reminded me New Orleans survived hurricane

Katrina. The faulty levee system is what led to death and destruction, after the storm had passed.

The United States Army Corps of Engineers were responsible for the maintenance of the levees, and they were negligent. Gabe, along with many other residents, were clear in their understanding. The United States government failed New Orleans.

The devastation witnessed by the country and the world was not a natural disaster. It was a man-made one. The levees didn't work as advertised. The government knew it and they failed to keep the water out.

"Well... what about this job? It's only for transportation. That's all we're providing, right?" I asked but I was really searching for reassurance.

"Nothing more. Nothing less," Gabe said, making his way back to his seat at the table.

Gabe looked at two guys sitting on the sofa. They were identical twins and carbon copies of each other. They had short red hair, freckles, and shared the same gap-toothed smile. They reminded me of Alfred E. Neuman, the poster child for MAD Magazine.

He pointed to the guy on the right. "That's Jayden," he said.

The guy shook his head. "I'm Hayden."

And as if he didn't even hear the man, he pointed to the other and said, "That's Hayden."

The twin shook his head too and said, "I'm Jayden."

I acknowledged both brothers with a nod of my head. Gabe then motioned toward the other two men in the room. They were standing near the makeshift bar in the back, drinking shots of tequila, from what my nose could tell.

"I'm Tony," he said. He held up his hand and waved. "But you can call me Tone. And this is Chuck."

Chuck gulped a shot of tequila while Tone did the introductions. His eye contact with me was short. All he said was, "Hey."

Never being a fan of men who didn't make and hold eye contact, I took the opportunity to go overboard in my greeting.

"Hey Chuck! How ya doin' fam!" I yelled. I waved at him just as Tone had waved at me.

Gabe called for everyone to join us at the table. They all stood as Gabe and I sat in the only available chairs. Everyone's attention was drawn to a large map of the city that was taped to the table.

"The new guy's an out of towner. He may need the visual," Gabe said, pointing to the map. "This is going to be simple. Our guy likes the executive protection package. In his mind, he's a big spender, who needs to be secure while moving from location to location. He typically goes to dinner, then to the Inter-Continental on St. Charles Street. We pick him up from the hotel, escort him to Harrah's—"

"It's only a few blocks away," Chuck interrupted Gabe with a shoulder shrug.

"That's right," Gabe said, moving his finger from the hotel to the casino on the map. "He texts me when his night is done and then we take him home. It's quick and easy."

After examining the map and reflecting on the plan Gabe shared, he must have sensed that I was less than thrilled with the plan. Maybe they all did.

"What?!" Gabe said. "This is a good plan."

I pursed my lips and squinted my right eye.

"I think the new guy..." Hayden said.

"...has a different idea," Jayden finished.

"Yes, it's a good plan. But I can't help but think it could be a little more theatrical. Maybe add a little flair to it. You said the guy likes to *feel* special, right?"

"Mmm hmm," Gabe said.

"Well then, for the money he's paying, make him feel special."

Tone did another shot of tequila rolled his eyes and said, "And how do you suggest we do that, new guy?"

I stood from the chair. I leaned over the map and examined it. "Is it too late to communicate a change of plans?"

Chuck, Tone, Hayden, and Jayden all huffed and groaned. But Gabe responded as if none of that happened.

"No," he said.

"Well then, let's get theatrical. Right now, it looks like it's just a cloud of men hovering around the man. The visual behind that is no different than a B-list celebrity with an entourage. Instead, let's use multiple cars. Two-way radios with earpieces.

"Start his night at his house instead of the hotel and play a shell game with him. He would probably love the air of misdirection. I'm suggesting Chuck and Tone pick him up from home and take him to the restaurant." I dropped my finger on the map in the French Quarter. "Right here. Dickie Brennan's Steakhouse on Iberville Street. It's upscale. Tell him it's gone through a full security protocol sweep, thereby 'guaranteeing' his safety.

"The two of you should park outside, where he can see you. It's all about perception, right? As soon as the dinner is over, take him to the hotel. At that point, we switch cars and coverage. That's where the twins will pick up the package and escort him to the casino.

"Once he's had his fun for the night, he texts Gabe, and we execute another coverage change to escort him home."

"That sounds like a lot," Hayden said.

"But it really isn't. And think about it, he wants to feel special. This will do it. Just the idea that he's getting this type of movement and protection might make his dick hard."

The men looked at Gabe as he pondered my suggestion.

"Ok, Mr. 'I don't fully know this city yet.' Let's do it," Gabe said.

The twins, Tone, and Chuck took their attention off of Gabe and set their gaze squarely on me.

Tone rolled his eyes. "You're the boss," he said.

Chuck walked over to the twins and grabbed a shot glass. "Well," he said, as he poured a drink. "If anything goes wrong..."

The twins interrupted in unison and said, "We'll just blame the new guy."

Chapter 16

Remo

Thursday, September 12th

Remo had been tracking down leads that ultimately brought him to the Fourteenth Street corridor, in the northwest section of DC. He heard that Red Lounge, a fairly well-known hookah bar was a frequent pitstop for Anthony, so he tried looking there first. He didn't have any luck. It was closed.

Remo stood on the corner. He looked around the busy intersection and inspected the different venues that were around. Remo then noticed a Tex-Mex restaurant across the street. There was a beautiful woman with smooth brown skin straightening up the outside seating area. She wore a fitted pair of black pants and a black dress shirt.

Remo looked at his watch. *One o'clock. I guess I can have a little lunch.*

Careful to track the oncoming traffic, he crossed the street.

Once inside and seated at the bar, Remo waved down a bartender. "I'll take a glass of red," he said. "Barolo, if you have it."

The bartender shook his head.

"Fine," Remo said. "Make it Merlot."

The bartender acknowledged his request with the nod.

Remo stood when the brown skinned beauty he observed outside approached him. The silver nametag, pinned to her shirt, spelled her name out in black ink. He pulled out a bar stool for her to have a seat.

"Hello, Krysti B," Remo said.

"Ok. I've got a little time."

Before either one of them could say another word, the bartender came back and placed a margarita in front of Remo. He shuttled off before Remo could grab his attention. It wasn't the red wine he ordered.

Krysti saw the confusion on Remo's face. "A margarita comes with every food order at the bar," she said.

Remo looked at the drink and then slid it over to Krysti. "I'll wait for the Merlot."

"You sure?" she said.

"Enjoy."

As Krysti took up the glass and sipped the drink without further hesitation, the bartender made his way back with Remo's wine.

"What can you tell me?" Remo asked.

"That's right! Anthony! Yeah, I used to see him a lot over there," Krysti pointed in the direction of Red Lounge. "Plenty of times, I would finish work and then head across the street for drinks and music."

"When was the last time you saw him?"

"Definitely over a year ago," Krysti said.

"That's what people are telling me. Gone for over a year. Ok, fine... but someone has to know where he is now."

"Could it be y'all are overlooking the obvious?" Krysti said between sips of her drink.

Remo knew what she meant.

"If he was dead," Remo responded, "I would have an easier time finding him."

"Sorry. That's all I've got for you."

Krysti pushed her bar stool away from the bar. Now standing, she gulped down the rest of the margarita. Krysti smoothed out her black pants and then waved down the bartender.

"Put this on my tab."

"That's kind of you," Remo said.

"No problem." Krysti walked off in the direction of the kitchen.

"Hey!" Remo called out. "You just said, 'Could it be y'all are overlooking the obvious?'"

"Yeah," she replied.

"Who's the *'y'all?'*"

Krysti shrugged, "Well... you're not the only one looking for Anthony. And what I shared with you is exactly what I told the other guy. "

Remo gave her a puzzled look.

"Timing is funny," Krysti said. "You're the second guy this week."

Chapter 17

Remo

T*he second guy this week?*

"What am I not seeing?" Remo mumbled to himself as he headed back to his car.

Remo parked a couple of blocks away from Red Lounge because he liked to walk. Since growing older, it was his way of building movement into his daily routine. He was also naturally paranoid and it was a great way to see if anyone was following him.

In cars, it's easy to lose track of a tail. But when walking, Remo could easily identify strangers and track them as they become familiar faces. Like the bald, clean-shaven Black male who had been behind him since he left the restaurant.

He appeared to be in his mid-thirties. It was hard for Remo to miss his six-foot two-inch frame. He was across the street and walked at a measured pace. The stranger's distance was consistent. He stayed about fifteen feet behind Remo.

Who is this person? Is he looking for Anthony too? Is he a professional?

Ultimately, Remo was trying to assess if he would have to

kill him. Questions ran through his head as he walked west on V Street.

Remo was only two minutes from his car. But at this point, he had more questions than answers and leaving without resolution was out of the question.

There was only one way to get the answers he needed. Remo took a deep breath.

"I guess it's time for a conversation," he said to himself.

Remo stepped off the curb. He walked across the street.

Chapter 18

Remo

Remo was now on the same side of the street as the man following him. He slowed the pace of his gait to the point where the guy lagged by only a couple feet. Remo reached in his pocket for the car key. When he pulled it out, he fumbled the key fob and dropped it on the ground. The stranger kept his pace. Just as Remo bend over to retrieve the car key, the man was about to pass him. The timing couldn't have been more perfect.

Without warning Remo swept the guy's leg to the front, causing him to fly in the air and land on his back. The back of his head smacked against the pavement. In that same motion, Remo grabbed the gun out of his ankle holster, leaving the car key on the ground.

Before the guy knew it, Remo was on top of him with all of his weight. Holding a gun under his chin.

"Amico, *friend...* you either start talking to me or in a minute, start talking to God. The choice is yours."

The man groaned. "I don't know what you're talking about! Get off me!"

"I'm giving you until the count of three."

"Damn man! I think I have a concussion! This shit is crazy!"

Remo rolled his eyes and exhaled deeply. "You know what... Three." He pulled the gun hammer back with the flick of his thumb.

"Wait! Don't shoot!" the guy shouted. "Ok! I was tailing you! But only because I'm looking for Anthony too. I overheard you talking to the waitress. I came by earlier in the week and I stopped by again to see if he had shown his face since. You were at the bar asking all the questions, so I came outside to wait for you to leave. That's the truth. I'm just looking for Anthony. That's it!"

"That's it." Remo echoed.

"Yeah... that's it."

He looked at the blood stream behind the man's head. Remo quickly ran his free hand over the guy's waist, back and ankles. He was unarmed.

"Are you alone?" Remo asked.

The unknown man furiously nodded.

Remo slowly lifted himself up and then pulled the man up from the ground.

Remo then looked around to see if they had drawn any attention.

"What's your name?" Remo asked.

"You don't remember—" he cut his words short. "They call me Beaux."

"Is that with an 'X'?" Remo asked.

Beaux smirked and nodded his head.

"Hmm... You don't look French. Well, listen here Beaux 'with an X,' you just came as close to death as you're ever going to get. Why don't you tell me why you're looking for Anthony? And I'll let you know if it's worth almost dying for?"

Beaux's reply was delayed by the ring of Remo's phone. He

looked at the caller ID and the number wasn't familiar. He held up a finger toward Beaux to put what he was about to say on pause.

"This is Remo," he listened intently. "Ok. Make sure the door is locked and stay away from the windows. Text me the address. I'm on my way."

Remo hung up the phone and then ran his hands along Beaux's pockets.

"Where's your phone?"

Beaux stepped back from Remo in resistance. But he also reached in his back pocket and yanked out his cell phone as a sign of compliance. He wasn't stupid.

Remo took a minute to dial his own number from Beaux's phone. Once it rang, he disconnected the call.

"Now I have your number. When I call, answer it. Don't make me come looking for you."

Remo reached down for the car key that was still on the ground. He brushed past the bleeding man as he walked to his car.

"Get the back of your head looked at."

Beaux watched as Remo hurried away. "Where are you going?"

"Don't worry about that. Just don't let me catch you following me again."

Remo sped off and Beaux stood on V Street. Bleeding.

Chapter 19

Beaux

A sense of relief washed over Beaux. His failed attempt at covertly following one of the most lethal men he had known didn't end in his death. That alone made it a good day. Beaux was also relieved that the man had not recognized him.

Maybe an acknowledgement of familiarity would come later. Maybe it wouldn't come at all. But one thing was for certain, Beaux needed to remain an unknown stranger to complete his assignment.

Heading back to his own car, Beaux brooded over the last time he saw Remo. The blood leaking down the back of his neck and staining his clothes only made him more committed to his goal. If he was successful, Anthony would be found and Remo would be put in the ground.

Beaux ultimately settled into the comfort of not being recognized, like he settled behind his steering wheel. With relative ease.

And why would Remo recognize me? Beaux thought to

himself. It's not like they actually met face-to-face. Beaux wasn't completely sure if Remo even knew of Beaux's existence. He had spent the better part of his life tracking Remo and not the other way around.

Beaux's one and only encounter with Remo came when he was fourteen years old. That's when he found out that the father he adored worked for a crime family... and Remo killed him.

His father claimed to work for a construction company but even at his young age, Beaux didn't buy it. He didn't know much about his father's work, only what his father told him. But he knew enough to know that hand-washing blood out of clothes nightly wasn't normal. Maybe Beaux's thinking was influenced by watching too many gangster movies.

Beaux's father reassured him that the hazards of construction work was the cause of the blood. But there was always so much of it. It didn't make sense.

The only thing that made sense to little Beaux was what he glamorized for so many years. Organized crime. Gangster movies. He had no idea what his father was wrapped up in, but in a sense, he knew.

Beaux set out one night to find confirmation. He wanted answers to his mind probing questions. Just like he followed Remo, he thought it would be a good idea to follow his father.

On that fateful night, Beaux snuck up to his bedroom window and watched his father standing outside of their apartment building. His father never looked back to see if he was being watched.

The rain was unforgiving as it pelted his father's umbrella, and it made the night darker than usual. Beaux's father was six feet and five inches tall. He weighed no less than two hundred and fifty pounds. He was imposing in stature and hard to lose in the nighttime murkiness. The man looked at his watch and then stepped off in the direction of Northeast DC. His old man didn't have a car, so he walked.

Beaux had to move quickly before he lost track of his father. He ran out his apartment, snatching his clear hooded poncho on the way out of the front door. Leaping down the staircase, three and four steps at a time, he cleared the three flights of the building in enough time to splash onto the sidewalk just as his father turned the corner.

Sticking to shadows and dark corners, careful not to be seen, Beaux crept behind his father all the way to his destination. *10th Street Auto Repair.*

"A car garage?" Beaux said to himself.

There was a blue and white sign centered above a gray garage door. They both accented the seafoam green brick structure with an alleyway along its left side. Beaux stood across the street and watched his father disappear into the alley.

There was a door for building access that Beaux's father used. Beaux carefully approached the door. It didn't have a window. Without seeing another way in, Beaux dashed around to the front of the garage. Standing in the rain, he examined the front of the garage, scouring for another access point.

Beaux saw a set of metal stairs that were outside of the building to the right. He ran up and to his surprise, the one-story structure had a small studio on it's top. And the studio had windows.

With his forehead pressed against the window, Beaux strained to see beyond the clouded glass. He tilted his head from side to side, trying to get a better view.

The room was barely large enough for the boxing ring at its center. Beaux was able to make out a lone punching bag suspended from the ceiling. The stuffing of the bag bulged against the frayed gray electrical tape wrapped around its body. There were free weights stacked near a bench and weight bar in the corner, opposite the punching bag.

Beaux couldn't hear what was taking place, but through the clouded glass, he watched it like a damaged movie.

Two men tossed each other around the studio. One was his father and the other was a man he had come to learn was Remo.

The much smaller Remo was no match for his father. In the few seconds Beaux had seen, Remo had been shoved up against the ring, then tossed into a shelf of boxing trophies, and punched so hard he stumbled onto his back.

Beaux's father would prevail and that gave the boy a sense of pride. He knew his father was a badass, but now he got to witness it.

Remo was slow to recover. When he finally came to his senses to turn over on all fours and scramble across the floor on his hands and knees, Beaux's father attacked the retreating man again. He dove at him. Now both men were on the floor.

They threw wild punches and kicks at each other. They rolled around. It looked like Beaux's father was trying to fight and Remo was trying to get enough distance between them.

That's right, coward. Run, Beaux thought. But then a chill went down his spine as the goal of Remo's retreat became clear. He wasn't trying to run, he was reaching for something beyond Beaux's view.

Beaux's father tackled the man again. This time, he had the upper hand and was in complete control. He had Remo pinned on his back. The fight was over, and Beaux's father could've ended it right then and there.

In an unexpected move, Beaux's father lifted his head. He scanned the room, maybe looking for something to restrain

Remo. And in the process of looking around, his eye passed the cloudy window.

Beaux's father locked eyes with an unmistakable face through the glass. He was staring at his son.

In that moment, the shock of realizing his son had followed him and witnessed everything that just happened paralyzed the man. And in that moment, Remo took advantage.

Remo thrusted his knee upward. He made contact with his opponent's testicles with such force that Beaux's father shrieked in agony.

Now free from the hulking man's grip, Remo bolted toward the item he had been reaching for. It was a gun.

Adrenaline must have kicked in for Beaux's father. In spite of the lingering pain, he pushed himself off the ground and charged at Remo.

It was all in slow motion for little Beaux. The rain. The running. The ring of the gunshot echoing through the air. Beaux gasped as he realized his father had been shot.

Stumbling toward the stairs, Beaux's father attempted a downward escape. Beaux could no longer see him. All he saw was Remo standing at the top of the stairs, aiming his pistol down, firing another shot.

Then Remo slowly and confidently took a step into the stairwell.

Hoping his father wasn't mortally wounded or dead, Beaux ran back down the outside set of stairs. He made his way to the corner of the building, next to the alley. After peeking around the corner, Beaux saw his father on the ground and lying on his back. His father's labored breathing terrified him.

The door was still open. Remo hadn't emerged from the building yet. And Beaux did the only think he could think of, he stepped into the alley to aid his wounded father.

The father watched as the son took three steps toward him.

Beaux's father mustered enough strength to yell out a one-word command to his oldest child. *Run!*

Beaux froze in his tracks. The message was heard, loud and clear. He took one final look at his father, turned around, and ran. Beaux didn't stop running until he got home.

And he never saw his father again.

Chapter 20

Remo

The evening sun parted through the nearly closed blinds. Dark yellow beams of light sliced through the room. Remo sat on a gray suede loveseat that was opposite a single chair of the same fabric. Metty sat in it with her legs crossed under her.

There were tear streaked mascara stains under her eyes. She had been crying. She wore a pair of navy-blue athletic shorts and a wrinkled black t-shirt. She was holding a ziplock bag full of ice up to her lip as water dripped down her arm.

"What happened?" Remo asked.

Metty's voice was muffled by her ice pack. Remo couldn't understand what she was saying.

"Do you mind?" he motioned for her to move the compress.

Metty slowly lowered her hand. Her eyes sank to the floor at the same time. Remo saw a small cut on her bottom lip. It was clear to him that she had never been smacked before. The ice pack was unnecessary, but understandable. The experience was most certainly traumatic for her.

"They came back. The ones you had the run in with the other night. But they weren't alone."

"The Romanians. They did this to you?"

"The woman brought her uncle and he had four men with him. They trashed the diner. The manager tried to reason with them. But the uncle ordered the men to rough him up too. I ran for the back door. One of his goons grabbed me and took me to the uncle.

"He wanted to know how to get to the person who assaulted his niece. I told him I didn't know. That's when one of his goons slapped me across the face."

Metty began to cry again, and I leaned forward.

"So let me get this straight. He wanted to find me?"

"Yes," Metty sobbed out.

"Shit!" Remo said.

He sprang off of the loveseat as if he had been shot out of a cannon. He ran over to the window and carefully peered out of an opening in the blinds he made with his fingers.

"Did I just walk into a set up?" he said. His hand rested on his waist for easy access to his gun.

"No!" Metty shouted. "I didn't tell them anything!"

"Then why am I here?" Remo demanded to know.

Metty willed her tears and sobbing to pause. "Because... I need your help. They said they would come back to the diner every day until I gave them information. I can't go through this every day. I need your help."

Remo considered the implications of her request. He knew that she couldn't go back to the diner. And if they knew where she worked, they probably knew where she lived. They may have been on their way to her place at that very moment. If she was left behind, she might as well have been as good as dead.

His eyes were still fixed outside of the apartment, scanning the street. Then it hit Remo. He had to help her. He was obligated.

"Why didn't you call someone else? Why me?" Remo asked.

Metty took a second before answering. "Because you were nice to me."

Remo looked back at Metty. "Well, pack everything you need in a duffle bag, Metasebia. You're coming with me."

No sooner than he finished his statement, she was on her feet and running into her bedroom. She ran between the bedroom and bathroom two or three times. It took all of fifteen minutes before Metty was packed and ready to go.

"Thank you so much," she said. They stood at the front door, ready to leave.

"No need to thank me. Perhaps I should be thanking you."

Befuddled, Metty asked, "Why?"

"You could've given them my number, but you didn't. You're either really dumb, or really loyal. I'm banking on the latter."

Chapter 21

Remo

Remo was staying at the Marriott Marquis in Mt. Vernon Square on Massachusetts Avenue. One room. One king sized bed. And now, one new guest staying along with him.

Since he had a tagalong, he needed to think and revise his plan. The running shower in the bathroom was helpful in that it drowned out the sounds of the street below, allowing him to focus on his thoughts.

Metty was looking more and more like a long-term project. *Maybe she could be put to work?* Remo thought. But how? With the Romanians after her, Remo shook that idea off. Then Remo acknowledged to himself that keeping the girl around meant the Romanians would also be tied around his ankle.

Remo had been in town for nearly a week, and he was no closer to finding Anthony. But he did find a new sidekick and a potential showdown. This wasn't what he expected.

He was jolted out of his thoughts by the sound of shuffling feet. Metty had walked out in what was probably her standard nighttime attire. She wore a pair of green, red, and blue flannel pajama pants. Her purple t-shirt bore the crest of Trinity Washington University, with *TRINTY* written to the left side.

Metty's unrestrained breasts couldn't have been larger than a handful. They wiggled against themselves as she walked. Remo's disciplined eyes didn't gawk.

Metty sat in the armchair next to the bed.

"What now?" she asked.

"I'm not sure."

"I'm sorry for messing everything up."

Remo shook his head. "This Romanian. He got a name?"

"Uziel. Mr. Uziel," she said.

"Is that his first or last name?"

Metty shrugged her shoulders.

"Okay, Mr. Uziel it is. I'm sure he gave you a number or something. To pass along when you found me."

Metty pulled her duffle bag into her lap and dug through it. After a couple of seconds, she found the folded piece of paper and gave it to Remo.

"Get some rest, young lady. The room is all yours. I'll see if they have another room on this floor."

Remo made his way to the door. He slung the DO NOT DISTURB door hanger on the outside door handle.

"Don't open the door for no one except me."

Metty's face flashed with fear. Remo could only guess that she didn't want to be alone.

"Don't worry," he said. "I won't be far."

* * *

Remo walked into the hallway, still holding the folded sheet of paper. He opened it and dialed the number from his phone.

He listened to four rings before the line was answered. The accent sounded like the couple at the dinner. Romanian.

"Hello," Remo said. "Is this Mr. Uziel? I heard you've been looking for me."

Chapter 22

Anthony

Gabe shuffled around a crowded restaurant. "This happy hour is packed." Gabe said.

"I know. People came out of nowhere tonight. Thursdays are usually quiet," I said.

"My shift is done, but I'll stay to help clean up."

"No need. I got it."

"I wasn't asking," Gabe said. "Besides, it's the least I could do. You're helping me out this weekend. I can help you out tonight."

I shrugged it off. "Ok. Speaking of this weekend... Sunday, right?"

"Yes sir."

I looked over at a mess of tables near the front door. "Since you're sticking around to help, take care of section two for me."

Gabe shot me a thumbs up and headed in that direction.

As he walked away, my phone chimed. A text message came in. It was from Coco.

Coco: *Hey hunni. I have GREAT news! We don't have to*

wait to see each other. Job is sending me back to NO for a conference. Last minute plan. I get to see my baby again!

Me: *That IS great news. When?*

Coco: *This weekend. Fly back in tomorrow. Hotel is paid for. I get reimbursed for the flight next week.*

This weekend, I thought to myself. The timing couldn't be worse.

Me: *This weekend is going to be really crazy for me.*

Coco: *And??? Are you saying you'll be too busy for me?*

Me: *Uhh... OF COURSE NOT!*

I had to change the direction I initially took the conversation, and in a hurry.

Me: *Just wanted you to be prepared to only see me Fri & Sat. Sun is a no go.*

Coco: *That's fine w/me. I come home Sun afternoon. Fri & Sat is good enough for me.*

Me: *Sounds good. Can't wait. See you tomorrow.*

My last response must have satisfied Coco. She replied with a brown thumbs up emoji.

I couldn't help but feel uneasy. Though unexpected, the fact that Coco was coming to town the very weekend I planned on helping Gabe felt ironic. She would be home by the time the action started, but it was still too close for my comfort.

Was the timing a sign? Should I pass on the Sunday night job with Gabe? The thought lingered. But it didn't matter because this time they would be no watching her leave from the perch of my window. I'll take her to the airport and walk her to the security checkpoint.

While the job is low risk, as Gabe put it, I wouldn't chance Coco being anywhere near the city when the time came.

For the sake of my nerves and my heart, she would be long gone and far away.

Chapter 23

Remo

Friday, September 13th

Remo walked down the street at a furious pace. Metty had a difficult time keeping up with him. He parked a few blocks away from the Seven-Eleven and they walked the rest of the way.

"Why couldn't you just pull into the parking lot?" Metty asked.

Remo didn't answer her. But he did slow down so she could catch up.

"Are you sure about this?" her voice quivered.

"Nervous?"

"Uh, yeah! I don't want to be anywhere near these people."

"Just do what we discussed and everything will be fine."

To calm her down, he took her arm in his.

"Ready?" Remo asked.

Metty stared at the front door as if she was about to walk through it and face a firing squad.

She took a deep breath. "Ready," she said.

Remo led her into the store. A bell rang from the unlocked door. The lights were off. There were tarps thrown over beige colored store shelves. Half-filled boxes were spread around the space. The store looked to be permanently closing.

Metty held Remo's arm even tighter. They passed three industrial refrigerators on their left. They were empty. There was a slightly cracked door that caught their attention a few feet in front of them. That's where they headed.

Just as they reached it, a man emerged. "Goon" was the only word that could be used to describe him. He extended his oversized hand, placing it on Remo's chest, in order to keep him at an arm's distance.

"Who are you?" His accent was thick and Romanian, like his boss's.

"You know who I'm here to see," Remo said.

A voice boomed from the other side of the door. "Gedeon! Let him in!"

"You heard the man," Remo said.

Gedeon took his time searching Remo. He didn't find a gun, but he did take Remo's wallet out of the inside blazer pocket. He opened it, read the contents, and then looked at Remo as if he was a puzzle to be solved.

Gedeon pushed open the cracked door to give Remo full entry into what appeared to be a stock room.

Pointing at Metty, Gedeon said, "She stays here."

Without looking back, Remo said, "No," and walked in the room.

Unsure of how to respond, Gedeon looked at Metty and then the back of Remo's head. He was already several feet ahead of Gedeon. All he could do was shrug his shoulders and concede.

"Sure thing... Mr. Ribisi."

Chapter 24

Remo

Remo took in the room with his eyes. Mr. Uziel stood over two individuals who were in chairs at a circular wooden table. The lighting was low. The room was sparse. The only other person present was Mr. Uziel's bodyguard. Remo was outnumbered but confident. Remo knew the numbers were still in his favor.

He looked at the couple seated at the table. The lady sneered, but her husband lowered his head and avoided eye contact.

"You two?!" Remo shouted. He pointed to the woman. "How's your nose?"

The woman's face went wide with shock. "The nerve!" she said to her uncle. "Uncle Uzzi-"

Mr. Uziel cleared his throat. "Mr. Ribisi, I would be careful if I were you. You are no longer relevant in Washington, DC. And this isn't New York."

"You're right. I'm not."

"Then for your own sake and the sake of the waitress... shut the hell up!"

Metty hadn't been paying much attention to the conversation. She fidgeted and looked around the room, searching for other exits. There were no other doors. She felt trapped.

Lost in her thoughts of despair, Mr. Uziel's thinly veiled threat snapped her back to what was going on.

Remo didn't like being yelled at. He didn't like it at all.

"Ok Uncle Uzzi... I'm only here to ensure that my dear girl is safe. Free from harm. You understand?" Nodding toward the couple, Remo said, "She, in no way, had anything to do with my altercation with them."

"Mr. Uziel," the crime boss said sternly. "My name is Mr. Uziel."

"I only want to have this conversation once, Uncle Uzzi." Remo motioned to Metty and continued. "Leave her alone. No more threats. Not from you, your family, or your—"

"My name is Mr. Uziel!" he shouted at the top of his lungs. His barreled midsection expanded and contracted with every breath. "You have no respect! You are nothing like your brother! How dare you come in here, giving orders and failing to extend the proper courtesy?

"Your waitress refused us information. For that alone, she should lose a hand!"

Gedeon wheeled out a small square shaped table. On the tabletop was a hammer, hatchet, rope, and black electrical tape.

"Just so you know, your waitress will lose a hand." Mr. Uziel turned to Gedeon, saying, "Bring her over here."

Gedeon walked toward Remo and the girl. Metty stood behind Remo. Remo stood as a fortress between the girl and Gedeon.

"Don't take another step," Remo said.

Gedeon stopped dead in his tracks and turned to look back at Mr. Uziel. By this time, Mr. Uziel had each hand placed on the sides of his stomach. He laughed uncontrollably. But Gedeon was frozen, waiting for direction.

"If your plan was to come in here, make threats and give demands, then Mr. Ribisi, you should have brought a gun."

Remo stood unfazed by the potential for mortal violence. "And you know what you should've done?" he said. "You should've searched the girl."

Before Mr. Uziel knew what was happening, before the couple could raise their voices in protest, and before Gedeon could move on Remo, they all lost the upper hand. From Metty's perfect position hidden behind Remo, she raised the front of her shirt, allowing Remo to snatch out a black Beretta, equipped with a silencer.

Remo pointed it at Gedeon and squeezed the trigger. It was one shot to the center of his body. He stumbled back and crashed to the floor.

The couple sat in shock. Remo looked at Metty and pointed to the rope. "Tie them up."

Remo then turned his attention to Mr. Uziel and stepped closer, with the gun leveled to his head. "Ok Uncle Uzzi, we need to talk."

Chapter 25

Anthony

Coco was back in New Orleans for her work trip. She and I walked through Jackson Square in the French Quarter, waiting for the time of our dinner reservation. It was as perfect time as ever to throw a curveball at me.

“Soooo... I’ve been thinking,” she said. “How would you feel if I moved?”

I wasn’t sure if I heard her clearly and asked her to repeat herself. She did. The thought of her relocating stopped me in my tracks. A bench was within feet of us near St. Louis Cathedral. I took the opportunity to sit down. Coco wasted no time in joining me.

"You're thinking about moving down here?" I asked.

"Mmm hmm."

"Don't get me wrong. I love you. Truly I do. But moving down here, just to be with me, doesn't make much sense."

"I guess that's why they don't call it 'falling in sense.' And when you think about it, has anything ever made sense?

"The circumstances that brought you to New Orleans

didn't make sense. Do you really want to reason your way through this?"

We sat no longer than a minute in silence. Well, in thought, for me. She was right. What made sense about the two of us being together? I'm sure any other woman whose life was threatened because of her association with another person would simply write that person off and never look their way again.

But after the shootout, the fire, Marco's death and my disappearance, here she was. She was still willing to allow me the privilege of being in her life. All I had to do was promise that I would never put her in danger again. And that was a promise I would die to keep.

"Hypothetically, when would this move happen?" I asked.

"Hypothetically," Coco mocked. "I'd do it in six months. That's enough time to downsize, pack, find a new place here, and hopefully a job. I'm not too worried about work. Good therapists are hard to come by. I'm pretty sure I can come across something."

Silence returned for a few seconds. *Hypothetically* my ass, I thought. She had a plan.

"Give me some time to think about it." I finally said.

"What do you need to think about?" she said incredulously. "Weekly visits," Coco said, "*Those* aren't sustainable. And they don't make sense. In order for our relationship to work and have any future, either I need to move down, or you need to come home. And you are a much better *you,* when you're here.

"You're a different man in New Orleans. We get to spend time with each other in public. You can walk the streets and be lost in a crowd without fear of being shot, I might add. Just two unknown and nameless people, lost in a crowd. It's perfect!

"And let's not forget that *you* left *me.* No warning. Not as much as a goodbye note. You just left. And if it wasn't for a freak accident, we wouldn't even be sitting here together. So don't tell me that you need some time to 'think about it.' You don't get to do that to me. You've already done too much."

You've already done too much, was suspended in my ears. Again, she was right. I spent time convincing her to move me from friend-zone to boyfriend. In the process, we became attached to each other. We fell in love, only for me to throw it away and then have a freak accident, as she put it, bring us back together again.

* * *

I had been in New Orleans for a year and three months. I had a place to live, a job to work, and developed a good friendship with Gabe. In my mind, my disappearing act had been a success. By this time, I only occasionally thought about the life I left behind.

I was at work on this particular day and Spence, the Cafe Roma delivery driver, had called out sick. As a result, I had to do the only thing that I had come to hate since moving down. And that was be the substitute delivery driver.

To add insult to the injury of a humongous food order, it had to be delivered to the city. Metairie deliveries were halfway manageable. But the ones that really got under my skin were the rides into New Orleans.

The party of forty-five was at a small bed and breakfast on Prytania Street in the Garden District. They ordered mozzarella sticks, spicy chicken wings, chicken fingers, six large Caesar salads, six large Italian salads, and ten extra-large pizzas. It was a lot to load, haul, unload, and then I ultimately had to make my way back to the restaurant.

To make matters worse, this was no ordinary weekend. It was the Fourth of July weekend. And with the Fourth of July, came the annual Essence Festival, which is one of the nation's largest music festivals. For these reasons, I didn't want to make the delivery.

I felt like I was carrying a feast for a clan from Game of Thrones and I'd have to fight through traffic like it was the Hunger Games.

The job took most of the afternoon. A sweat soaked t-shirt clung to my body as I loaded the food into the van and then set out to battle traffic. What was ordinarily a twelve to fifteen minute drive took an hour and a half.

Without incident, I completed the delivery and then headed back to the restaurant. I hadn't even crawled two blocks before my phone rang. "Cafe Roma" flashed across the glowing screen.

"Hey man," Gabe said, "How far are you from the shop? What's your ETA?"

"Are you joking?" I said.

"Ok, you're still in the city then? Alana got busy and didn't charge the order until a minute ago. She either mixed up the numbers or they gave her a bad card."

"Have her call them and get it fixed," I said.

Gabe hesitated. "Well... she messed up the phone number too. Did it work for you when you got there?"

"Didn't need to call. They were out front setting up tables," I huffed into the phone. "I'm turning around."

I hung up the phone without waiting for a response.

Sitting at a red light at the corner of St. Charles and Erato, my impatience got the best of me. As soon as the light turned green, I honked at the two cars in front of me. The car that was at the light must have gotten the point. They pulled off and made a right turn on St. Charles. But it was obvious that the car immediately in front of me didn't.

I expected them to drive straight or make a turn, but instead, they inched out into the intersection.

By the time my brain registered how slow they were going, it was too late. My foot had already pressed firmly on the gas pedal.

What happened next shouldn't have been a surprise. The front of my delivery van collided with the back of the car in front of me.

Five minutes later, I was standing behind what appeared to be a car full of women, in town for the festival.

The driver hopped out wearing a yellow and white sleeveless maxi dress. Her skin shimmered like crystalized honey. Around her neck, hung a red Essence Festival lanyard with a rectangular laminated media pass that read *PRESS*.

Taking a quick minute to inspect the damage on the vehicles. It was negligible on my end. But the bumper of the car had a football sized dent. Surprisingly, the driver wasn't upset.

"They're going to stop offering me insurance on these rentals," she said as she leaned against her car.

"My damage isn't worth a claim," I said. "What about you? You want my info?"

"Don't need it. The rental is fully covered. I can bring this thing back on two wheels, with a missing door, and walk away without a care," she paused. "But if you feel like you just *have* to give me your info, we're here for a couple more days." She motioned to the other women in the car before continuing.

"I work for a radio station in DC and got all access credentials for the crew. If you want, you can come hang with us. Bring some friends. I have extra passes."

I caught everything she was throwing. But I wasn't sure if I wanted to be stuck babysitting festivalgoers for the rest of the weekend. On the other hand, the young lady had every right to call the cops, file a report, and call the insurance company over our run in. Careful not to appear rude or ungrateful, I suggested an alternative plan.

"That sounds good. But I'll be working like crazy for the next few days." It wasn't a lie. "Why don't you give me the best number to reach you? When I'm free, we can plan something."

"Let me get my card," she said as she walked back to her car.

I turned around and headed to the van as well. After three steps, I heard my name called. "Jelani!"

I thought it was weird because I didn't recall telling the woman my name. How did she know my...?

"Jelani!" was screamed again.

But this time it made sense. The sound was familiar. My name was no stranger to the cadence that called it. I knew the inflection.

I slowly turned around to see the driver of the car standing near the front door. And climbing out the back door was the frame of someone I ghosted long ago. It was Coco.

She looked as beautiful as the last time I saw her. She ran to me, and I didn't know what to expect, so I stood there. Coco wrapped both arms around my body and squeezed out what little air was left in me.

"Oh my God! Oh my God!" she shouted.

Her words melted into tears. By this time, the entire car had emptied out. The four other women watched with opened mouths, not able to comprehend what was going on. They didn't understand why Coco cried hysterically while she clung to me. A virtual stranger who just rammed the back of their car.

How is it that out of all the people visiting New Orleans during Essence Festival weekend, I would *run into* the main person I had been avoiding? Literally.

* * *

Coco and I took a break from pondering what-ifs and started reminiscing about that fateful day. The delivery. The girls trip. The car accident. The reconnection. And how it led to this very weekend.

And if it wasn't for a freak accident, we wouldn't even be sitting here together, she had said earlier.

She was right. I couldn't be the one to stand in the way of our future. Not again. Not this time. If fate brought us back together, who was I to stand in its way?

"Ok," I said.

Cautiously monitoring her optimism, she sheepishly repeated, "Ok?"

I nodded my head, "Yeah. Ok. Let's do it. I would love for you to move down."

Coco sat next to me but jumped in the air and landed in my lap. She kissed and hugged me. The smile beaming from her face told me we made the right decision.

"I was selfish to leave you. I was wrong to distance myself. The best thing that's happened to me since I've been here was running into your friend's car. So yeah, come on down. But first, let's eat."

Chapter 26

Remo

The stock room of the Seven-Eleven had fallen quiet. Remo was in complete control. Metty tied the couple to their chairs and placed the electrical tape over their mouths. The wife struggled a little bit against the ropes, but it was useless. Metty did a surprisingly excellent job tying the knots.

Remo pulled an empty chair in front of Mr. Uziel and sat down. With his gun aimed at the portly man.

Remo said, "Sit."

Mr. Uziel fell back and slumped into his seat. The brow of his forehead was furrowed. His round jaw was clenched.

"You're going to pay for—" Mr. Uziel said before he was cut off.

"Shut up," Remo said. "This meet and greet has been nice, but I want to talk about more important matters. I'm looking for Anthony."

"What are you talking about? I don't know anything about Anthony Ribisi!" he said.

"Well, I have it on good authority that you do," Remo

bluffed. He then cocked his gun. "Let's try this again. Where is he?"

The seriousness of the situation settled in. Mr. Uziel shifted in his seat.

"Wait...wait...wait! Come on man. Put the gun down. Let's talk about this."

Remo shook his head from side to side. He then walked back to the couple still tied in the chairs. Remo stuck the barrel of the gun against the shoulder of the rope-bound man.

"I'm going to count to three. Either talk or it'll be physical therapy appointments for him from now until he dies."

The man was frozen in his seat but eyes widened in shock. His wife bucked against the ropes in a poor attempt at kicking and screaming.

"One..." Remo said.

"Please!" Mr. Uziel begged.

"Two..."

"I swear on my wife and kids, I don't know anything about Anthony!"

"You know what..." Remo said to himself, but loud enough to be heard throughout the room. He moved the gun from the man's shoulder to forehead. "Three."

"WAIT!" Mr. Uziel yelled at the top of his lungs. The scream took all his breath. He was wheezing for air and panting like a dog after a long walk on a hot day.

"I'm listening."

"Look, I don't have any information on Anthony. Nobody has seen the man since after your brother's restaurant went up in flames. But I heard that Johnnie set up a few gambling houses in Maryland. He's been slowly trying to rebuild his father's legacy..."

"But..."

"But there have been challenges. Every house has been

robbed. People have been killed. And I heard no one in his camp can get a handle on it.

"Johnnie has people looking for Anthony too. He would kill to have him in his corner again. With Anthony, your nephew can rebuild the gambling business without fear of being robbed. He needs Anthony, at the very least, for security.

"His hangout is off of New York Ave. Queens Chapel Road, I believe."

"Johnnie's been a feckless imbecile ever since he was a kid. It's a miracle he hasn't gotten himself killed yet," Remo said.

"Nevertheless, I bet the lives of my family that Johnnie's been looking for Anthony. Whatever he's found out will bring you closer to finding him. I'm sure of it."

"The lives of your family, you say? Let's see how much you mean that."

Remo turned his attention back on the bounded couple. With two quick shots, he put a bullet in each of their heads. Their bodies slumped as blood poured down their bodies, staining their clothes red and puddling on the floor beneath them.

Mr. Uziel screamed and surged forward in agony. He launched his body out of the chair and landed on his knees. All he could do was stretch his arms out to his dead family members.

Remo cocked his gun again walked to the sobbing man. He took a fist full of hair, pulled him off the ground, and stuck the gun under his chin.

"You need to clean this mess up and get rid of the bodies. I know you have the means. From now on, you'll leave Metty alone. If anyone comes near her, me, or anyone else I'm halfway fond of, I'm coming back. And next time, it's your mother and grandfather."

Mr. Uziel was too distraught to respond, but Remo knew that the message was received.

"Don't be too upset, Uncle Uzzi..." Remo let go of Mr. Uziel. He turned around, grabbed Metty by the hand and started making his way for the exit. "I'm feeling generous. That's why your wife and kids aren't part of the deal. They're safe, for now."

Chapter 27

Remo

Remo and Metty walked back to the car. The Seven-Eleven was already in the distant past. The shock of witnessing the murder of two people wore off quickly for Metty. Maybe it was her desire to see Uziel pay for what he had done to her. But whatever it was, she quickly adjusted to her new reality.

Remo was first to break the quiet between them. "Alright hun. It seems we're at the end of our road. I think you're safe now."

"What do you mean?!" Metty shot back.

"Uziel has been handled," Remo said. "Now you can forget about gangsters, gambling houses, and guns. Go home. Have a nice life."

Remo's word felt like an offense to Metty. They stopped her in her tracks. She held an incredulous look on her face.

"You've gotta be kidding me! What am I going to do now? I don't have a job to go back to. No real friends. And my family can't do anything for me."

Remo kept walking, so Metty yelled, "Where am I supposed to go?!"

Remo called over his shoulder and he caught a glimpse of Metty. "Don't be so dramatic. You can always go home."

In that moment, he saw a lost little girl.

Pity made Remo stop walking. He turned to face her.

"Why do you want to stick around?" he asked.

Metty searched for an answer. "I don't know. I just feel safer when I'm with you. That's all I know."

It became Remo's turn to search for a response. He didn't have one.

Remo looked at his watch. "Ok," he said.

Metty's sadness turned to glee. She ran to Remo and wrapped her arms around him.

"Thank you!" she exhaled out.

"Don't thank me yet. If you're going to stick around, you'll have to work. Starting tomorrow, you're going to help me find Anthony."

"How... how am I going to do that?" she stuttered.

Remo pulled out his cell phone and dialed. "By doing exactly what I tell you."

Chapter 28

Beaux

Saturday, September 14th

Metty and Beaux drove up New York Avenue, headed towards Bladensburg Road. Their car stopped at every red light along the way.

"Are you for real?" Metty chuckled. "You spell with an 'X,' huh? What are you, French or something?"

"Why does everyone keep asking that?" Beaux said.

"Never mind. Your response tells me everything I need to know." She continued laughing.

"Whatever. Just keep your eyes open for Johnnie."

Beaux drove five miles below the speed limit. He was going just fast enough to not get on the nerves of the drivers behind him, and not so fast as to garner unwanted attention.

"Any idea why Remo is so interested in finding Anthony?" Beaux asked.

"I didn't bother asking," Metty said. "All I know is that this Johnnie fella is probably looking too. So now we're keeping an eye out for both."

The car slid to a stop at another red light.

"What about you?" Metty asked. "What's the interest?"

"Anthony and I go way back. And I'm having some problems."

"And what, he can help you sort them out?"

"Something like that."

The car pulled away from the intersection.

"Is that a Taco Bell?" Metty said, pointing up a block ahead.

"Looks like it. You hungry?"

"No," she said. "I've got to tinkle, and I've been holding it."

"Tinkle?!" Beaux said with a laugh. "Say no more."

Beaux made the right turn into the parking lot and backed into a space. "Don't take forever, please."

Metty rolled her eyes as she opened the door. She slammed it hard enough to rock the car.

Sitting in the parking lot, Beaux started scrolling through different radio stations. Frustrated that he couldn't find anything that he wanted to listen to, he looked up to notice the McDonald's across the street.

"That's where I need to be," he murmured to himself.

And that's when he saw him. Or at least he thought he did. He lifted the cover off the arm rest compartment and shuffled through the contents until he found it. Pulling out a four by six photo, he held it up.

"Shit. Johnnie Ribisi? Yeah. I see you."

Beaux grabbed the camera sitting in the back seat and watched Johnnie through the lens. Johnnie walked out of the McDonald's with four bags of food, hopped into a waiting car, and sped up the street. But not before Beaux could write down the license plate number. He shoved the piece of paper in his pocket.

Beaux exited his car and continued watching Johnnie's vehicle through the lens, until it made its way up New York Avenue. He watched as the car made a right turn and was then out sight.

Just as Beaux got back in the car, Metty came out of the Taco Bell. She rushed toward the car, drying her hands with brown paper towels.

Once Metty was settled, Beaux started the car.

"Ok," Metty said, "did I miss anything?"

Beaux glanced at her quickly and then back to the road as he was pulling out of the parking lot.

"Miss anything?" He repeated. "No ma'am. Not a thing."

Chapter 29

Anthony

Sunday, September 15th

We agreed to meet on Reynes Street. It came to a dead end, and I sincerely hoped that wasn't ominous foreshadowing. I sat a wooden bench atop a knoll that led back down to the street. In front of me was the Mississippi River. If I wanted to, I could have stepped right into the water. I watched the river water slosh against the rocks beyond the grassy levee.

Behind me and at the bottom of the hill was the Lower Ninth Ward. Turning around to see that the height of the riverbank towering over the community below left me feeling uneasy.

Renovated houses were scattered between dilapidated shacks and grass covered lots. Devastation from the Katrina flooding was inescapable. After the hurricane, water rushed down this very same hill into the community below. It virtually created a lake, covering neighborhood.

"Jesus," I said aloud. The thought of it gave me chills.

I stood from my seat and looked to my right at the Central Business District off in the distance. The night was illuminated by the skyline. All the buildings burned with light. The beauty of downtown New Orleans and its business district was on full display.

My attention was diverted to three cars driving towards me. The first car came to a stop and Gabe hopped out. We walked toward each other. I walked down the hill as Gabe walked up.

"Early, I see," Gabe said.

I nodded my head.

The other two cars rolled to a stop as well. No one exited. I assumed the twins were in one car, and Chuck and Tone were in the other.

"I'm here. That's all that matters," I said.

We walked past my car, which I left behind, and opened the doors to his.

"Yup," he said. "That's all that matters."

We sank into our car seats, shut the doors, and then drove back down Reynes Street.

As we drove away, I turned around for another look. I couldn't shake the frightening thought of being chased by an overflowing river.

Chapter 30

Chuck & Tone

Chuck drove up in front of Dickie Brennan's Steakhouse. Tone had already spotted Mr. Rookard standing out front. The man was impeccably dressed. He wore a white and gray seersucker suit, accented by a lavender bowtie.

Tone exited the car and escorted the man to the back passenger door. "Good evening, Mr. Rookard," he said. "Enjoy your dinner?"

"I sure did. It was perfect," Mr. Rookard said. "You guys have outdone yourselves." He slid in the car. The first thing the overcautious man did was look for the seat belt.

Once Tone was back in the car, he checked his watch and nodded at Chuck. They were off to the hotel.

Chapter 31

Mr. Rookard

Mr. Rookard stood outside of the Intercontinental Hotel on St. Charles Street. He had already run up to his suite. The man was quick. He was so fast that he was back down before Chuck and Tone could drive away. The only change was now he sported a black aluminum attaché case. One side of a pair of shackles was connected to the handle of the case. The other side was tightened around his wrist.

Mr. Rookard tugged against the cuff as he watched Chuck and Tone disappear into the night. This happened as the twins arrived. And before he knew it, Hayden was already out of the car and opening a door for him.

Hayden looked at the handcuff and said, "Looks like you have some new jewelry this month, huh?"

"Of sorts," Mr. Rookard said with a smile. "With the new security plan, I felt like I wanted to gamble a little differently tonight. I'm bringing the big guns out!"

After patting the briefcase, he took his position in the back seat. Hayden smiled back at the man through the tinted widow.

"Nothing wrong with a little change of plan," Hayden said out loud. "Absolutely nothing."

Chapter 32

Anthony

Gabe and I patiently sat in our car a block away from the Harrah's Casino. When it was time, we'd drive around to the front and collect Mr. Rookard. But first, Chuck and Tone would take the man to the hotel. The twins were responsible for getting Mr. Rookard from the hotel to the Casino.

"Let me ask you something," I said. I didn't wait for him to answer. "How long you been working with these guys?"

"Why does that matter? I've only been working with you for a short amount of time. Why don't you ask what you really want to know?"

"Which is?"

"Do I trust them? And I do. We've done a lot of work together over the years. They haven't failed me yet."

"I guess. But Chuck and Tone... I'm not too sure about that pair."

Gabe grabbed the handheld radio, switched to a different channel, and began speaking. "Gemini, come in."

After a few seconds, the response came blaring from the unit. "This is Gemini, how can I help you?"

"What's your status?" Gabe said.

"Sitting outside the hotel. The po'boy is being delivered. Wild Boys just pulled up with him."

"Copy," Gabe said. He tossed the radio to the side. "I'm not too sure about that pair either. That's why the twins have kept their eyes on them since they picked Rookard up from home.

"Just like your Washington, DC politicians say, *trust... but verify*. I always verify and they always come through."

Chapter 33

Mr. Rookard

Once inside the massive king suite on the twenty-fourth floor of the Harrah's Casino and Hotel, Mr. Rookard took in his surroundings. The expected trappings of a luxury hotel suite were present. There was a plush white sofa and armchair set with four red accent pillows in the center of the room. The wet bar behind it was stocked with every kind of alcohol imaginable. There was also soda, San Pellegrino, multiple three-hundred-dollar bottles of Gaja Sperss barolo wine, and Dom Perignon.

After a minute, Mr. Rookard spotted what he was looking for. It was a gray floor safe in the southwest corner of the room. There was a rectangular cherrywood table in front of it. And between the safe and the table stood the pit boss and cage cashier.

Mr. Rookard wasn't on a traditional casino floor. Because of this, the curated space made every effort to provide as close of an authentic gambling experience as the real thing. Even if it was only the four players in the room.

He placed his attaché case on the table and in front of the

casino employees. Retrieving a silver key from the inside pocket of his blazer, Mr. Rookard freed himself from the cold steel against his wrist. He laid the case down, spun the numbers on the combination wheel, and in a matter of seconds, lifted the top to expose the beauty inside. Diamonds.

The contents were protected by black foam. Each diamond was set in its own perfectly fitted hole. There were three of them. The center diamond was ten carats, and it was flanked by two smaller five carat stones. A battery-operated light flickered from the top part of the open case and beamed down as soon as it was opened. The light perfectly reflected from the diamonds in every direction, leaving both men at the table with their eyes wide in amazement.

"I call them the Holy Trinity," Mr. Rookard said.

He nodded to the pit boss, giving him permission to inspect the jewels. From under the table, the pit boss pulled a gemscope and mini diamond carat scale.

One by one, the pit boss placed the diamonds under the gemscope and then onto the scale to confirm their size. After careful examination, he returned each of the stones to their positions in the case.

He looked at the cage cashier. "Give Mr. Rookard a million in chips."

Without delay, the cage cashier provided the gambler with a tray of chips totaling the requested amount. At the same time, the pit boss closed and locked the attaché case, turned around and placed the case into the safe that was behind him. Mr. Rookard watched until he was certain that his diamonds were secured inside. Then he walked off to the awaiting table of gamblers.

"Gentlemen," the dealer said, "you all already know the house rules."

It was a statement, not a question. And everyone nodded in unison.

"Great. Then let's play some blackjack."

* * *

After nearly three hours, Mr. Rookard was no longer the fashionably dressed man who started the night. His tie was gone. His shirt was unbuttoned to the point where it exposed a white v-neck t-shirt underneath. His eyes were red from alcohol consumption and his hair was disheveled.

The pit boss walked by and looked over Mr. Rookard's shoulder.

"Looking kinda low on chips, Mr. Rookard. Do you need to make a trip to the cashier?"

Mr. Rookard couldn't tell if it was concern or condescension in the man's voice. Either way, he didn't like it, so he didn't reply.

That's when the pit boss followed up with what Mr. Rookard knew for certain was condescension. "Oh well, that's ok. I'm sure you can just pray to your Holy Trinity. I wonder which will help you, the Father, the Son, or the Holy Ghost."

Chapter 34

Anthony

Mr. Rookard sat in the back of the car as I drove away from the casino. His face was stoic. I couldn't read his mood. He slumped in his seat.

"Everything ok with you back there?" I asked.

Mr. Rookard didn't respond. I looked over to Gabe.

"Must not have had a good night," Gabe said.

I shrugged off Mr. Rookard's demeanor. I drove up Canal Street toward City Park because that's where Gabe instructed me to go.

Gabe told me that our passenger had a lady friend he liked to end his night with after his time at Harrah's. Sometimes he went home, sometimes he went to his friend's.

She was about to be very disappointed, I thought to myself.

We hadn't been rolling for long. We had just come to the corner of Canal and Carondelet and the dazed man spoke.

"That shit was crazy." Mr. Rookard struggled to lean forward in his seat. "It was surreal."

I let the man talk.

"I'm a cash man, but tonight I was inspired. I tried something different."

"The case?" Gabe asked.

"Yeah. The case. And it's worth..."

"It'll be ok," I said, looking at our passenger in the rearview mirror. "You can always get it back next month."

"Next month? No sir. I'm good."

He lifted the case from the floorboard so that it was visible.

"I almost lost these bad boys tonight. I'm taking my diamonds, my extra million, and I'm never doing that again!"

"Wow!" I said. "You actually ended up on top! Good for you. How'd you do it?"

"I don't know," Mr. Rookard said. "I was so deep in, I thought everybody was counting cards except—"

Mr. Rookard's statement was cut short by the explosion of glass. The back window burst into countless tiny shards. I felt a bullet whizz past my head. It left a perfect bullet hole in the windshield in front of me.

At the sound of the shot, Gabe jerked the car to the left and then brought it back to make a hard right turn at the corner.

We both whipped our heads around to see a black minivan barreling behind us. The van moved faster by the second.

Both Gabe and I held our breath and watched until the black minivan did the inevitable. It made a right turn behind us.

Chapter 35

The Minivan

Inside the black minivan were two men dressed in black denim jeans, black long-sleeved t-shirts, and black boots. Both men covered their entire head and face with opaque black stockings to conceal their identity. They also wore black latex gloves. As if that wasn't enough, black androgynous costume masks further concealed their identities.

As the minivan made the corner, the driver banged his fist against the protruding dashboard in frustration.

"Stop that fucking car!" the driver yelled.

The driver had great control of the vehicle, allowing them to catch up to the car they sped behind. They were nearly side by side.

The passenger hesitated slightly. Then he unbuckled his seatbelt and quickly dove headfirst into the second row of seats. Now in the second row, the passenger buckled himself up again. This time, without hesitation, he wrapped his hand around the door handle and yanked the sliding door open.

Carefully leaning out of the speeding minivan, the

passenger took aim at the back driver-side tire of the car. Three shots was all it took.

There was a loud screeching of tires against the asphalt. The sound of metal and fiberglass crunching rang through the night air.

"Hold on!" the driver yelled.

The second-row passenger held on for his life as the driver hit the brakes and did a complete one hundred and eighty degree spin. They now faced the car they once pursued.

The car was up against the sidewalk and wrapped against a tree. It was time for the masked men to get their prize.

Chapter 36

Anthony

Gabe swore loudly. He wrestled with the seat belt until he was able to unlatch it. Looking over his shoulder, Gabe called out to his passenger, "Rookard?"

Nothing. There was silence.

I was low in my seat and couldn't see our client. The quiet in our car made me uneasy. "Mr. Rookard!" I yelled out. "Are you still with us?!"

Still... no response. Not a sound. At least not one I was looking forward to.

The nighttime street was just as quiet as our car, until I heard the sliding of minivan door. It opened just as quickly as it was slammed shut. Then there were footsteps. They shuffled closer and closer to the crash site.

I wanted to know what was going on with our client, so I popped up just long enough to spy a glance.

Mr. Rookard had to be in shock. The chase. The bullets. The crash. He was face down against the floor of the car. His body now suffered from uncontrollable tremors.

I didn't see blood and he didn't look to be injured. Convinced that he was still alive, I threw my body back into my hiding position.

On the way back down, I saw them. Dressed in all black, approaching the car, and thrusting their firearms in our direction.

"Shit! Probably about thirty yards away," I said.

Bullets smacked against metal and obliterated the windows.

Gabe crouched so low he could've been under the steering wheel. He groaned in frustration.

"That means thirty yards until they light our asses up. Would certainly be nice if we could shoot our way out of this. But nope. Somebody didn't want to carry guns. Ain't this a bitch?"

"Maybe when they stop to reload, we can make a run for it?"

Gabe shook his head. "We won't get ten feet."

He was right. We were trapped.

That's when the bullets stopped and one of the men yelled out to us.

"I'm going to count to three! By that time, one of you needs to walk that briefcase out to us! I don't care who it is! Give us the briefcase and you live! If not, you all die!"

"They're going to kill us anyway," I said.

Gabe was lost in his thoughts. He didn't hear a word I said.

"I know that voice." He said incredulously. "I can't believe this!"

Gabe slung open his door and flopped out of the car. He landed on his back and then struggled to get to his feet.

Instinct kicked in and I sprang after him.

Not being bulletproof, I had know idea how I would help him if bullets started flying again. But there I was with Gabe. Instead of sitting, we were now standing ducks.

Staring at the masked men, Gabe's fists were clenched. He was enraged.

"Hayden?! Is that you?!"

The men looked at each other and then back at us. They simultaneously pulled their masks off. Shear black stockings stood between us and their faces. We could easily see, it was the twins.

Hayden and Jayden. While Gemini was keeping an eye on Chuck and Tone, no one was keeping an eye on Gemini.

"The case!" Hayden said.

"And the money!" Jayden added.

I could smell Gabe's anger like it was a post workout stench. His red face and eyes told me that his blood was boiling.

"One!" The twins counted in unison.

"Gabe?" What's the play here man?"

He was silently focused.

"Two!"

"Gabe!" I said again.

"Three!"

That's when two shots rang out. There was a slight pause and then two more.

Both Hayden and Jayden let out agonizing cries. Their knees exploded as they toppled over.

Their guns flew out of their hands and clacked across the ground, a few feet away from their bodies.

I snapped my head in the direction of the gunfire expecting to see Chuck and Tone, or worse, the cops. But I didn't see anyone.

It took a second, but I was finally able to make out a hulking man standing in the shadow, against a much larger tree. He stepped out, placing a handgun back in its holster.

It was the face of a man I hadn't seen in years. Smitty had

just saved our lives. I don't know if I had ever been as happy to see him. Gratefully elated, couldn't describe the emotions I felt. And then out of nowhere, gratefulness turned into confusion.

I was lost, trying to figure out how in the hell he found me.

Chapter 37

Anthony

Back at the Reynes Street levee, Smitty and I listened as the Mississippi River sloshed against the rocks.

"Anthony, you need to come home. I booked a flight for tomorrow morning."

"What's this about?" I asked.

"Does it matter? I'm here and I'm letting you know that you need to come home."

"Well, thanks for visiting. But this is my home now. I hope you have a nice ride back to DC."

I turned to walk back to my car.

"You don't get it, do you?" Smitty said.

I continued walking until I got to my car and reached for the door handle.

"Anthony," Smitty said as I opened the door. Then as if he reached down from the bottom of his diaphragm, what came next sent a chill down my spine.

"Jelani Anthony Jones!" The bellowed yell was probably heard blocks away. "Don't you dare disrespect me!"

At that moment, I froze. Partially out of respect, but mostly out of fear of what would happen if I didn't. I then turned around to face Smitty. By the time my body spun, he had already closed the distance and was towering over me.

"Everything has gone to shit since you left," Smitty said, "and Johnnie can't fix it. He can't put the pieces back together again. Either he doesn't know how or doesn't want to admit it. Either way, that makes him a danger to himself and everything he touches.

"I've finally gotten him to a place where he can accept that he needs your help."

"Are *you* asking me to come back or is Johnnie asking?"

"Wrong question."

"Ok," I said, shrugging off Smitty's misdirection. "Then let's start this from the beginning. How did you find me?"

"Ahh..." Smitty said. "Now you're asking the right question."

Gabe's car crept down the dead-end street and pulled up behind mine. He hopped out with a messenger bag. He approached the two of us and handed me the bag. When I looked in, I saw that it was filled with twenty, fifty, and one-hundred-dollar bills.

"Seems a little heavier than expected," I said.

"Yeah. Suddenly we had fewer people to split it with."

"The twins?"

"Yeah... they had to run to Scotland or something to handle some family business. They won't be back here for a very long time. If ever.

"The nerve of those guys. Come to find out, the dealer from the private game would text them whenever someone hit it big. The twins have been robbing players for months! Just so happened that when they got word Rookard kept his diamonds and made extra money, they decided to go rogue."

After giving me the bag, Gabe brushed passed me and walk up to Smitty. He extended his right hand.

"Thank you. Was good as dead if you hadn't shown up when you did. You looking for work, big man?"

They shook hands.

"Don't mention it. And no, I've already got a job."

Breaking up their little meet-n-greet, I cleared my throat.

"Oh yeah. You want to know how I found you," Smitty said. "It was easy. I followed the girl and she led me straight to you. I've been tailing you for days.

"Your problem isn't your history in DC. Your problem isn't that you fell out with the family. Hell, it ain't even that you decided to hide all the way down here.

"Your problem is that Anthony Ribisi left a void. There's a black hole in your place that's sucking up everything in its path. This new reality is creating a bunch of frustrated gangsters with inflated egos trying to fill the void. It's not just Johnnie and his crew. There's even a biker gang, if you can believe it. They're riding around the city causing mayhem.

"And when it finally dawns on them that they'll continually fail at being you, then they'll get frustrated at your very existence. How long do you think it'll take before they realize you're alive and might be entertaining the possibility of coming home? They won't like that. They'll come after you."

"That's bullshit. I'm dead to those people." I said.

Smitty let out a laugh that echoed through the sparsely populated neighborhood.

"You're dumber than I thought. They've been trying to fill your shoes ever since you left. They can't. Once they know you're not dead, like really dead, they'll come looking."

Smitty paused and visibly considered his next words.

"You asked how I found you. I told you I followed the girl. And it was easy. Simply put, either you come home on your own to clean this mess up—"

"It's not my mess," I interjected.

"Either you come home to clean it up or they'll come, looking to force you back. They won't want you to help them, but they'll want to kill you and get you out of the way. As long as they continue to be horrible at what they're doing, you'll always be a threat.

"Look... it's good to see you, Smitty. Really, it is. I appreciate that you came all this way. But it's not my problem."

"You're not hearing me," Smitty said in frustration. "I followed the girl, Anthony. Do you want them to follow the girl too?"

With that, Smitty stepped away from me and walked back to his rented black Nissan Altima. As he climbed in, the entire vehicle rocked.

After cranking her up, he spun the car around, sped down the street, and left a cloud of dust trailing behind.

Smitty left me standing on Reynes Street alone with Gabe. He left me to the sound of the Mississippi River's waves. And he also left a lingering question, echoing in my head.

Do you want them to follow the girl too?

I exhaled a breath. Could I honestly keep my promise? Keep Coco from harm? Not if what Smitty had shared was true.

Chapter 38

Anthony

The bartender at Negril Cafe didn't have to ask our drink orders. A second visit made us regulars.

The shots of bourbon began as soon as we sat down at the bar.

"DC, huh?" Gabe said.

I drank my shot. "Yup."

A second one appeared out of thin air in an instant.

"Gambling houses, huh?"

"Yup," I said again.

"And this girl?"

I nodded my head.

"And you left because?"

"That's already been explained."

"I beg to differ, my good man. All you said was that you hopped in the car and just ended up here.

"You've yet to tell me why you stayed and even more, why you never went back. Sounds to me like you're running from something. And from the looks of it, that something has tracked you to New Orleans."

I shifted in my seat a little bit. Either the bar stool or Gabe's assessment made me uncomfortable. It was probably both.

"Sounds like they need you. Maybe you should go."

I looked down at the bar. Gabe hadn't touched his first shot yet and I was on my third.

"Yeah... you're running. You're hiding. Probably scared shit-less. And that doesn't sound like you," Gabe said.

"That's not fair, Gabe. You don't know my situation."

"The situation?" Gabe chuckled. "I barely know *you*! But from the bit I do know, it's clear to me that you can own the situation and not let it own you.

"You didn't ask for my advice, but I'm giving it anyway. Go back, Jelani. On your terms. And make the bastards regret pulling you back from this beautiful city of New Orleans. You think you can do that?"

The idea of returning after being gone for so long actually terrified me.

Johnnie wasn't the only one I needed to sit with. There was also Johnnie's twin sister, Jena. I would have completely under-stood if she stabbed me at first sight.

Maybe Gabe and Smitty were right. Maybe it was time to go home. If not for the people I've been running from, then at least for myself. I should run toward closure instead of away from it.

I also wanted to make sure that Coco was protected. Smitty hit the nail on the head. If following her was a way to get to me, then she was in danger.

With too many thoughts in my head, I said, "Maybe you're right."

That was all I could muster. And to that, Gabe finally picked up his shot glass. "I can toast to a 'maybe.' In that tiny word, many great things begin."

Chapter 39

Anthony

Monday, September 16th

Either Smitty wasn't paying attention, or he pretended to be more concerned with the magazine in his lap. Walking down the aisle, I could see he was in a window seat. It wasn't until I plopped down in the same row that he acknowledged my presence.

"Kind of you to make the flight," he said.

"Kind of you to leave me a ticket. Right on top of my pillow. Nice touch."

"I do what I can."

There was an empty seat between us. But not just that. There was a three-row radius around us, behind and in front. All the seats were empty.

I motioned to the seclusion with my hand.

"Why didn't you just charter a private flight?"

"I like space. And it's the most privacy I can buy on my budget," Smitty said.

I laughed as I buckled my seatbelt.

"Well, I'm here now, so get to it. What have I missed?"

"What do you know about MC Clubs?"

I shrugged my shoulders.

"Biker gangs," Smitty egged on.

When I didn't answer, he grinned. "Yeah... I need to get you caught up. You've missed a lot."

Chapter 40

Anthony

Smitty and I walked into a damp and moldy warehouse. I was relieved to see a few tables and chairs, because there was no way I was going to lean against the walls.

Smitty was a few feet in front of me. I was shocked that no one heard us walk in. The heavy metal door slammed shut behind us. Its loud bang echoed throughout the space. Our arrival had been announced. Necks belonging to unfamiliar faces snapped in our direction.

Two strangers sat at a wooden table. There was a third, off to the right and behind them. He was looking out the window with gigantic headphones covering his ears as he bopped his head to music.

The two at the table stood after seeing Smitty and walked over to us.

"Hey Smitty," one of the guys said.

Smitty motioned in his direction, saying, "This Axel."

We shook hands.

"That's Blake by the window... and this is Squid."

Just then, Squid approached close enough to violate my personal space.

"This is?" Squid asked.

I looked at Smitty and said, "I don't think I like this one's tone."

By that time, Blake noticed what was going on and made his way to the commotion. "Hey man. I'm—"

"Blake," we said in unison.

Squid's fingers rang out with the loud snap. "Oh! You're Anthony! The Black Ribisi? You're the one we've all been waiting for.

"The way I hear it, you're supposed to be Johnnie's brother. But that's funny. I don't see a resemblance. Anybody else think they look like siblings?"

Smitty stepped in between me and the unnecessarily aggressive Squid. He placed a hand on his chest and moved him back a couple feet. Squid's undersized body had no choice but to comply with Smitty's brute strength.

"Trust me, Squid. You don't wanna do this."

At that moment, the familiar bang of the front door sounded from behind. We all turned around to see Johnnie making his way toward us.

He struggled past us with both arms wrapped around pine green canvas garment bags. They were body slammed on the table.

"Squid... Listen to Smitty," Johnnie said. "That's the only warning you're going to get."

Johnnie patted Smitty on the shoulder as to indicate a job well done. He then threw both arms around me with a vice-grip like squeeze. It was unexpected.

"Damn man. It's been too long. I'm so happy that you're finally home."

Johnnie released me from his embrace. "Let me ask you, do

you need to get settled? Is it too early to discuss a little business?"

"You wanted me back. I'm back," I said. "No need to stand on ceremony. Let's get to it."

Johnnie turned and looked to the assembly of men.

"You heard the man," he said with a grin. "Business it is!"

Chapter 41

Remo

The silence in the hotel room was cut in half by the humming of a small black refrigerator hidden within the wardrobe closet.

Remo sat in the armchair against the balcony, scrolling through his phone. Metty sat on the edge of the bed across from him. Her eyes, fixed on Remo, as if stuck in cement.

"You know... you never said you was a Ribisi," Metty said.

"There are a bunch of things I haven't mentioned." Remo continued scrolling in his phone.

"I'm just saying," Metty said. "It's not that I'm mad. I haven't even brought it up until now. I just think it wouldn't have hurt to know."

"It wouldn't have helped either. Besides, it's not like I wear my family name on my sleeve."

"Really? Why? It seems in this town, people do things for you if you're a Ribisi. Once they know who you are anyway."

"That's precisely why I choose not to broadcast it."

Remo scrolled in his phone for another few seconds.

"There you are," he said. He continued to inspect his screen.

"You're related to Anthony, huh? How?" Metty asked.

"Technically, I'm not. But since you want to continue down this path, Marco was my baby brother."

The room fell back to the hum of the refrigerator.

Metty shifted in her seat with an uneasy twist of her lower body. "Oh... I'm sorry. I... I... didn't know."

"Of course, you didn't, my dear. Because I don't broadcast things. Besides... we weren't on the best of speaking terms when he died."

"I'm still sorry. Even more so now," she said. "When did you two talk last?"

Remo looked up from his phone for the first time during the conversation and gave the question some thought.

"Uh..." he said. "It's been a really long time. I can't really say for sure."

Metty's eyes went wide in astonishment. "What?"

Remo went back to looking at his phone. "Yeah," he said. "And it wasn't a pretty conversation."

Remo's memory of the night had not faded, even though the events took place over two decades prior.

The four men were soaking wet from the torrential rain. They walked around the boxing studio, surveying the damage. The men were careful so as not to add more expenses to their tab. They knew there would have to be financial compensation.

It was appropriate that they used a boxing gym for their meetings. Boxing was organized chaos. It was regulated homicide. Two men would enter a controlled environment and try to kill each other, hoping that the referee wouldn't let it happen.

The walls of Finley's Gym were literally papered with images that told this story. Fliers from old fights covered every inch of the walls and even the ceiling.

Regional stars and national superstars all graced Finley's ring, and at one time or another, had enjoyed some level of training there as well.

That sense of boxing history and nostalgia was disrupted by the unorganized chaos of broken glass. Trophies were strewn about and blood was smeared across the floor.

It was ironic that the man who used Finley's Gym to fight his way out of poverty and live a productive life lost his life in the very same place.

That irony was not lost on Marco and he had grown increasingly agitated thinking about it. What pushed him over the edge was the puddle of blood gathered at the bottom of the stairs. The door was still open, but the body had been removed.

Marco broke the silence.

"Brother... what have you done?"

Remo didn't respond.

Jack Lowinger, a tall lanky man with blond hair, had entered the boxing ring. He had hazel eyes, a strong jaw, and a cleft chin. Strong physical features leaders would kill for. He drew the attention of men and women in every room he walked in.

And Jack was a shrewd entrepreneur, always looking for ways to make money. He had a way of anticipating trends and taking advantage of them, just at the right time.

Standing with his arms casually hanging over the top rope, Jack said, "You do know this will impact us in two ways,"

"How so?" the decades younger Remo asked.

Marco used Remo's response as an opportunity to spar with him.

"For starters," Marco said, "after we pay for the mess you made, we will never be able to use Finley's again."

"He's a good man and only lets us meet here out of the kindness of his heart," Jack said.

"I think the five grand a week helps," Nick Nick said sarcastically.

Dominic Nicholas donned his usual uniform, even in the middle of a rainy night. Two-piece suit, perfectly starched white shirt, straight tie, and spit polished black shoes. His black hair was slicked back and his Italian accent was ever present.

Marco wasn't amused. "But if we're killing people in his gym, it'll need to be fifty grand a week!"

Before Marco could get going, Jack interjected. "And secondly, once the word is out that he's gone and that one of our own killed him, we will be vulnerable. A laughingstock, I might add. They will come for us."

"Who will come for us?" Remo asked incredulously.

"Everyone," Marco said.

Nick Nick walked to the top of the stairs and stared down at the open door.

"I don't think you have fully grasped how much fear that man put into our enemies. I couldn't hold them all off by myself if I tried. Things will become very challenging for us."

"It's so much more than that," Marco said. "He was one of us. How do you do this to one of your own? Tell me something, Remo."

The room fell quiet again.

Frustrated at Remo's silence, Marco belted out, "Say something!"

"I—I—I'm sorry," Remo said just above a whisper. "I didn't mean to kill him. We were supposed to talk, and things got out of hand."

"And what did you need to talk with him about?" Nick Nick asked. "I mean, alone."

Remo walked to the stool near the punching bag. He sat with his elbows on his knees and his hands holding up his head. He took a deep breath before trying to explain. "You know how he didn't want us to know anything about his personal life? He said it was to protect his family and I get that."

Marco shrugged his shoulders and said, "What does this have to do with anything?"

"It's his wife. I know her. We bumped into each other some weeks ago and after connecting the dots..." Remo paused and thought about his next words. "Marco. It's her. It's Angel."

Marco didn't need to hear another word. He had all the information he needed to fill in what was missing.

There was an amorous history between Remo and Angel that dated back another fifteen years. A history that included falling head over heels and then making the hard choice to go their separate ways.

In that time, Angel found love with a man who hadn't and wouldn't push her away as Remo had done.

Their paths had been ripped apart and serendipitously came back together. The odds of that happening left Marco stunned.

After he processed through the hypothetical storylines that he'd mentally cooked up without asking for details, Marco's rage returned. The flash of red in his eyes wasn't from the lack of sleep.

"This was avoidable. But no... you couldn't control yourself because of a woman?! And now we're going to be in an unimaginable position because you had to think with your dick!" Marco seethed with disgust. If it was one thing he abhorred, it was a lack of control that led to tragic consequences.

Marco sighed. "Ok. There's nothing else to discuss. I can't

even think straight with you around. I need you out of my sight for a while."

"For how long?" Remo asked.

"I don't know."

"And where should I go?" Remo then protested.

"Once again, I don't know. I don't care," Marco said. "Maybe the family in New York is an option. But for now... there's nothing here for you."

* * *

That was the last time the brothers spoke to each other.

Remo was stuck in the memory.

"I regret almost nothing in this life," Remo said as he came back to his present day. He looked up just long enough to say, "But don't take for granted that you'll always have another day to see the people you love. You'll look up one day and find that you have no one left."

He turned his attention back to his phone. After pressing dial, he waited while listening to a ring on the other end. Finally, someone picked up.

"Hello," Remo said. "Yeah, it's me. I got your text. I'll be there in an hour."

Chapter 42

Anthony

The six of us huddled around a stack of garment bags centered on the table.

"It's a simple thing," Johnnie said. "In order for us to reopen gambling houses and protect ourselves from the bikers, we need money. And a lot of it.

"I have a plan that will give us enough capital to finance three houses and buy enough security that'll last at least a year.

"In a year's time, profit will have grown to a point where we can set everything on autopilot and make even more money. And I've saved the best part for last.

"Not only will I be able to get the houses up and running again, but there will be enough money to more than likely pay each of you a million dollars, at least."

"Bullshit," I said. "Sounds too good to be true."

"It's not," Johnnie said.

Blake spoke up. "The only way we'd make that kind of money is if we robbed a bank." He chuckled. "I know you're not talking about robbing a bank, right?"

"Not 'a bank,'" Johnnie said. He held up three fingers. "We're going to rob three banks. At one time."

"Then I really call bullshit," I said.

"It's not," Johnnie said again.

He fished a folded piece of printer paper out of his pants pocket. As he unfolded the sheet and laid it on top of the garment bags, everyone could see a hand drawn map.

"This is the Gallery Place and Mount Vernon Square areas of downtown," Johnnie stuck his finger on the map.

"And if you look at these two dots along Tenth Street... that's a Bank of America near Pennsylvania Avenue to the south. There's also one to the north. It's near the Convention Center, by K Street. And the lone dot to the west—"

Squid interjected, "That's the Bank of America at the Metro Center train station. Fool... I bank there."

"Sorry man, then we're about to rob you," Johnnie said.

Squid dismissed him with the wave of a hand. "Whatever. All you've done is show us you know how to draw a triangle between three banks. How is it possible to stick them all up?"

"I know a guy who works the armored truck route," Johnnie said. "He told me it starts at the Metro Center location, moves south to the Pennsylvania Avenue branch, and then back north to the Convention Center bank before heading to another part of town.

"Within forty minutes, the truck will have made three cash pickups. I have been assured it'll be carrying no less than eight million dollars."

Axel let out a high pitch whistle. "That's a lot of bread."

"Yes, it is. That's enough to pay each of us and have plenty for the gambling houses.

"All we have to do is hit the truck as soon as it makes that last stop in Mount Vernon Square," Johnnie said.

"Impossible," I said. "I'm assuming that an armored truck

comes with armed guards. As well as triggers for alarms. It'll never happen."

Johnnie rolled his eyes.

"My guy tells me that protocol is for the guards to give up the loot if ever a victim of armed robbery. There's a higher value placed on life because the money is federally insured. So I'm not worried about them. Flash a nine-millimeter and trust me, they'll step back.

"As for alarm triggers, there aren't any."

"This guy must be high on meth. You're trying to tell us there's NO security?" Axel said.

"Well... I didn't say there wasn't security," Johnnie took a deep breath. "These trucks are equipped with a state-of-the-art video surveillance system. There are cameras on each side of the vehicle and in the front. There's also one above the back door and two inside the truck."

"Figures," Axel said.

"There's also a 360-degree camera mounted on the top of the truck that provides a bird's eye view of the everything happening around the vehicle. All the footage is livestreamed to a command center that's probably miles away. In another state, maybe.

"When a truck is hit, they know immediately and have local law enforcement dispatch the cops."

"Tell me more about this wonderful plan of yours," I said. "It sounds like, as soon as we approach the truck, then we're as good as caught."

"My plan isn't 'wonderful,' it's perfect. They can get all the video they want. We'll be camouflaged to the point of invisibility.

"Anthony? Is today not the third Monday in September?"

"It is."

"And what did we do every year as kids on the third Tuesday of this month?"

It took me a little while to figure it out and I didn't like where it was going.

"That's right," Johnnie said without waiting for my response. "It's the city's annual Christmas in September convention at the Convention Center."

Everyone looked at each other in complete confusion.

"Let me help y'all out," I said. "It's the city's unofficial start to the Christmas season.

"There's going to be Christmas arts and crafts, Christmas storytelling, Christmas food and drink tastings—"

"...and it wouldn't be complete without the annual Parade of Santas," Johnnie said.

"Just skip over Halloween and Thanksgiving. Damn," Squid said.

I snatched up one of the pine green garment bags and let the hand drawn map float to the ground. Holding the bag with one hand, I unzipped it with the other. My fear was realized. "You've got to be kidding me."

But I knew it wasn't a joke. And it kind of made sense. I threw the bag back on top of the pile and watched the red and white velvet Santa suit slide from out of the garment bag.

The smile on Johnnie's face was blinding. "This is how we'll be invisible, fellas. We'll all be Santa and march in the parade. There will be thousands of Santas to disguise us.

"We can break from the pack when they make the left turn off Seventh Street, rob the truck, and then slide right back into parade before anyone knows what hit them.

"Now, there are some specifics we should go over to make sure it's done right. But come on... tell me this isn't brilliant!"

"Yeah, sure..." Squid said. His sarcasm couldn't be contained. "Dressing like Santa is some Einstein level shit."

Johnnie looked at the group of us, "I'm open to any idea that's better."

It sounded like a genuine request for plans that we thought might work. But instead of getting ideas, Johnnie got silence.

"Well," Johnnie said, "hearing no new ideas or serious objections, I guess it's 'Ho ho ho' motherfuckers."

Chapter 43

Priest

Priest and Liza sat at a wobbly table in Harvey's Hangout. The only two in the room. They huddled side by side in rickety chairs that creaked with every movement.

Liza's elbow was on the back of Priest's chair as she ran her hand through his hair.

Priest pulled an ashtray close and lit a cigarette. He offered it to Liza.

"I told you I'm trying to quit, babe."

"That's right," he said. He took a long drag on the cigarette before extinguishing it in the ash tray. He blew the smoke away from Liza. "You think this is doable?"

"Nothing's impossible," she said with a grin.

"I'm being for real. There are a lot of moving pieces in DC. I have the Broken ready to move in, but sometimes I've gotta wonder—"

"Wonder what?" she cut him off. Her hand moved from Priest's hair to his back. "This isn't the time to doubt yourself babe. You have the Broken. Those guys would walk off a cliff for you.

All you need now is a better understanding of the landscape before etching your moves in stone.

"From what you've told me, DC used to be managed by committee, right? Each representative was responsible for their own thing. Well, the committee no longer exists and now all the left-behinds are eating each other.

"There isn't a crew strong enough to control the city because they all seem to be fending off attacks from each other. Timing is perfect. They are too busy fighting and too weak to sustain what they're doing over time. No one will be able to beat us."

"But they soon will," Priest said.

"No. They won't," Liza said. She was emphatic. "They won't."

"They will." Priest said.

"Well, then let them come. You're close to finishing off the little gambling racket. Take drugs and prostitution next. Squeeze every last one of them until the bitches can't breathe. You have an army. Who's going to stop you?" Liza's eyes widened with inspiration, a thought, and then snapped her fingers. "All you need is someone who knows the local landscape. If you get some intel, it'll make the takeover much easier."

"Someone who knows the landscape, you say?" Priest said with a kiss to the side of her head. "You know... you are absolutely the best advisor a man could have."

At that moment, Harvey swung open the door that separated his office from the rest of the bar.

"Aye Priest! You taking phone calls here now too?"

Liza cut her eyes in suspicion. "Hmm. Who's calling, babe?"

Priest got up from his stool, kissed Liza again and said, "Exactly what you say I need. A local landscaper."

Chapter 44

Priest

When Priest emerged from Harvey's office, Liza had company with her—Harvey, the Enforcer, and Maddox. Priest had been anticipating the call he received and made sure everyone was available to lay out their next steps.

"It's time to put the pressure on the Ribisi kid," Priest said. "He's back."

"When?" Harvey asked.

"I don't know. But what I do know is that he has the experience and backbone to put up a fight. He won't be able to beat us, of course. But he will annoy the hell out of me. So now is the time to strike. Hit him quick and fast. Elimination is the goal."

Maddox kept his gaze down at the table in front of him until that moment. That's when he looked at his brother and let out a sigh of frustration. "Elimination? Another murder? Based on information you got from someone no one here has ever met? Looks to me like we're being used to do someone else's dirty work," Maddox said.

Priest rolled his eyes in annoyance. He turned to his brother and said, "That might be the case."

"And you're cool with that?"

"If a stranger wants to deliver DC to us on a silver platter, I don't see anything wrong with that. You either step up and get with the program or find yourself another city to ride in. Because sooner than later, DC will be ours."

"I'm not sure I want to have anything to do with this."

Maddox had gotten on Priest's last nerve with his insubordination. He was ready to spill the beans on Maddox and how he hadn't earned his patches the way the other brothers had.

But that knowledge was just between Priest and Harvey. Letting that information fly, in a room full of patched in bikers, would certainly put his brother's life in danger. And Priest didn't want that. He just wanted his brother to comply.

Priest decided to go in a different direction. "Look man! What's your problem?! When you were patched in like every other man in this club, what did you think we was going to do? Sell Girl Scout cookies?

"What have you been looking at your entire life? Did you have blinders on? We watched our father and grandfather run the Broken. We knew what was going on."

"That was before we started killing people, Priest!"

There was a look of amazement between everyone in the room. The only one on the outside was Maddox.

"Holy shit," Harvey said. "The kid really does have blinders on. Kid, the Broken has been killing people for generations. This is business as usual."

Priest used the lull in conversation to take advantage of the moment.

"Maddie. What if we could do this without bloodshed?"

Maddox scrutinized his brother's words as they hung in the air.

"Really?" Maddox asked. "How?"

"My contact tells me there's a chance for a parley. Are you familiar with that term?"

"I'm not an idiot. I know what a parley is."

"Ok, good. I'll let you set up a parley with them. Maybe the Ribisi kid will see how futile it is to fight us. He can't possibly be in the mindset for all out war."

"Parley?" Maddox asked.

"Parley," Priest repeated. "No one has to die. And it'll be because of you. Lives will be saved."

"I guess I can do that."

"Good! I knew we would come to an agreement.

"Ok everyone!" Priest yelled out to the crew. "That's it for now! I think we've made good headway here."

Feeling accomplished, Maddox was the first person to leave the bar. Liza and the Enforcer followed right after. Leaving Priest and Harvey alone.

Harvey grabbed his vest, swung it on his body and approached Priest. "A parley?"

"That's what I said."

Harvey's bellowing laugh bounced off the walls. "Your brother is more stupid than I thought."

"Yes, he is," Priest said. "And that's a shame."

Chapter 45

Anthony

Smitty and I stood on the sideway, a few feet away from the front door of the warehouse. He fumbled through his pocket and pulled out his car keys.

"That's the stupidest idea I've ever heard of," he said.

"Yeah," I said in agreement. "But the more I think about it, the more it looks like it might work. It's stupid, but it's doable."

"Oh God. Ok Saint Nick. Just don't get stuck in no chimneys."

I let out a reluctant laugh. My cellphone rang. Then my heart started doing jumping jacks as soon as I saw the caller ID. I stepped away from Smitty to take the call.

"Hey babe!" I said through the smile on my face. "Yeah. Miss you too. But look, I can't talk right now. We'll talk soon. I just need to take care of something real quick. Oh yeah... I have a surprise for you."

I didn't give Coco much time to respond. She didn't know I was back in town. I'm sure she would've had a trillion questions. And I would've slipped up and spoiled the surprise. I felt like it was best to get off the phone as soon as I could.

I held the phone with both hands and spoke into it as if I was talking directly in her ear. I told her that I loved her and quickly disconnected the call.

Walking back toward Smitty, I was partially on cloud nine. Only partially because I noticed a set of keys flying in the air toward my face. Ducking out the way, I caught the keys at the same time.

"What are these for?" I asked.

"It's so you can get around town." Smitty pointed to the black Ford Fusion in front of us. "I'm not your damn chauffeur. And the two silver keys are for the basement apartment beneath my place. I figured you needed a place of your own."

"Thanks man. I really appreciate it."

I started walking to the car when Smitty called out to me. "Anthony! Are you going to see her? I know she'll be really excited."

I just waved goodbye to the brother and hopped in the car.

He was somewhat right. I was going to see her. But not the *her* he was thinking of. It was clear from his joyful demeanor, he assumed I was going to see Coco. But first, it was time I faced Jena.

She was the mother of my child. A child I had never seen. That's who I was going to see. And I was sure she would be less than excited to have me resurface, after years of ignoring them.

Chapter 46

Anthony

It took a minute to get reacquainted with the area. Having been gone for so long left me feeling like a stranger. The drive from DC to Rockville, Maryland helped a lot.

It still amazed me at how the city and its suburbs steadily expanded. Breathing life into a forgotten about area. In my youth, I would've never seen this many new apartments and homes along Rockville Pike.

I pulled the black Ford Fusion up to the front of what looked to be another newly built multi-purpose building. Plenty of shops, restaurants, and an apartment, all crammed into the same space.

Sitting behind the wheel, I grabbed a piece of paper from the cup holder to double check the address.

"Rockville Town Square. Yup. That's it."

I took a deep breath and got out of the car.

My legs felt like a mix of jelly and molasses. Jiggly and trudging at a snail's pace with each forced step. I didn't know what to expect.

In spite of the unknown, I was committed to facing the

consequences of my cowardice. And it frightened me. But what frightened me more was not being strong enough to break the cycle of a son living with an absentee father.

Was I kidding myself? Had that ship already sailed?

Now it was a matter of taking advantage of my return, possibly salvaging whatever semblance of a relationship that I could.

What would happen if I never told Jena I was back? How would I ever look her in the eyes again? And most importantly, what would my child think of the man who ran out on him?

It was clear to me that fear made me run away, but it was also fear that brought me back.

I scrolled through the touchscreen intercom until I found her name.

J. RIBISI.

This was the moment of truth. Whether a kiss on the cheek or a punch to the chin... I had to get what was coming to me.

I looked at her name until it felt like I was lost in time. And the longer I stared, the more doubt crept in.

"This woman probably hates me," I said to myself. I looked back to my car. "Nah... I can't do this."

I punked out. Walking back to the Fusion, disappointment welled up inside of me.

I reached the vehicle and before I could grab the door handle, I caught a glimpse of my reflection in the window. The image of the man I saw wasn't one I recognized or remembered. Who was this guy?

Anthony Ribisi was fearless. Jelani Jones was just as cold. But the person in the reflection was a shade of what I used to be. And I didn't like him.

I made a split-second decision to not let fear win. Turning around, I decided to walk toward the edge of the cliff. I was headed to press her door buzzer. I would fall or I would fly.

Either way, I committed myself to feeling the rush of air against my cheek.

I rang once. I rang twice. After waiting nearly a minute, I pressed the button a third time. There was no response.

Standing back a few feet, I tilted my head and looked up the face of the building like I could figure out which window was Jena's.

No such luck. But I did feel better about not tucking my tail between my legs and scurrying away. It was honestly a relief that Jena wasn't home. I attempted to be present and take my lumps. But I was so happy that I didn't have to.

I turned around to finally head back to the car. That's when relief was snatched out of my body and the air was knocked out of my lungs.

Jena Ribisi now stood before me in stunned silence. Her olive skin was smooth and blemish free. Mouth agape. The dark strands of her brown hair with auburn highlights had been pulled back into a ponytail.

Jena's right hand held three plastic red and white Target bags. And her left hand held a small hand belonging to a little boy. He looked to be approximately two years old.

There I stood, face-to-face with Jena. And for the very first time, my son.

Chapter 47

Remo

Remo and Metty parked in a familiar neighborhood. Sitting in the back seat, Metty swiveled her head from side to side.

"I remember this area. I was just here the other day."

"Really?" Remo said.

"Yeah. With—"

Metty's sentence was disrupted by the tapping of a finger on the passenger side window. She jumped.

The dark-skinned man wore blue jeans, a gray v-neck shirt, and a blue blazer with gray pinstripes.

While his bright smile, velvet smooth skin, and overall physique said he was in his mid to late forties, his eyes looked worn. Tired from a hard worked life.

Remo rolled the window down halfway.

"Get in," he said, waving the man toward the open passenger seat in the front.

After the guy got comfortable, he looked at the girl.

"It's ok," Remo said.

"If you say so. And where are my manners?" he twisted his

body and extended his hand over the seat to Metty. "I'm Kenneth Dowd. My friends call me KD."

"Well, I'm Metasebia," she said in response, after shaking his hand. "My friends call me Metty."

Remo rolled his eyes and sucked his teeth, "Are we done?"

"Don't be mad," KD said, settling back into the seat. "The ladies love KD and KD loves the ladies."

Metty giggled.

"KD! Where are we?!"

"You were right not to trust Beaux. You wanted me to follow him and he led me to the same spot almost every single time.

"You see that building over there? I've sat on it for a while now. That's a hang out. And Beaux's been casing it too. Probably looking for the right time to break in."

"How many?" Remo asked.

"Four. Maybe five. And you'll never guess who was with them."

"Anthony?"

"Mmm hmm. Not just him. My old rookie too."

"Smitty is with him?" Remo asked.

"Yup. But they're not there now."

Remo let out a groan. "Why didn't you call me when they were here?!"

"Because you didn't tell me to call you when they were. Next time, be explicit with your instructions."

"Get your ass out," Remo said. "Is that explicit enough for you?"

KD didn't budge. He looked back at Metty. "You really do have some pretty eyes."

Metty giggled again.

Remo swore and then groaned. He shuffled in his blazer

and pulled out a rectangular shaped envelope. He tossed it to KD.

KD held the brick up to his nose and took a long sniff. "Now I can leave."

"Yeah, yeah, yeah. To hell with you."

"Love you too, Remo."

KD let himself out the car and started walking back to his own vehicle.

Remo rolled down his window, grabbing KD's attention. "Hey detective?"

"Yes?" KD said.

"Are you sure?"

KD didn't say anything. He just looked across the street. A familiar face walked pass the front door, holding what looked like a crowbar.

It was Beaux.

Remo's eyes bulged in disbelief. He looked back at KD and pointed his index finger at him.

"Good work. Love you too, man."

Chapter 48

Anthony

Her apartment keys clinked against the sides of a heart shaped crystal bowl she tossed them in. She did it without looking.

Jena led me down the long hallway. The first room we encountered was the kitchen. We walked in.

After setting her son... our son... in the highchair at the kitchen table, she walked back to me and grabbed the bags that I took from her on the way up.

"Thank you," she said. Her tone was indecipherable.

Standing in her apartment, looking in her face, I had no idea what thoughts ran through her head.

"Don't mention it," I said.

She placed the bags on the marble countertop and fished around, drawing out each item, one at a time. Her back faced me. Other than the sound of ruffled plastic, the room was quiet.

"How... how old is he?" I managed to stammer out.

At the sound of my voice, Jena stopped fishing. She held herself up with her hands against the countertop, buttressed by both arms. Jena's head hung so low that from behind, all I saw was her back and shoulders. She looked headless.

Jena let out a deep sigh, turned around and leaned against the counter. "You don't give a damn about this boy." She paused before mocking me. "'How old is he?'"

She huffed out a sigh of exasperation. "You've got some nerve. Well, since you care so much, let's do the math. It takes nine months to bake a baby, right?

"If you add to that the time that you disappeared and then magically popped up again, that would make him about twenty months."

"I can explain," I said.

"He's almost two years old, Anthony!"

"Just let me explain."

"Were you dead?! I don't think you were dead."

"No," I said. "I wasn't dead."

"Then there's no explanation for what you did!" Jena walked over to the boy and snatched him out of his chair.

She marched straight to me, shoved him into my chest and let go. I grabbed him before he dropped to the floor.

"You're so good with words, Anthony. Explain it to him because I'm not listening."

And with that, silence returned. I felt like a storm ravaged island after the passing of a hurricane.

She was done and she was right. There was nothing I could say. No reason. No explanation.

The silence was broken by the sound of the boy's giggle. It was almost as if he knew his mother handed me my ass and was laughing at me. I deserved every giggle he dished out. Just like I deserved every word his mother said.

"You're right," I whispered.

"I know I'm right," she said walking to me with her arms held out. "Gimme my son."

She snaked her arms between me and the boy and started bouncing him in the air. Her attitude changed as soon as she connected with him.

"How's my big man doing?!" she asked him. She smiled bright and her voice bounced as she bounced the boy. "Yes! You're my big man!"

She carried him to the window and peered out for a few seconds. Then she came back to me. "Marco," she said. "I want you to meet someone."

Almost responsively, he held his hand out to me. I put my index finger in his tiny grasp.

"I want you to meet your father," Jena said. "This is your daddy."

Our son smiled and then giggled again. The anger his mother unleashed on me wasn't in him. He was too young and just a baby. His needs were simple. Protection, care, and love.

Things that as his father, I never gave him. And yet he held no resentment. He just had giggles for me.

I felt like shit... like I was on the bottom of a homeless person's hole ridden and tattered shoe.

My face was flushed and I unsuccessfully tried my best to will my eyes from watering.

"Hey Marco," I said through the lump in my throat. "It's nice to meet you."

The next sound startled me somewhat. I heard the front door of the apartment slam. Keys jingled and then there was a familiar clink against crystal.

The thud of footsteps came in succession, moving ever closer to the kitchen. Then a man appeared in the portal between the hallway and the kitchen.

"Oh! Hey! I didn't know we had company," he said.

We, I thought to myself.

Jena squealed and bounced the baby at the sight of the man.

"Look Marco!" she exclaimed. "Daddy's home!"

Chapter 49

Remo

KD was right about Beaux. Remo and Metty watched him return to the warehouse with a crowbar in hand.

Beaux hurried past the front door to a window that was to the right of it.

They watched as he used the crowbar to pry open the window. The window slid open with ease. Apparently, the geniuses left without locking it.

"You see this shit?" Remo said to himself.

Metty struggled to sit up and then propped herself between the two headrests, "I'm completely lost. We were in this area just the other day. I don't get it. What am I missing?"

"It's simple," Remo said. "Beaux can't be trusted. He's working with someone else. But who?"

"Beaux can't be trusted? But with everything that's going on, you can?"

Remo turned around and looked at Metty incredulously. The tone of distrust sliced through him.

"I'm just trying to make sense of this, Remo. The last time Anthony was seen, the city was a war zone and he was at the center of it. He disappears and everyone thinks he's dead. Then he comes back right when the world is looking for him? This stinks. I have no idea what I've gotten myself into."

"To be fair... I gave you a chance to leave some time ago," Remo said.

"Fair enough. But what the hell is going on? Why are we sitting across from a warehouse that Beaux is breaking into? And why is everyone hell bent on finding Anthony?"

Remo turned back to the warehouse. "You know... Marco wasn't the only one who raised Anthony. Since his biological father was... well, he wasn't around. Marco and Nick Nick were largely responsible for taking Anthony from a boy to a man.

"My influence was from the shadows. I gave the boy a little polish and pizazz. I offered him a different perspective on work and life. And in order to not rock the family boat, I had to do it from New York.

"I'm back now because I know a trap when I smell one. Anthony will need my help."

"What makes you so sure? How do you know?"

"It was a message from the beyond," Remo said before turning to look at Metty. "My brother Marco told me."

Chapter 50

Beaux

Beaux wiggled his way, headfirst, through the window he managed to open.

Once inside, he poked his head out to see if any passersby witnessed his break-in. Seeing no one, he retreated into the building.

Beaux looked around the dimly lit room but couldn't see much. He took his phone out of his pants pocket and flicked on the flashlight. He immediately saw a table at the center of the room.

Standing over the table, he lifted one of the garment bags and looked inside.

"Santa?" he thought to himself.

Examining the costume, Beaux noticed a few sheets of papers had fallen to the floor when he grabbed the garment bag.

It looked important enough to take pictures. One was a hand drawn map of the Gallery Place in the Chinatown area. Three circles were connected by three lines. Forming a triangle.

Each circle was drawn around a three-letter inscription, "BoA."

He had an idea of what he was looking at, but did a Google map search on his phone just to be sure.

"Just what I thought," he said softly. The circles indicated specific Bank of America locations.

The second sheet of paper only listed three things. *1) Metro Center. 2) Pennsylvania Avenue. 3) Convention Center.*

The branch locations, Beaux thought to himself.

It all made sense. Beaux was certain that the crew intended to rob three banks. And now he knew which banks and the order in which they would be robbed.

Beaux put everything back and started taking more pictures with his phone.

Careful to exit the same way he entered, Beaux climbed out of the window that he had pried open earlier. Once outside, Beaux retrieved his phone again and dialed.

"Hey. Yeah... I've got it. They're robbing three banks. From what I gathered, it's going down tomorrow. When they're all done, they'll probably come back here."

Beaux began walking away from the building.

"Am I sure?" he asked. Beaux then pulled his phone away from his face and looked at it incredulously. Returning the phone to the side of his face, he then said. "I didn't stutter, did I?"

Chapter 51

Anthony

The man who just let himself in Jena's apartment could have been my twin. Did she pick him intentionally? He could easily replace me as little Marco's father. The similarity of physical characteristics was scary.

His name was Brandon. He sat across from me at the dining room table shoveling a grilled Chic-Fil-A chicken sandwich into his mouth.

The aroma of waffle fries seeped out of the white and red paper bag. The bag was slightly torn open for easy access. Between bites of the sandwich, he dipped the fries into honey mustard sauce and swallowed them whole.

It took every ounce of discipline not to roll my eyes. I stood there and mimicked the annoyingly wide grin on his stupid face. The idea that he believed he was the father of my child made me sick to my stomach.

"You know," he said with a full mouth, "I never come home on my break."

"You don't say?" I said with fake astonishment.

"I work at the Bestbuy down the street." An air of embarrassment flashed across Brandon's face. "It's only temporary, you know."

I shrugged. If he knew I didn't care, it probably would've brought a sense of relief to his ego.

Brandon grabbed a couple napkins. He wiped the grease and salt off his fingers. Then his mouth before looking over his shoulder and leaning into the table.

Brandon whispered, "You know, we've met before. At the restaurant. Not long before you left town. You were busy and all. I know you don't remember."

"Why are we whispering?"

"Well... it's this bullshit job I have. I know Jena would be upset if she knew I was asking, but if you hear of any work, let a brother know."

"Work?"

"Yeah, man. Work. I'm not stupid. I know all about the Ribisi's." He leaned back in his chair, wiping his face again. "And I'm damn near family now.

"You've gotta have something cooking. If you don't, then why in the hell did you come back? You've been gone for a long time."

"Look Brandon, I don't know what you think you know. But you're—"

Our conversation was cut short by Jena walking into the room. She held Marco against her body with one hand and had a powder blue kid's bowl in the other.

"Don't you have to get going?" Jena said.

Both Brandon and I stood up from the table.

"Yeah. I guess you're right," I said.

"I wasn't talking to you," Jena said.

"I've gotta get back to work," Brandon said after kissing Jena and Marco.

Brandon walked back to the table to retrieve his jacket from around the back of his chair. "Good to see you again, Anthony. Come by any time. Hopefully we'll see more of you around."

"Anthony's always pretty busy," Jena said. "I don't know about that."

"I'll do what I can," I said.

Brandon walked out of the room. We heard his footsteps take him through the apartment to the door. Then came the slam.

Jena walked to the table and placed the bowl in front of the highchair. It was identical to the one in the kitchen. She gently placed the kid in the chair.

"I'm going to ask you a question," Jena said, stirring the green soup-like content in the bowl. "It's a simple question, so don't lie to me."

"That's not how simple questions are prefaced."

"He's been trying to get in with Johnnie for almost a year. He thinks the family is what it used to be. But it isn't."

Jena stopped feeding Marco long enough to say, "Did he ask you for a job?"

"Yes."

"Are you going to give him one? I'd rather you didn't."

"I'm not here to work, Jena."

"Yeah... right," she huffed. "If you're not here to work—"

"Why in the hell did I come back?" I asked.

I was being as honest as I could. I hadn't returned for work. I return to keep Coco safe. And no one would understand that but me.

Jena walked over to me. She took her hands and cupped my face. This was the first sign of intimacy I received from her since I walked in the front door.

"If you don't know why you're here," Jena said. "You better figure it out before it's too late. Before someone gets hurt really bad... or worse."

Chapter 52

Anthony

Blinded by darkness, I pawed the wall, looking for the light switch. The borrowed apartment was mine for now. But I didn't know where anything was, including the light switches.

With the living room lights finally blazing, the first thing I did was walk through all the rooms, flipping every switch I could find.

Taking stock of the area, I looked under the sofa and bed. I open the closet doors for a quick inspection and checked out the laundry room as well.

No one was in the apartment. I was alone.

I noticed a door at the back of the kitchen, marched to it, and twisted the knob. It was locked.

"Ok. I'm good," I said to myself. But I still unlocked and opened the door, peering outside into the dark backyard.

I used the flashlight on my cell phone to brighten the area. A six-foot wooden fence encased the property. A lone grill sat in the center of the yard.

I double checked that I had locked the door after closing it and walked into the bedroom. My luggage from the New Orleans flight was at the foot of the queen-sized bed. Smitty must have delivered it.

I sat on the bed and kicked my shoes off. The firm mattress was comfortable, but not comfortable enough to put my mind fully at ease.

Knowing that I was staying in a basement apartment at Smitty's house helped more than anything. But there was still an anxiousness I couldn't shake.

The anxiety was at war with exhaustion. I had been running nonstop since New Orleans, without taking a minute to rest. My eyelids hung heavy, but my mind shifted to the one thing that would ease my anxiety.

"I know what I need," I said.

My phone was still in my hand. I swiped across the face of the phone until I came across the call log.

Recent calls. There was one name at the top of the list. "Coco."

I leaned back to think about how I would explain my return to DC. I mentally outlined my words. I plotted out a reasonable timeline for seeing her again. And I speculated whether she would immediately come back to New Orleans with me.

The pillow behind my head was softer than the mattress. And way more comfortable too.

Somewhere between the blinking of itchy eye lids, I figured it out. I knew what I was going to say. I knew what I needed to say.

I willed my heavy eyes lids open long enough to tap her name, initiating the call.

Placing the phone between my right cheek and shoulder, I listened to the ring on the other end. With my eyes now closed, I kept listening and waiting for Coco to answer.

Waiting. Listening. Drifting.

* * *

Coco's voice erupted through the earpiece of Anthony's phone. "Hello!" she shouted.

She heard long and deep breaths, which led her to one conclusion.

"Jelani! Are you asleep?! Answer me if you can!"

It was no use. Even though she had been on the receiving end of a phone call, she was the only one awake between the two.

"Ok," she said. "Get your sleep, sweetheart. I'll speak with you soon. Good night. Love you."

Chapter 53

Anthony

Tuesday, September 17th

Startled by the ringing phone, my body jerked forward.

"Hey! He... hello!" I shouted into the receiver.

"It's me," Smitty said. "You get some rest?"

I stretched my body before answering his question. Looking down, I was wearing the same clothes from the night before.

"Yeah. I'm good," I said. My voice trailed off in disappointment when I realized I had fallen asleep before talking to Coco.

"Glad to hear it. You've got thirty minutes."

"That's not a lot of time."

"It's enough. Meet me out front."

* * *

I was outside in twenty-five minutes. And it was a good thing, because they were early. The tinted black Mercedes-Benz Sprinter van made its way around the corner and came to a screeching halt right in front of me.

Smitty was behind the steering wheel.

The cabin door slid open and Johnnie stuck out his arm to hoist me in. He was already fully dressed in his red Santa suit. Axel and Blake were half dressed. I hopped in.

The door slammed shut as Johnnie tossed me a garment bag.

"Suit up," he said. "We've got a parade to get to."

Chapter 54

Anthony

Standing at the Mount Vernon Square metro station on the corner of Seventh and M streets, we watched as the crowd grew. Families scurried along the parade route to find their perfect spot. Traffic had yet to be diverted. All sizes and colors of Santas dodged oncoming cars as they crossed the street.

"Everybody ready?" Johnnie asked.

We all nodded our heads. Well, maybe not everyone.

Three elderly Black women stood on the corner. All with graying hair. Squid was preoccupied with the trio. He inched closer to get a look at the signage and pamphlets they set up on the small table nearby.

Each woman wore a full-length black skirt with a white blouse under their waist length jackets. One of them also wore a gray scarf wrapped around her neck.

After catching a glimpse of one of the signs, I knew the interaction wouldn't go well. One sign read: *JESUS LOVES THE SINNER... BUT HATES THE SIN.* Another sign read: *PUT CHRIST BACK IN CHRISTMAS.*

I walked over to monitor.

"Jesus loves you, Santa," the lady with the gray scarf said.

"You don't say?" Squid responded. Fumbling around through the different pamphlets, Squid continued, "Whatcha got here?"

"Feel free to take whatever you need, Santa, and as many as you want. Share the Gospel of Jesus Christ!"

One piece of literature caught his eye. He picked it up. "Tell me a more about this one," he said.

The lady said, "Yes... *Breaking the Addiction of Porn and Masturbation.* Pray to Jesus and he can help you."

Squid flipped through it for a moment and then handed it back to the lady.

"Nope. I'm good with that one. I broke those addictions long time ago."

"Praise God!" One of the other women exclaimed.

"See..." Squid stepped in and talked just above a whisper. "People have no idea how much pornography can get ahold of you. It creeps around in your brain." Squid pointed to his head. "It has you thinking all kind of crazy things."

"Tell it, young man! Tell it!" the third lady said.

"But I broke it!" Squid continued. "And it's an everyday struggle, you know what I mean? Just talking about porn can take my mind to different places. Like right now... I just can't stop staring at your sixty-year-old titties."

The three women jumped back and shrieked in horror.

"Ok... that's enough," I said as I pulled him away by the arm.

By the time we got back to the guys, Squid was laughing uncontrollably.

"You have your fun?" Axel asked.

"Hey! There it is," Johnnie pointed out a white armored truck with blue letters that spelled out BRINKS. The truck sat at the traffic light, waiting to make a left turn.

Johnnie turned to us and said, "We need to get in place. Let's go."

As we walked toward the bank, which was just a few blocks away, we bustled our way through the growing crowd.

In the process, Squid bumped into a little boy who was walking in the opposite direction, with his mother. The boy couldn't have been more than eight years old. He held a stuffed animal... Rudolph the Red-Nosed Reindeer. And Squid knocked it clean out of his hands.

Blake saw it. I watched as he doubled back and picked up the stuffed animal from the ground. The little boy smiled and his mother thanked Blake.

"I can't wait to see you in the parade, Santa," the little boy said.

Blake smiled back and let out a hearty, "HO! HO! HO! You be a good boy! Now Santa's gotta go finish making Christmas toys!"

The boy waved as his mother dragged him away to find a place to stand along the parade route.

"Finish making Christmas toys..." I thought to myself.

Maybe we'd have energy for toys after the truck robbery.

Chapter 55

Anthony

Only forty yards away from the armored truck parked outside of the Bank of America on K Street.

"Ok! Let's get the front of the line together... to my left!" I heard the instructions over the loudspeaker. I looked over my shoulder and saw the parade was about to start. The mass of Santas had formed at the corner of Seventh Street and Mt. Vernon Plaza.

The armored truck was directly in front of us. There was a guard at the back door of the vehicle. A second man stood at the front door of the building. I could see a third man through the glass windows that lined the front of the bank. The large man carried six bank courier bags with ease. He held two courier bags by the handles in each hand. Two additional bags were strapped to his back.

As soon as he walked out of the building, his partner stepped inside the door and turned his attention to the people in the bank. Probably to make sure no one snuck up on them.

The guard at the truck opened the back door as his partner

approached. In one motion, the bag carrier tossed the bags in the truck and then swung the extra bags from his back and tossed them in as well.

By that time, we closed the distance between us and the bank. Axel was closest to the front door. Johnnie, Squid, Blake, and I were a couple steps behind. Closer to the guards at the truck.

The bag man looked at his partner. "That's the rest of 'em. I'll get Mitch."

He turned around and headed back toward the bank. Being a nice and respectful Santa, Axel held the door wide open for him. But Squid wasn't as nice and respectful.

Running at full speed, Squid crashed his shoulder into the back of the guard. The man left his feet and flew past Axel, who slammed the door shut. Retrieving a U-shaped padlock from within his Santa suit, Axel quickly fastened it to the door handles. Locking the two guards inside, leaving only one guard at the truck and all of its money.

Johnnie had already pulled a Glock 17 out of his Santa suit and shoved it in the guard's face. "Don't you move," he said.

The guards inside the bank began banging on the glass doors with their fists. But it was too late. We were already inside the truck. As we ripped white cotton stuffing from the belly of our Santa suits, we quickly replaced it with courier bags from the bank.

We moved as fast as we could. The truck's 360-degree video surveillance most certainly had broadcasted our activities to their command center and the cops were on their way.

"Let's go!" Johnnie yelled to us from outside the truck.

I was ready. Axel and Blake were ready. But Squid was trying to stuff one more bag into his suit. And it wasn't working.

"Leave it man! We've gotta go!" I said.

"Yeah. Come on," Blake added.

Squid ignored us as the sound of squad car sirens were blaring off in the distance.

I grabbed Squid by his arm and spun him around. "We don't have time for..."

Before I could finish my sentence, Squid jammed his Sig Sauer pistol in my face.

"Back off!" he said.

With my hands raised in the air, I did just that. There was no telling whether Squid was bluffing or not. He shoved the gun back into his Santa suit and continued wrestling with another bag.

With the few seconds of silence we had, I thought about Squid's miscalculation. Threatening me with a gun? He should've just pulled the trigger.

Then gunshots rang out. Two of them. I heard the crackling of shattered glass dancing along concrete pavement.

We all crouched low. I peeped out to see that the gunshots came from the guards. They wrestled against the door, banging the metal handles against the iron of the U-shaped locks. It wouldn't be long before they were free.

Johnnie didn't hesitate. He struck the guard he covered with the side of his gun. Once the man went to the ground, Johnnie then kicked him under his chin. I was certain he shattered his jaw.

I pulled out my gun and fired at the other guards. I aimed at the ground near their feet with the hopes that they would retreat into the building. It worked long enough for Axel, Blake, and Squid's greedy ass to hop out of the truck. Johnnie followed my lead with gunfire of his own to provide cover for me. Without hesitation, I chased after the gang.

Walking briskly to the corner of K and Tenth Streets, we heard the wailing of cop sirens from the other direction... Ninth Street. Just as they screeched to a stop in front of the bank, we hit the corner and turned up Tenth Street. With all of the bags stuffed in our suits, we couldn't run. Walking as quickly as we could, we made it to Massachusetts Avenue.

I chewed my lip as I watched seven police officers, on foot, turn the corner in pursuit. They ran at top speed in search of five armored truck robbery suspects dressed as Santa Claus. Their pace went from a sprint to a jog, to a slow walk until they stopped at Massachusetts Avenue.

Now caught in the parade route. The look of befuddlement on their faces truly amused me. Maybe Johnnie was brilliant after all. We slowed our pace to a steady stride. After a five block lead, our pursuers were completely out of view.

The police desperately searched for five men who robbed an armored truck. Dressed as Santa Claus. Unfortunately for the cops, they were searching through a sea of them.

Chapter 56

Anthony

We rumbled into the warehouse like bowling balls rolling down a lane. Crashing into the front door as if it was a pin.

Laughs and jeers echoed throughout the space. The excitement could not be contained.

"Wasn't it a great plan?" Johnnie asked. His need for approval was ever present. But in this case, it was well deserved. The plan worked. No one was arrested or shot. And we made it back with the money.

"Yes sir. You are the man!" I said.

Johnnie pointed to Axel.

"Hey! Call Smitty. Tell him to get his ass over here so he can get his cut."

"He's gotta get that van from out back too. We can't have it lingering around," Axel said.

"Right," Johnnie said. "Blake, get the table set up."

Squid took a drill to the padlocks on each of the banks courier bags. As he demolished the locks, Johnnie and I dumped mounds of money on the table.

"The table's ready to go," Blake said.

I walked behind Blake and stood over his shoulder.

"What do we have here?" I asked.

"The Safescan 2885-2. It counts fifteen hundred bills a minute."

"You don't say." I looked up to see Johnnie and Squid stuffing the Santa suits in a green metal barrel.

I was thrilled at our taste of success, but something had bothered me the entire ride back to the warehouse. It was Squid.

Squid put his gun in my face and in doing so, violated a simple rule of mine. Never point a gun at anything you don't intend to destroy. And he put his gun in my face.

I wanted to address the issue as soon as possible, so I approached Squid and Johnnie, eyeing the gun inside Squid's waistband. I wasn't sure if it was the only gun on him until I remembered getting dressed in the van earlier. At one point, he had stripped down to his boxer briefs. I knew for a fact it was his only gun.

Drawing closer to both men, Johnnie must have sensed something wasn't right with me.

"Aye. You good man?"

I shoved Johnnie out of the way and lunged at Squid. In a split second I had his gun in my left hand and my gun in my right. I held both of them against Squid's chest. He threw his hands up immediately.

"Woah! What the hell is going on?!" Johnnie shouted.

The commotion was swift yet loud. Blake jumped up from the table.

Axel ran over to us with his hands extended. "Anthony!"

Johnnie recovered himself and carefully approached me. "You wanna tell me what this is about?"

"You need to pick your crew more carefully," I said.

"What do you mean? Everything went great," Johnnie said.

"It was going great. Until this fool pointed a loaded gun at me in the van."

Johnnie turned his attention from me to Squid. He closed eyes and took a deep breath. With gritted teeth, he then looked at Squid again. Johnnie placed his hands together in a prayer posture and said, "Squid. Please tell me you did not point your gun at Anthony."

"I was trying to get more money and he was rushing me."

And with that, I took four steps back. I hit the magazine release for both guns, dropping the loaded magazines. I carefully pulled back the slide on the first gun, ejecting the bullet that rested in the chamber. And then I tossed the empty gun to the corner of the warehouse. After a second, I did the same with the other gun.

I couldn't wait to knock Squid out.

Chapter 57

Priest

Priest, Harvey, Maddox, and the Enforcer quietly crouched outside of the warehouse with the rest of the Broken Brotherhood.

Priest and Harvey peered through the window.

"They look like they're going to kill each other," Harvey said.

"Good. It'll save us the hassle," Priest said.

Maddox overheard the comments and twisted his face in disagreement. "Wait a minute. What you do you mean? Isn't this a parley?" he asked.

Priest and Harvey looked at each other. Priest then nodded to the Enforcer.

The Enforcer ran off toward the motorcycles parked around the corner.

"I made an executive decision, Maddox. No parley. Instead, we're going to run the table, kill these bastards, and take their money. Do you have a problem with that?"

Maddox hesitated and didn't offer a response.

"Maddy. Do you have a problem with it?" Priest asked again.

The Enforcer came back to the brothers, carrying a forty-pound tactical battering ram. It was the same kind you'd find SWAT using to break down a door.

Priest looked at Maddox. "This is it. We handle this right, and we'll run this place. I'm assuming you're with us. Because if I have to assume otherwise..." Priest shook his head from side to side to indicate it would be a bad move on his part. "When he knocks down the door, if you're not the first one through, I'll shoot you where you stand."

Priest wasn't bluffing... and Maddox knew it.

Chapter 58

Anthony

"Nobody's scared of you," Squid said. He welcomed my challenge.

"Good," I said.

"Come on y'all," Johnnie said. "We've got all this money. Let's calm down and count it up."

"Nah. I'm good," Squid and I said at the same time.

There was an awkward silence.

Blake walked over to me. He placed a hand on my shoulder. "You don't have to do this," he said in my ear.

I smiled and said, "I know."

It was at that moment I recognized a hard truth. It was a bitter pill to swallow. I had fooled myself into thinking that I returned to Washington, DC a changed man.

I was even more foolish for thinking that this job with Johnnie wasn't a road that would lead me to this moment. Because here I am, back to being Anthony Ribisi.

I wasn't a victim of muscle memory taking over and recapturing my second nature. No. This was me being me.

Johnnie squeezed out a deep sigh of frustration.

Johnnie cursed and then said, "Axel, Blake. Come with me. I'll call Smitty and tell him we have the van.

"Gentlemen. You've got fifteen minutes, twenty tops, to work this out. Knock over what you want, but stay away from the money pile. Don't knock that over."

Johnnie frantically walked out of the back door. Axel and Blake followed him.

Squid and I stared at each other. Six feet of space stood between us. As soon as we heard the back door slam shut, Squid made the first move.

He bolted at me, throwing his body through the air. His shoulder crashed into my stomach. The force of the blow sent me to the ground. The full weight of his frame landed on top of me. He wasn't on top of me for long because the momentum from his attack caused his body to roll another foot or two.

But the damage had already been done. The wind had been knocked out of me. I flopped around like a fish gasping for air. While I flopped, Squid looked to take advantage of my incapacitation. He pushed himself off the ground and charged at me again.

But this time, I slid to my right and in the process, kicked him between the legs—right in the nut sack.

Squid howled. He crumpled over immediately. I could only imagine, but the pain must have been unbearable.

Now standing over him, he attempted to crawl away from me. I looked past him and saw where he was headed.

There was a metal pipe in the corner of the room.

Squid moved so slow I was able to walk past him at a regular pace. I reached down and picked up the pipe.

"Is this what you're looking for?"

I placed my foot on Squid's back and with a thrust of my leg, pushed him to the ground. He was face down. I used the same foot to roll him over on his back.

Jabbing Squid's chest with the pipe, I said, "You've been a pain in my ass ever since I got back. How long did you think I'd let that ride?"

Squid's eyes bulged. His face was covered in sweat. My foot was still on him, and I could feel his body trembling.

I lifted the pipe above my head, ready to bring the full force of the makeshift weapon down on him. But the thundering sound of metal on metal grabbed my attention.

It was torn away from Squid and placed on the front door of the warehouse. The door now hung off its hinges and a wild hulk of a man with a mohawk ran in followed by no less than twenty others. All of them wore motorcycle jackets. I assumed this was the MC gang Smitty told me about.

Handheld cannons were being waved around. Everyone had a gun. Everyone except me. Well, except me and Squid.

I reached for it but it wasn't there. Then I remembered that I threw our guns to the other side of the room. Save the pipe, I was unarmed.

The gang parted, like the Red Sea, to let a scraggly, long-haired man walk through. The leader, I surmised. A younger version of him stepped from out of the crowd and joined him by his side.

"The infamous Anthony Ribisi? This was easier than I thought," the man said.

Looking at the numbers and thinking through my options, I decided not to be antagonistic. Escaping wasn't on my radar. I knew that ship had sailed. But patience would hopefully win out and provide me an opportunity to live.

"Who are you guys?" I asked. But I already knew.

I still held the pipe in one hand.

"Who are we? We're a reckoning that's been a long time coming."

"Yeah... that doesn't tell me shit."

The decision to not antagonize went out the window. The stranger didn't respond to me. Instead, he nodded to Squid, who was still on the floor.

The hulk with the mohawk grabbed Squid and lifted him off his feet. At the same time, two smaller men grabbed me by my arms. A third snatched the pipe out of my hand.

The stranger approached the dangling Squid. "Where are the rest?"

Squid grunted between the flailing and kicking of his legs.

"It doesn't matter. I want you to find them. Tell them we took the money and killed Anthony."

The walking muscle discarded Squid like a crumpled piece of paper. Squid slid across the floor on his back.

"If they have a problem with it, tell them to come find me."

Squid propped himself up on his elbows but beyond that, he didn't move.

The stranger was handed the metal pipe and pointed at Squid.

"Leave," the stranger said.

Squid was still frozen in time. And the stranger scratched his head with the end of the pipe. His impatience erupted in an unexpected way that wasn't good for me. He crashed the pipe against the side of my head.

I heard a thud. There was a ringing in my ears. The pain and trauma of being struck with a blunt object forced me to my knees. I was barely conscious.

"Get out of here!" Echoed a voice in my head.

Even with blurred vision, I could see the sense of urgency in Squid's movements. He turned over on all fours and scurried to his feet until he was in a full sprint out the front door. Then the attention was back to me.

The most I could do was get into the fetal position as I was mercilessly beaten by this man, whom I've never met. I protected my head as much as I could, but the pipe still pummeled my body.

I felt the breaking of skin. The bruising of muscles. Bones crunched with every hit. I willed myself to remain conscious and wouldn't give him the satisfaction of seeing me pass out. He would have to killed me. And it felt like that's exactly what he intended on doing, until the young man ran to my defense.

He grabbed the stranger's arm. "Priest! Stop!"

Priest, I thought.

"You're going to kill him," he said.

"Yeah," Priest replied. "That's kind of the point."

"Don't do this," the younger man pleaded. I silently agreed with him.

Priest didn't seem convinced. He took his gun and thrusted it into the younger man's hands.

"You're right. I won't kill him. You do it." Priest said.

The room fell silent. The younger man must have had an aversion to murder. He recoiled at the thought of having to shoot me.

"Gentlemen! Tonight, Maddy pops his cherry," Priest yelled out to the crowd with a grin plastered across his face.

Maddy was the other man's name. And then it made sense. This was a sibling rivalry.

Maddy took a few steps back as he protested a second time. Shaking his head, he said, "I'm not a murderer."

Short of patience, Priest reached out and grabbed his younger brother by collar of his motorcycle jacket. He yanked him closer with a neck-snapping force.

"You ever hear the saying 'kill or be killed'?"

His grip grew tighter. Maddy struggled against his brothers' strength. He ultimately wrangled free and jumped back, creating a separation between them. Then Maddy did something I didn't expect. He aimed his gun at his brother.

The energy in the room vibrated at a higher frequency. In an instinctual reaction to the threat posed toward their leader, members of the gang lurched forward. But Priest extended his arms out toward the men to indicate that he didn't want them advancing another step. The men stopped.

Priest never broke eye contact with his brother. He remained calm. There was no anxiety in his voice. "And I thought you said you weren't a murderer."

Disregarding his brother and the pistol aimed at his chest, Priest motioned to the rest of the gang. "Brothers... bag up the money and let's go. Maddox has some work to do here."

The gang cleaned us out and was gone in less than five minutes.

Maddy and I were left in an empty room. Gun in hand, he turned toward me. What was he waiting for? I was broken and bleeding. I was nothing but a discarded man, unable to do anything but lie on the floor and wait for death. Consciousness slipped away with the passing seconds.

I struggled to keep my eyes open. I then heard the *CLICK* of a cocked hammer. After that, the last thing I heard was a slight whisper from Maddy.

He said, "I'm sorry."

Chapter 59

Priest

Priest sat on his motorcycle, outside of the warehouse. Harvey stood next to him.

"I swear... if he doesn't shoot him, I'll kill 'em both."

"Stop it," Harvey said. "We both know you're not going to kill your brother."

"Shh," Priest said. "You hear that?"

"What? I don't hear nothing."

"My point exactly. Tell the road captain to get everyone ready. After I end this, we leave."

Priest hopped off his bike and walked toward the warehouse.

He was ten feet from the door before a gunshot rang out from the building. It stopped him cold in his tracks.

Then there was a second shot. A smirk crawled across Priest's face.

Before he could take another step toward the building, Maddox emerged hold his brother's gun.

"You did it," Priest said.

Without saying a word, Maddox threw the gun at his brother's feet.

When Priest bent over to pick it up, his face was met with Maddox's right hand. The uppercut sent him reeling backwards.

A few members of Broken Brotherhood rushed over to Priest to help him up.

"No. No. I got it," he said, so that he'd be left alone.

"I guess I deserved that," Priest said.

Maddox walked over to his bike and cranked her up.

"No. You haven't gotten what you deserve. Not yet."

Chapter 60

Johnnie

Johnnie and Blake ran to the front door of the warehouse but Smitty pushed them back. Like a sentry, he guarded the door. It was much like Smitty's old club bouncer days.

Squid and Axel remained on the sidewalk, not looking at all interested in going near the building. Or Smitty.

"Let me in! Is he in there? Is he dead?" Johnnie said.

"Stand back, Johnnie."

"What do you mean, 'Stand back'? This is my warehouse!"

"I'm not going to tell you again."

"Hey man. Maybe you should calm down," Blake said to Johnnie.

"I don't have to calm down! Who the hell does he think he's talking to?" Johnnie said.

"I get it," Smitty said. "But I'm just following orders."

Johnnie scratched his head. Befuddlement flashed across his face.

"Orders?" Johnnie said. "But you work for me."

"Don't be stupid," a familiar voice from a distant past sounded from behind.

"Uncle Remo?" Johnnie said before turning around. More confusion set in. "I'm lost. What the hell is going on here?

Johnnie stumbled back on his heels as Remo brushed past him. Remo walked up to Smitty and patted his shoulder.

"You're parked in the back, right?"

Smitty nodded.

"Ok," Remo said. "Go get my boy. You know where to take him."

Then Remo turn his attention to Johnnie.

"Nephew... What are you doing? You might be in over your head. You should get out. Now."

"How many years has it been? And that's what you got for me?"

"That doesn't matter. I need to get Anthony out of here before someone actually succeeds in killing him."

"He's alive. Good!" Johnnie said. "Leave him with me. Don't you have to go back to New York or something?"

"Why should I leave him?" Remo asked. "Does he *work* for you too?"

Finally hitting the mark of his frustration, Johnnie lashed out. "You can't just pop up after years and think you can run shit!"

"Yes, I can. And no... I'm not leaving Anthony with you. You're the reason he nearly died."

Smitty returned, wiping what looked to be Anthony's blood from his hands onto a brown rag.

"We're ready to go. But he's in bad shape."

"Go," Remo said.

Remo pulled out his phone and dialed. "It's me again. We'll be there soon." Remo stopped and looked at Johnnie. "Don't worry. I will."

Remo disconnected the call and asked Johnnie to walk with him.

"What's going on, Uncle Remo? What are you doing here? How bad is Anthony?"

Remo didn't say a word. He let Johnnie squirm in the intentional silence.

Then he walked to his car. Johnnie followed.

"Uncle Remo?"

There was no response.

Johnnie called out again, "Remo!"

Remo turned around once he reached the car. His nephew was on his heels.

"I don't have time for the questions or the bullshit. Just know that I've been in town long enough for people to tell me things.

"From what I hear, I think your father would be very disappointed. And from what I see," Remo motioned to the residual mayhem left around them. "I know he would. You should stop... before things get out of hand."

"Everything is under control," Johnnie said.

"Really? Including the Broken Brotherhood?"

Johnnie hesitated. There was no response.

"Never mind," Remo said. "Don't bothering answering that question. The Broken Brotherhood has your number. And from what I can tell, they have your money too."

Chapter 61

Metty

Thursday, September 19th

Metty sat at the center of a U-shaped counter and scanned the kitchen that was bigger than her apartment. The white mug in front of her rebelled against the black marble counter beneath it.

She wore navy blue and white flannel pajama pants and a Howard University hoodie with the same colors. Metty didn't attend the school, but enjoyed going to their homecoming concerts and parties every year.

Staring straight ahead past the sink and out of the large rectangular window, she was lost in the greenery outside. There was a field of grass beyond the other side of the window. And after the grass came a forest of pine trees, standing at attention.

She broke her gaze just long enough to pull the white mug from the marble, placing it to her lips. After taking a sip, she heard footsteps walking toward the kitchen from her right. It was Remo. He was with the owner of the gigantic kitchen.

Metty nodded at Remo first and then turned her attention to her host.

"Good morning Mr. Lowinger," Metty said, carefully rhyming his name with "singer" to pronounce it correctly. But she still missed the mark.

"Ger," he said. "Low-in-GER. Just think of Ger-man."

Metty lowered her eyes and said, "Sorry," just above a whisper.

The man grabbed a French press coffee carafe that was sitting on the countertop near the door.

"Don't worry about it," he said. "Let me get that for you." He refilled her mug. "Besides, with a name like mine, I insist on being called Jack."

Metty looked at Remo. He closed his eyes and nodded his head in approval.

"Thanks for the coffee, Jack," Metty said.

"You're welcome." Jack placed the carafe down in front of Metty. "What do you think of the house?"

"It's absolutely beautiful," Metty said. "Must've cost a fortune."

"Not really. Not when you're in control of the concrete and cranes."

"Oh. You're in construction," Metty's words trailed off. Then her eyes became wide with excitement. "Oh! Lowinger Construction! You have cranes all over DC with your name on them!"

Jack smiled. "When I was a kid..."

"Oh boy," Remo interrupted. "I'm sorry, hun. He always has a story."

Jack stopped talking, shot him a glance, and then rolled his eyes. "When I was a kid... my mother didn't have money. My father split before I was five and my mother had to work three jobs to make ends meet and put food on the table. And to keep a roof over our heads." He motioned toward the ceiling above him.

"Must've been rough," Metty said.

"In the worst way. But something tells me you can relate. My mom worked three jobs. And we were still evicted."

Jack looked at Remo and facetiously asked, "How could that be?"

He turned his attention back to Metty, he said, "She worked her fingers to the bone to rent that measly apartment. Hard work, was paid weekly, and that still wasn't enough to live. That's what happens to the working poor.

"I learned at a very young age that security comes from ownership and I made up my mind that I would own. Not rent, borrow, or beg. But own.

"So yes... you see my cranes all over the District. I worked hard for that."

"This man," Remo said, "has singlehandedly changed the skyline of DC. Forget the Capitol or the Washington Monument. Now all you see are his ugly ass cranes spread throughout the city."

"That's right. It's my own Crane City," Jack said.

"And no one will ever evict you again," Metty added.

"Precisely." Jack grabbed a mug and poured himself a cup of coffee.

"Metty?" Jack said. "Would you be a doll and check on Anthony? Remo and I need to finish our talk."

When Jack wanted privacy, being direct was never a problem for him.

"No problem," Metty said. She slid her stool back from the marble counter and then took the mug and coffee carafe in each hand.

Metty walked to the door, but spun back to the men before walking through. "What if he's awake? What should I do?"

Jack, being the arbiter of directness, simply said, "I think the polite thing to do would be to introduce yourself."

Chapter 62

Remo

"To old times," Jack said. He raised his mug of coffee.

Remo let out a chuckle. "Old times? Not quite."

Jack sighed in exasperation. "If not like old times, then why are you here? I haven't seen you in over a decade and the boy, I haven't been face-to-face with him since he was almost a teen."

"Don't get ahead of yourself," Remo said.

"Don't you hold us back," Jack replied. "Haven't you ever thought of getting the crew back together? A new and improved version, maybe."

"For starters, Marco is dead."

"Didn't I say new and improved?" Jack said. "Sorry for your loss, by the way."

Remo shrugged off the belated consolation.

"And as for Nick Nick," Jack continued, "it's a shame he was a murderous backstabbing traitor. I'm glad that rat is dead."

Remo reflected on Jack's comments about Nick Nick's death. He wrinkled up one side of his face.

"Umm... yeah. Nick Nick."

Jack walked to the sink and dumped the rest of his coffee.

"I'm just hoping we could lay low for a few days until he's rested," Remo said.

"And then what? Leave town? You should consider staying. Right now, I'm pretty much working alone. And I'm tired of cleaning money for imbeciles, babies, and wannabe gangsters. At least with you around, I'll have a peer to commiserate with while getting paid."

"You're already paid," Remo said.

"Who doesn't want more money?" Jack said.

Remo rolled his eyes and said, "I'll give it some thought."

"Liar. But you know what... I've kept an eye on the kid over the years. Up until he disappeared, that is. He's impressive. You know who he reminds me of?" Jack said.

Remo didn't acknowledge Jack's comment. Something in the silence connected the dots for Jack.

"Wait a minute," Jack said. "He doesn't know?"

Remo rolled his eyes. "Marco never told him and I haven't either. Let's leave it at that, because there's a lot you don't know."

"What's not to know? Anthony is a chip off the old block. His father was fearsome and so is the kid."

"Anthony doesn't know much about his father. He was very young when..." Remo's words trailed to a silent pause. "He absolutely doesn't know his father worked with us. Let's keep it that way."

"Come on, Remo. History is a cycle, and it always repeats itself."

* * *

Remo thought back on the first time he had ever seen Anthony. They hadn't officially met. And he was Jelani then.

Angel Jones, Jelani's mother, stood under the shaded canopy of a cherry blossom tree. Her youngest son played just a few feet away from her.

The little boy rolled around on the ground, turning a patch of grass between the Jefferson Memorial and the Tidal Basin into his personal playground.

"Stay where I can see you!" she yelled out. "Stay clear of the water!"

After a few seconds, he screamed back, "Okay mama." He was now on his feet, running in circles and tossing the blossoms that had fallen from the trees into the air.

Angel looked at her watch and then spun her head in both directions. She was waiting on someone.

A few minutes passed before she let out a sigh of relief. From the same direction as Jelani played, she watched as Remo approached her.

The boy and the man had not known each other. That moment would come soon after. But for now, Remo walked past the kid and didn't think anything of it. Jelani continued playing, lost in his own world.

Remo stopped within two feet of Angel. This was the first time he had shared the same space as her in almost fifteen years. They were estranged up until this moment.

As she stepped out of the shadow of the tree, the glow of the sun reflected off of her freckled, honey brown face. The mix of green, yellow, and brown in her hazel eyes captivated Remo. All over again.

He wanted to hug her, but since he had just murdered her husband, the idea didn't feel right.

Angel broke the ice and lunged at Remo, wrapping both arms around him. Uneasy and unsure, Remo gave into it and hugged her back.

Now that he was close enough, he looked deeper into her

eyes. They were bloodshot red and puffy. She had been crying. Probably not sleeping. And Remo pretended not to know why.

But Remo knew why Angel had called him out of the blue. She asked to meet with him. Remo had no illusion to the reason behind the meeting. She didn't want him back. She wasn't over her missing husband. She needed help and figured Remo would be the one to help her.

Remo patiently waited for the favor that she would inevitably ask. But holding her in that moment, he took his time to inhale the flavor of her natural pheromones.

Remo thought he had broken the addiction to Angel's bodily scent. He was wrong.

Gathering her composure, Angel extended her arms and gently pushed away from Remo. In truth, she was merely steadying herself against Remo's sturdy physique.

"It's been years," Remo said.

Angel nodded her head.

"Never thought I'd see you again," Remo continued.

Angel was doing a painstaking job of holding in her tears. "And you still came," she said.

Remo rolled his eyes as to signify he didn't have any choice in the matter. "You called. Did you expect anything different?"

"No," Angel said. "I guess not."

The time for small talk had come and gone. Remo decided to rip the band aid off the raw wound and just get to the matter.

"So... why'd you call?" he disingenuously asked.

Angel didn't immediately respond. Instead, her body was invaded by tremors. She had done a yeoman's job at holding back tears—up until that moment. Remo's question unleashed a torrent of emotion that she couldn't defiantly stand against. Tears flowed freely. Violently.

"I don't know where he is," Angel said through sobs.

"Your husband?" Remo asked.

"Yes," Angel said through tears. "I know it's crazy coming to you with this, given our history and all. But I didn't know who else to turn to.

"It's not like him to vanish. Something is wrong. And I know if anyone can find out what's going on, it's you. Help me find my husband, Remo."

The soft spot for Angel hadn't dissipated. But what she was asking for, Remo couldn't help her with. No matter how much he still wanted her.

She was distraught and looking for her missing husband. Remo knew where he was. But neither him nor the waters at the bottom of the Tidal Basin would share their secrets.

Just then, Metty came rushing back into the kitchen.

"Hopefully history won't repeat itself this time," Remo said before looking at Metty. "Yes?"

Her eyes jumped between the two men. "It's Anthony," Metty said. "He's awake."

Chapter 63

Anthony

My head pulsed with a throbbing pain unlike anything I've ever felt. I tried to prop myself up, but moving just made it worse.

The first person who tumbled through the door had the face of a distant memory.

"Uncle Remo?" I said. I thought I was dreaming.

He walked to the bed and asked, "How are you feeling?"

Before I could answer, two more faces surfaced in the room.

The woman was a mystery to me. But the man was vaguely familiar.

"Where am I? How long was I out?" I asked.

"You're safe. That's all that matters. How's your head?"

"I've had better days," I said.

Looking at the older white man, I tried to place his face. He approached the other side of the bed. "You gave us a pretty good scare, kid," he said.

"I gave myself one too."

"You probably have a bunch of questions," Remo said. He

looked at the other two and said, "Let's give him some space to rest."

Everyone nodded in agreement. As they began walking away, it hit me.

"Mr. Lowinger?"

The white man stopped and turned around. "It's been a long time, kid. You've looked better."

"I bet," I laughed, wincing in pain. I looked past him at the young woman standing behind him. "You're new. Eritrean?"

She incredulously placed a hand on her hip. "What is it with you and Remo? I'm Ethiopian."

Chapter 64

Anthony

"You don't have to check on me every thirty minutes," I said.

Metty sat in a brown leather swivel chair across from the bed. "I know," she said. "But Remo insists."

I swung my legs over the side of the bed and placed them firmly on the floor. My body was still bruised, but the pain had started to subside. It could have been the pills Lowinger gave me.

Supporting my body with my arms against the bed, I pushed forward and stood straight up. Lightheaded, I scanned the room before taking a step toward the window that was to the left of Metty. "Who put these pajamas on me?"

"Wasn't me," Metty said, as we laughed.

"Where are we? Do you know?"

Metty shook her head. "Somewhere in Virginia, I think."

"Upperville, to be precise," Remo said from behind us. He stood at the door with Mr. Lowinger and another man.

"Doc. Should he still be in bed?" Mr. Lowinger said.

"That's a good idea," the doctor said. "You're nowhere near a hundred percent. Don't push it when you don't have to."

I turned around, shrugged my shoulders as I made my way back to the bed. My balance was off. I stumbled after taking my first step. It was a good thing Metty was nearby. If she hadn't sprung out of her seat to help me, I would've fallen flat on my face.

With Metty's assistance, I made it back to the bed.

"Sit up and take off your shirt," the doctor said.

For the next fifteen minutes, the doctor performed a standard physical evaluation. He flashed a light from a pen in my eyes to see how my pupils dilated. Then he listened to my lungs with his stethoscope. Afterwards, he took my temperature and finished by taking my blood pressure.

"Vitals seem fine," he said. The doctor reached in his pocket, pulled out a pill bottle and shook it. "Vicodin. Your body is doing a great job healing itself. So only use this if you're in severe pain."

"Sure thing, Doc."

With that, he spun around, shook hands with Remo and walked out the door. He passed Lowinger on his way out.

I tossed the pill bottle in the trash can.

"The golf cart is charged up and ready to go," Mr. Lowinger said.

Remo looked at me and said, "You have ten minutes to get yourself together. Then meet us out front.

"I don't golf," I said.

"Neither do I, but I'm sure you have questions," Remo said, "and answers can be offered on the golf cart in ten minutes."

Chapter 65

Anthony

Lowinger maneuvered the golf cart across the perfectly manicured grass. Seated next to him was a brown duffle bag that was large enough to hold an adult male body. Remo and I sat in the back two seats.

We came to a tree-lined gravel road. The road went from smooth to bumpy. Jack pointed out structures as we drove by them. Remo didn't look impressed. I was certain he had been there plenty times before. But for me, I had never seen such a thing.

"This place started as a plantation. The original structure was a farmhouse built in 1889," Lowinger yelled over his shoulder. "As we moved into the 20th century, different owners added different pieces.

"That's the barn over there," Jack continued pointing. "I had to rebuild it."

Jack then pointed out a redbrick hanger in the opposite direction. "And those are the stables."

We rode pass a small pond just beyond the barn. The water shimmered as the late morning sun danced along its surface.

The path we rode made another transition. We had gone from grass to gravel, and now rolled along a dirt road, which took us into a heavily wooded area. I looked back at the barn and the stables as they shrank in the distance. Soon after, a fortress of trees blocked them from my view. The woods surrounded us.

"You haven't asked yet," Remo said to me.

"Not sure I understand you."

"I came back to DC right when your life is in danger. And you don't think anything of it?"

Pondering the question, I said, "Yeah... I gave it some thought."

"And?"

"Look... I don't know what's going on. New Orleans is a pretty good setup for me. It's an escape from the fights, the guns... and the almost getting killed, you know. It's madness.

"And I have a lady who doesn't mind coming to visit. She's even thinking about moving there. I hadn't been back more than a couple days and I'm robbing cash trucks. Oh... and I get the living shit knocked out of me by a motorcycle gang.

"I'm not too sure I'm remotely interested in why you're back or what it has to do with me. I just want get back to New Orleans and leave all the madness of running and gunning in the past, if you don't mind."

The golf cart came to a stop at the foot of a dark brown hill that looked to be made of dirt and hay. It was at least thirty feet in height. There was a slight stench of manure as well.

Mr. Lowinger grabbed his duffle bag and was the first one out.

"We're headed just on the other side of the compost pile," Jack said.

Remo and I hopped out and began to follow.

"I've known you since your childhood. If you think for one

minute I don't have your best interest at heart, then you're wrong," Remo said between steps. "It's just that you and I are like fish and this kind of world is our ocean. The madness, to use your word, affirms who we are."

I heard what Remo was saying, but I don't think I was listening. That was largely because the next sounds I heard stopped me in my tracks.

"Hold on, y'all! Are those guns shots?!"

Chapter 66

Anthony

The sound of gunshots grew louder with every step. Once we reached our destination, the reason for them became apparent.

Along with a barn and stables, Jack Lowinger also built a private shooting range on the inner most part of the forest, adjacent to his property. In front of us was a fifty-yard tract of dirt, about thirty feet in width.

At the end of the tract was a wall made of tree logs, dirt, and packed mud. Human silhouettes were scattered throughout the homemade gun range as targets.

Jack reached into his duffle bag and pulled out two pairs of earmuffs and tinted glasses for protection. "You'll want to put these on before going any further."

We did just that and followed Jack's lead.

Another shot rang out. There was a man, who looked to be around my age, standing behind a six-foot table littered with firearms.

From where I stood, I saw and counted at least six semiautomatic pistols, four revolvers, two AK-47s, an AR-15, and an M16 rifle

My eyes widened with excitement. *What the hell!* I thought to myself.

Remo read me like a book. "Leave the madness behind," he said. "Yeah... right."

The guy behind the table noticed us walk up just as the slide to his pistol locked open. His magazine was empty. He dropped the magazine out of the gun, caught it with one hand, and placed it on the table along with the gun.

Snatching the eye and ear protection off, he yelled at Jack, "You trying to get some practice in old man?"

"Old man?" Jack said as he placed his duffle bag on the table. "Don't think your father can't outshoot you!"

"You wish," the young man said.

Jacked unpacked his own personal arsenal, which included a container of ammunition.

I looked at Remo and finally spoke up. "Ok. Who wants to tell me what the hell is going on?"

"Come over here," Jack said, waving us over.

"Hey Uncle Remo," the young man said. The two of them embraced.

"It's been a few years. You look good. Strong!" Remo said.

"That's what Special Forces will do for you," Jack said with the widest grin. Pride beamed from his face. Then he turned to me, saying, "You two probably don't remember each other. You were kids when you met."

Pieces of the past started to fall in place. The flood of images helped me recollect one of my favorite childhood memories.

And Jack and his son, they were there.

* * *

I was the only Black face in the room. Even at eleven years of age, the weight of that distinction wasn't lost on me. I was the only Black face and the reason for the celebration.

The dining room was full of Ribisi family and friends. They sang to me. *Happy birthday to you...*

It was the only birthday party I ever had. And it was a surprise party at that. Marco had planned the whole thing.

The room had been decorated with blue, yellow, red, and green streamers, and helium balloons of the same colors. The food was from the restaurant and completed with my favorite dessert, a Carvel ice cream cake. It was the best birthday ever.

"That's not how you sing the song," Remo yelled from across the room.

Projecting loud enough that the room was forced to sing along, Remo began, "*Tanti auguri a te.*"

The room burst into laughs.

I sat at the head of the lengthy dining room table with the ice cream cake in front of me. Clasping my eyes shut, I made a wish, and blew out the rainbow-colored wax candles.

I knew my wish wouldn't come true, but I made it regardless. I hopelessly longed for an overworked mother to walk through the door and claim me as her own. Or even a father who I never got a chance to know.

One by one, the family approached to wish me happy birthday. They all came with a card and gift of some sort. First came the adults and then the children.

I didn't have many memories of Marco's wife, but this was one of my favorites. Mama Amalia was what I called her.

Sitting next to me at the table, Mama Amalia cleaned the ice cream off my face as she received my birthday cards for me.

"*Grazie*," she would urge me to say.

The last adult to approach was Mr. Lowinger. He was accompanied by his son and had a hand on each of the boy's shoulders. I had briefly seen them around the restaurant and the house from time to time.

The boy held a box wrapped in white paper with a purple ribbon tied around it.

"Junior, this is Marco's other son," Jack said.

This was our first-time meeting. We just stared at each other. Junior broke eye contact first and flashed the most confused look at his father.

"Anthony," Mama Amalia said. "Dove solo le tue maniere?"

Where are your manners? I quickly translated in my head. And she was right. The least I could do was introduce myself.

"Hi. I'm Anthony." I extended my hand.

Junior placed the gift on the table and did the same. We shook hands. "Hi. I'm Junior."

Marco walked over to the four of us. "So, what did he get you?" Marco said after winking at the boy's father. "You should open it!"

I looked at Mama Amalia, concerned that it would have been rude to launch into tearing wrapping paper off the gift so soon. But she nodded her head, as to indicate that there was nothing wrong with it, at all.

After unwrapping the gift, Mama Amalia wasn't pleased. If I couldn't tell by the look she gave Marco and Jack, it was clear when she sucked her teeth, stood from her seat, and walked away. I, on the other hand, was ecstatic.

The picture on the box was of an automatic toy sniper rifle. From what I could tell, the toy came with two clips, one hundred foam bullets, a bipod, and scope. The box also advertised the toy's three shooting modes.

I would be able to shoot one bullet at a time, individual bullets in faster succession, or a rapid-fire mode that shot multiple foam bullets.

Junior pointed to the rainbow-colored bullseye targets on the box. “We can hang those out in the backyard.”

Before he finished his thought, I was already headed out the back door.

* * *

"It's Junior, right?" I said.

"Yes sir. And I remember you from the birthday party. When dad introduced us.”

“I remember you giving me the best birthday gift I ever received. Looks like much hasn’t changed with you.”

Junior motioned toward the table of guns. "Since you're here... any of these beauties calling out to you?"

I scanned the table and picked up a handgun. After inserting the magazine that was lying next to it, I chambered a round of ammunition.

"You're always bearing gifts," I said. "This is the one, right here."

"Ok... Keep in mind that these aren’t foam bullets,” Junior said with a grin. “Ready? Let's shoot."

Chapter 67

Anthony

We spent the whole day at the shooting range. Then we went back to the house to unwind in the den. The atmosphere was warm and full of laughter. It was something I missed since Marco's murder.

Jack and Remo were at the bar. Jack was busy making drinks. Junior and I sat at a small round table in the corner of the room that was closest to the bar. Metty sat in between the two of us.

"You already know each other?" Metty asked.

"Not quite," I said.

"We met once. A long time ago," Junior added.

"Small world," Metty said.

"Small indeed," I said back to her.

Turning my attention to Junior, a thought had crossed my mind. "What's up with that huge hill of dirt next to the shooting range?"

"Oh, you noticed."

"Couldn't help but notice."

That's when Jack walked over with four drinks on a silver

tray. He placed three down on the table for me, his son, and Metty. Then he grabbed a chair from the bar area and came back to join us. Remo came with him.

"Composting is very good for the environment, Anthony," Jack said. He shot a glance and a grin at his son.

I took a few seconds to look around the room. Confusion set in, but I tried to play it cool. "That's interesting. I thought that was a compost hill. But I haven't seen a single recycling bin around here, not in any of the rooms. And I haven't seen any organic waste disposal in the kitchen either. So why do you have a compost hill that large? From the looks of it, there's nothing here to compost."

Remo spoke up, "You ever hear of thermophilic composting?"

I shook my head. Metty did the same. "No."

Jack said, "Compost heaps are made up of all types of microorganisms. It's pretty much a heap of bacteria. And they're categorized a few different ways.

"You have psychrophiles, mesophiles, and thermophiles."

"This already sounds like too much information. I'm guessing the thermophiles are where I should be paying attention," I said.

"Exactly," Jack said. "These different types of bacteria can grow at various temperatures. But thermophiles generate, grow, and maintain at the highest heat levels."

"Which are?" I said.

Junior interjected, "Anywhere between forty-five to fifty-five degrees Celsius."

"At least," Jack said.

"Temperature ranges can get as high as a hundred and five degrees Celsius," Junior said

I rubbed my chin as my face wrinkled. "Guys, I didn't go to

school in Europe. Who uses Celsius degree measurements?! Can you give it to me in American?"

Remo raised his voice. "Two hundred and twenty-one! One hundred and five Celsius degrees is two hundred and twenty-one degrees in Fahrenheit."

"That's well above the point of boiling water," Jack added.

I shrugged my shoulders. "Ok. You have a compost heap that has really hot bacteria in it. So what?"

"Well," Jack said. "Many farms use thermophilic composting to not only compost organic food waste, but to breakdown fat and protein from dead livestock.

"It would take a fifty-pound carcass, for example, about ten days to decompose and be completely broken down. A carcass as heavy as, let's say, two-hundred and fifty pounds, would then take approximately three months."

The purpose of the compost heap slowly started to make sense to me. They talked in the context of animal carcasses, but I was sure they had been more creative than that.

"What's left over after decomposition?" I asked.

Junior pulled his drink away from his mouth just long enough to say, "It cleans the bones."

"And if you turn the soil again to get the heat back up," Jack said, "you can let the dead matter sit a little while longer. Then the bones will become hollow and brittle, which is easy enough to crush to dust."

Remo cleared his throat. "This concludes our lesson on thermophilic composting. I hope you learned something today."

"I did," I said in response.

"Which is?" Remo said.

Looking at the father and son duo, I said, "It's simple. Stay away from men who own private gun ranges and compost heaps. You may never be heard from again."

Chapter 68

Johnnie

"It's been days since we've heard from him," Blake said. "Do you think he's even still alive?" Blake sat at the familiar table in the center of the warehouse, which was their command center and hang out.

"If he was dead, Remo would've been here by now," Johnnie said.

"You think he'd go through the hassle just to let us know?"

"No," Johnnie said. "He'd come to set the place on fire." His tone communicated that he wasn't joking.

That's when Axel spoke up. "So who do you think took the money? Remo or the bikers?"

"Definitely the bikers. Remo wouldn't have mentioned the money if he took it. And stealing money isn't his thing."

"Do we go after bikers? How do we get the money back?" Axel said.

Johnnie grabbed a trash bag and started cleaning up pizza boxes and beer bottles scattered around the space.

"How do we get the money back, Johnnie?" Axel asked again.

Johnnie continued cleaning.

Blake shifted uncomfortably in his seat. Maybe it was the silence. Maybe it was the blank look on Johnnie's face. "Johnnie?" Blake said.

Tossing the trash bag to the floor, Johnnie faced the frustration of not having answers. "I don't know!" He yelled out in exasperation. "Damn it! I don't know!"

Johnnie's words bounced off the walls and reverberated throughout the room. The silence was ushered in after his proclamation.

Then that same silence was disturbed by a completely different sound. Pounding broke through the front door.

Blake got up from the table, crept to the door, and looked through the peephole.

"It's Squid," Blake said. "Looks like he has company."

Johnnie was still deflated on the other side of the room, so Axel spoke up. "Let 'em in."

Blake slid the bar on the lock back and turned the knob to allow Squid and his guest access to the space.

The mystery man was someone they had never seen before, but he had seen them. It was Beaux.

"What's up, Squid? Haven't seen you in a while."

Squid brushed by Blake. "Yup. Not since y'all left me to get my ass beat by Anthony. But that's ok. I'll let y'all make it up to me another time."

Blake closed the door and secured the lock.

By this time, Johnnie had regained his composure and made his way over to Blake, Squid, and Axel.

They stood at the table. But Beaux remained by the door.

"Who's that?" Axel asked, pointing to Beaux.

"He's someone who's going to help us get right again," Squid said. "Anthony's nowhere to be found. We have no direction. And from the look on everyone's face, the money must be gone."

"Direction?" Johnnie said. "I set the direction."

"Well, you're doing a hell of a job," Squid replied.

Johnnie rushed at Squid. Blake was the first to jump between the two of them and then Axel did the same.

The tussle lasted only a few seconds. But that was all the time Beaux needed. He was still leaning against the wall, near the door. While the guys were preoccupied with trying to tear each other a part, he slid the bar on the lock and no one noticed.

"Get your hands off of me!" Johnnie yelled, as he broke away from Axel's firm grip.

"Look... I'm not here to fight with you, Johnnie. I don't mean to make it seem that way." Beaux approached the group and Squid gestured over to him as he continued, "But a gift has fallen into our lap. You want to be the King of DC, I think he can help. He has connections and all they want to do is meet us."

Attention was placed squarely on the new guy, Beaux.

"Is that so..." Johnnie muttered. His eyes snapped to Beaux's face. "Well, who are you?"

"My name is Beaux. Spelled with an—"

"No one gives a damn how it's spelled," Axel said. "Why are you here?"

"As Squid said, I can help. I have connections. And my connection is eager to be your benefactor."

"For what? What does he want in return?" Johnnie asked.

"Yeah... nobody is willing to give up something for nothing. Squid, you brought him in here. What's this man's angle?" Axel said.

"I don't have an angle. It's just an offer. You can get your entire operation funded by this person and then do what you want with the money. If you want to go back to gambling houses, so be it. But if you want to do more, then he'll support that too."

"Sounds good to me," Blake said.

"What are you saying?!" Mocking Blake, Axel said in a whiny voice, "Sounds good to me."

"What does he want?" Johnnie said.

Beaux looked around. "He only wants a tiny cut. He'll be happy with forty percent of what you take in monthly."

"Forty percent? You've got to be kidding me."

"That's less than half," Beaux quickly said without blinking an eye.

"And what else? An offer that bold can't possibly come without additional strings," Johnnie said.

"He only wants an opportunity to advise you on your moves."

"What I'm hearing is that he wants forty percent and to tell us what to do," Axel said. "I have a better idea."

Axel pulled a gun from inside of his waistband. "I think we heard enough. Johnnie, let's rebuild and establish our own dominance. We can shoot him and then rob this 'benefactor.' Looks like this is a middle man. Let's go after the one with the money."

"Hold up," Johnnie said. "Wait a minute. I think I'm interested in hearing more."

Axel's impatience with Johnnie had grown. But Johnnie uncharacteristically kept his cool.

"You want to hear more? You've got to be out of your mind!" Axel said.

"You heard what I said. Last I checked, I was in charge. If you don't like it, leave."

Blake spoke up, trying to turn the temperature down. "Come on guys. I'm sure we can work this out."

"Nah Blake. Johnnie has been letting his emotions cloud his judgement for months. It's time we had new leadership. Fresh blood."

"New leadership? Who do you mean? You?" Johnnie was incredulous.

The energy at the center of the room had been ignited. There was inescapable tension. It was so consuming that the only one to notice the opening door was Beaux.

Beaux didn't move, not even when an older man crossed the threshold of the doorway.

He was impeccably dressed in a navy-blue three-piece suit. Walking past Beaux, his limp was aided by a sleek black walking stick. His cane had a shiny sterling silver skull for its handle.

The man's mustache and beard were silver. It shined as well, along with his hair. It was long enough to pass the collar of his suit jacket, resting just above his back.

There was an incredibly beautiful older woman on his heels. Her blood red skirt and blazer matched her shoes. As did her lipstick.

While Johnnie and Axel squared off at the center of the room, Beaux managed to allow the two extra people in for a ringside view of the fight.

Blake's attention was grabbed by the sound of the door slamming shut. But he was too late. The older couple now stood in the room.

"Hey. Guys. Who's that?"

"Who's who?!" Johnnie shouted with indignation. "Who the hell are you talking—" Johnnie snapped his head around and was the frozen in place. After a minute, he was released from his catatonic state.

"How can it be?" Johnnie asked aloud. "You're supposed to be dead."

The man stared at Johnnie but didn't say a word.

Instead, the woman spoke up. "I guess I was wrong, Nick Nick. It doesn't look like he pissed himself."

"Don't worry, Marina. There's still enough time for that."

Chapter 69

Anthony

Jack wiped the table off after the evening of food, drinks, and camaraderie. Metty came over with a wet rag in her hand.

"You don't have to do this, dear."

"It's ok. Keeps me busy," Metty said.

Jack shrugged his shoulders and stepped away from the table. Tossing his rag in the sink, he made his way over to me and his son.

Looking at Junior, he said, "So he hasn't asked yet?"

"Nope. Not yet." Junior responded.

"Well, maybe he doesn't really care to know."

"That could be it, but I'm not sure."

"Are you guys entertaining yourselves?" I asked.

"He's still asking the wrong questions." Jack called out to Remo.

"No, he isn't. He's just taking his time," Remo said.

"Good God!" I said. "Ok, I give up! Someone please tell me about that arsenal of guns. It was like I died and went to pistol heaven. What's the damn deal?"

"Good. Now we get to talk fun," Junior said.

Jack pulled a chair next to me and sat down. "I assume you're familiar with ghost guns, right?"

"A little," I said.

Jack continued, "All of our guns are phantoms. According to the government, they don't exist. They don't have identifiers or serial numbers, and they're all built, piece by piece, one by one, and by hand."

Junior interjected, "At one time, you could find the blueprints online. You'd be able to purchase the main components, trigger and hammer, already assembled. Then with a good 3-D printer, carve the rest out of metal and assemble the gun yourself."

"The feds didn't like that, for obvious reasons," Jack said. "The online blueprints had to go bye bye."

"Banned," Remo chimed in. "A half measure, really."

"Sounds like it," I said. "What sense does it make to ban the blueprints? They've already been out there. Ain't no yanking them back."

"And?" Jack prodded me.

"And if I can still get access to the gun parts, I can still make guns."

"Precisely," Jack said. "They pulled the blueprints, but never stopped people from selling the gun kit. It's not hard to build these untraceable guns. And it's even easier when you're working with someone with a military background and extensive weapons training."

Junior waved his hand in the air. "Dad used an outside person to do it in the past. It was some hermit in Fairfax County. But after I came home from my second tour, it just made sense for me to take over. It minimized the liability of an extra person with knowledge of our shop."

"We did this for decades," Remo said. "Long before Junior went off to war."

"We?" I said with a confused look on my face.

"Yes. Me, Jack, Nick Nick, and Marco."

"We built and sold untraceable guns to whoever would pay. The operation spread up and down the east coast."

"Hold up," I said. "What about Marco's gambling houses? Was gambling a front for the guns or guns a front for the gambling?"

"Neither," Remo said. "The gambling houses was just cuz Marco wanted something to do. What you didn't know is that he had much larger investments."

"Larger investments? What do you mean? Marco was practically the largest guy out there. Gambling made him a giant in DC."

"I didn't know he was so small minded," Jack said to Remo.

I was too confused to take offense at Jack's comment. I knew he wasn't being mean. He was prodding me to think outside of the box of gambling, but I had grown accustomed to that space. I caught myself looking at the men around the room. I was almost hoping they would give me the answer I was seeking. But they just stared back at me.

I don't know when the focus of my vision went from the men in the foreground to the images in the background, but it did. The cloud of confusion slowly lifted. Clarity set in.

Framed pictures of giant cranes with the "Lowinger" name emblazoned on them, hung on the wall. Next to the cranes were framed blueprints of various neighborhoods in Washington, DC.

Petworth. The U Street and H Street Corridors. Navy Yard. Brookland. There was a humongous blueprint of the Gallery Place and Chinatown area, where much of DC's gentrification began.

It made sense. Gambling was a way for Marco to do what he loved. But selling ghost guns allowed him to invest in Lowinger. And investing in Lowinger allowed him to have a hand in building the city.

Jack saw the lightbulb shining bright above my head. "I think he gets the picture," he said. "Gambling made Marco a giant? But the guns gave us the ability to *make* DC. There's no corner of this city that hasn't paid us."

Remo said, "You and Johnnie helped put the gambling houses on autopilot. That freed up Marco and Nick Nick to work with Jack."

"And even though Remo and Marco weren't on the best of terms, Remo stayed involved, but from New York," Jack said.

"I tried," Remo said. "But it was difficult."

"It's even more difficult now to do anything," Jack said.

"What do you mean?" I asked.

Remo continued, "It's like you said, Marco was a giant. The only one stupid enough to cross him was the man who built everything with him. Nick Nick.

"But with both Marco and Nick Nick dead, things have changed. There's really no one to continue this work. It's just Jack and his son. Even if I stayed in town, there still wouldn't be enough hands."

My eyes widened at the thought of what was coming next.

"I feel an ask coming on," I said.

"This one's smart," Jack said sarcastically.

"Well," Remo said. "What do you think about staying in DC? Just long enough to pull off a job big enough to float the construction operation for the next few years.

"As good as Junior is, we can't maintain production. With the increase of new federal laws, gun sales have decreased. The pipeline of money to the Lowinger Construction has dried up."

I held my hands up. "I can't help you. I'm a quick study, but I don't know the first thing about making guns."

Jack shook his head. "You're not hearing me. We're well beyond guns."

"Yup," Junior chimed in. "We could build from now until the end of next year and come nowhere close to bringing in the amount of money needed. Nobody's buying."

"Well, whatever your alternative is, I hope is a better plan than robbing banks. That didn't work out for me, at all," I said.

I laughed, somewhat to myself, but I also attempted to pull the other men into my self-deprecating joke. It didn't work. Instead, the men looked at each other and then back to me.

I got the feeling that a bank robbery was exactly what they wanted.

Chapter 70

Johnnie

"Forget this," Axel said. He spun around on his heels and pointed his gun at Nick Nick.

Like the chain reaction of dominoes, everyone drew guns. It was cause and effect.

Beaux had a gun in each hand. One pointed at Axel and the other at Johnnie. Blake and Squid pointed guns at each other.

But Nick Nick and Johnnie did nothing. Johnnie just stared at Nick Nick from across the room. Just over Nick Nick's shoulder, he watched the last time they were together. The buried memory played like a video recording.

Johnnie felt himself pull the trigger of the gun, all over again. He watched the bullet slam into Nick Nick's body. The body spun around from the impact. He saw Nick Nick lying motionless on the ground. But there was one thing Johnnie didn't see—he didn't see Nick Nick die.

This entire time, he just assumed Nick Nick was dead. And he has assumed it with no real proof.

"Why don't we all calm down?" Nick Nick said. He slowly

raised his hands in the air to show everyone he was unarmed. One hand dangled his cane.

"I know this is a lot to take in, Johnnie. But I just want to talk. I can explain everything. Then we figure out where we go. I'm not going to insult you by asking for forgiveness. But can an old and young man have a conversation? Hmm?"

Johnnie didn't move a muscle or say a word.

"Johnnie," Nick Nick said again.

Johnnie remained stoic.

Nick Nick looked at the men around the room.

"Gentlemen... if you want the money you've just recently lost, put your guns down."

Axel furrowed his brow and pursed his lips. "How do you know about the money?"

"Axel, right?" Nick Nick said, pointing his finger toward him. "I know where the Broken Brotherhood is, and I can lead you right to them. Let me lead you right to your money."

"How so?" Johnnie came out of his trance to speak for the first time.

"Dear boy... I know everything about them because I sent them to you. I've been directing them this whole time."

Chapter 71

Anthony

"With all due respect," I said, "you're out your damn mind. I've done the bank robbery thing. I'm not doing it again."

Junior took the first crack at trying to convince me. "Look Anthony, this really isn't a bank robbery. We can pull this off without stepping foot in a bank."

"I've heard that before," I said.

"Or an armored truck." Remo replied.

I turned my head slightly toward Remo, saying, "Weren't you the one who had to rescue me after the last job? I was bloody and unconscious. It probably would've been worse if you hadn't shown up when you did."

Jack let out a long sigh before he spoke. "You've been through something horrible. I get it. But if you're scared, just say it. Because I have yet to hear a reason why you can't do this job."

"That's exactly it. I am scared. I left town and everything was good with me. I had a little job. Got my lady back. Life was good. This isn't who I am anymore.

"Nick Nick tried to make me choose once. It was either jump in with both feet or have nothing. That's not much of a choice. Because if I must choose, then I choose my life."

"Stop being so dramatic," Remo said. "Nick Nick never had your best interests at heart. Truth be told, we can do this job without you. But we don't want to cut you out."

"If you can do it without me, then do it without me." That was it. My mind was made up. There was a chance for me to leave the life alone. And I was going to take it.

Remo walked away, leaving me in peace. Jack and his son didn't say another word. Metty knew enough to not even enter the fray. I won. At least that's what I thought.

Still seated at the table, I heard footsteps walking from behind. It was Remo. He reached over my shoulder and slammed my cell phone on the table.

"Call her," he said.

I pretended not to know who he was referring to. "What?" I said.

"Call her!" he said more forcefully. "You say you want to leave the life. Then call your lady and leave.

"You've been in DC over a week. Have you seen her yet? Have you even talked to her? What are you waiting for? Does she even know you're in town?"

"I... I..." was all I could stutter out.

"That's what I thought. You need to stop playing games, Anthony. All of this back and forth won't do anything but get her killed."

His words stung, but not because they were hurtful lies. They were very close to the truth.

It wasn't a big deal for Coco and me to go days without talking. Sometimes we even went weeks.

Daily phone calls can feel like a chore in long distance relationships. We agreed early on not to read into lapses of time between talking.

But that's when there was distance between us, not like now, when in the same city. I had been in town long enough to talk with her and see her. But I hadn't reached out. I was too busy. Wrapped up in a life I claimed I wanted to abandon.

That was a problem. Remo knew it.

And deep down, so did I.

Chapter 72

Smitty

Smitty sat at on a dingy forest green bench on Madison Drive NW, between Third and Fourth Streets. Facing the National Mall, he waited for his late afternoon appointment. A familiar face that came into focus as it got closer.

She approached Smitty and he slid over to make room on the bench. She sat down. "Hey Smitty," she said.

"Hey, Bri," Smitty said. He threw his arm around her and pulled her in for a hug.

Sabrina Galloway and Smitty had been friends since high school. He affectionately referred to her as "Bri." It was an abbreviation of her name. And only Smitty could use it.

Their friendship had been tested soon after Smitty graduated from the Metropolitan Police Department's academy. Sabrina had been in a relationship with a man, who over time, became disinterested in her. But instead of simply walking away, he decided to take his unhappiness out on her. The relationship devolved from loving to abusive in a matter of a few months.

After avoiding her childhood friend for weeks, they accidentally bumped into each other at the same spot that they had chosen to have their little meeting today. It wasn't long before Sabrina was sobbing in Smitty's arm. She shared everything she had been going through and how it had emotionally wrecked her.

This newly minted police officer couldn't bear thought of a man treating Bri in such a manner, so he decided to have words with him. The conversation quickly became a test of physical will between the men.

Sabrina's soon to be ex-boyfriend ended up in the hospital with a broken nose, fractured ribs, and a deflated lung. And Smitty walked away without a scratch.

After the incident, Smitty was given an official reprimand. It also tainted his reputation within MPD. The rep followed him all the way to his unceremonious departure from the department. For Smitty, it was worth it. And he'd do it all again. That's how much he loved his Bri.

The golden-brown skin surrounding Sabrina's eyes was puffy. The whites of her eye were reddened. She held tissue in her right hand.

"You been crying?" Smitty asked.

Sabrina shook her head. Her mane was full of coiled and twisted locks of fluffy dark brown hair with auburn streaks. The hair bounced and shook as her head moved from side to side. "No," she said. It was an obvious lie.

"Something bad happened to Wes. I know it," Sabrina said. "Can you help me find him?"

"I wouldn't be here if I wasn't going to try."

Just then, another familiar face caught Smitty's attention. It was Coco. They locked eyes as she jogged by. Coco was still moving at a jogger's pace, but ran backwards and jogged in place, in front of Smitty and Sabrina.

"Hey Smitty!" she said. "Long time no see."

"I'll be right back," Smitty said to Sabrina.

He stood from the bench and walked over to Coco. "Coco. How you been?"

"I can't complain," she said, still jogging in place. She did an excellent job at maintaining her pace and breathing. Coco nodded her head in the direction of Sabrina. "Who's that? New girlfriend?" Coco's grin couldn't be wider. "You're always working so hard. About time you had some fun!"

Smitty laughed at the insinuation. "No. God no. That's a very dear friend. Well, client now."

"Oh. You're working? Surprise surprise."

Smitty let out another chuckle.

"Well... I guess I'll let you get back to *work*. It was good seeing your face, big man." Coco motioned towards Sabrina again. "She's a cute one over there. Looks a little sad though. But I'm sure she has you in her corner to make things better. That's a lucky girl."

Smitty acknowledged Coco with another laugh. Then he said, "Stop it... Jelani's luckier to have you, in my opinion."

With that, Coco waved and jogged away. Smitty walked back to the bench.

Before he reached Sabrina, Coco did the same backwards jog to where she previously was and then stopped running.

"Smitty... you just said that Jelani is luckier to have me. How do you know about me and Jelani?"

Smitty's eyes widened and brought both hands up to his face. Even though the sound was muffled, he could be heard.

"Shit!" Smitty exclaimed.

Chapter 73

Coco

Coco no longer ran at a measured pace. She now ran at full speed until she reached her car. Running usually cleared her mind, but not this time. She was consumed with trying to figure out how Smitty knew about her relationship with Jelani.

Jelani had resigned himself to cutting off everything and everyone from his past world, except Coco of course. But if that was the case, it didn't make sense that Smitty would know anything.

Had the two of them been in contact? If so, why would Jelani keep it from her? Coco's thoughts took her from Louisiana to DC again. Maybe Jelani had made his way back home and Smitty knew.

She thought about his missed call from the other night. She thought about how they hadn't spoken in some time. Ordinarily that wouldn't bother her, but the idea that either Jelani had been talking to others in DC or had potentially returned, worried her.

Once she got to her car, she hopped in the front seat and

pulled her phone out. She looked for Jelani's phone number and called it. There was no answer.

She thought to call Smitty to talk with him again, but knew she wouldn't get much more out of him. His response to her question told her everything and nothing at all.

There was only one other person she thought to call. One other person who might be able to shed light on what was going on.

She scrolled until she reached the R's and found a familiar name, Johnnie Ribisi. She dialed the number and listened to the phone ring, over and over again.

No answer. The outgoing message of the voicemail came on.

This is Johnnie. Do what you do.

"Hey Johnnie. This is Coco. Jelani... uh, Anthony's friend. I know I'm calling out of the blue. But call me back when you can. I have something to ask you."

Chapter 74

Anthony

The silence in the room was interrupted by my ringing cell phone. The phone was still on the table. The screen faced up.

Remo read the name flashing on the display.

COCO.

"Go ahead," Remo said. "Answer it."

I thought the timing was coincidental. We just talked about Coco and my desire to leave the life and start a new one with her.

An idea that was directly challenged by my uncle. And now she was calling. A piece of me wanted to answer the phone, but another piece of me didn't.

The phone continued to ring as I weighed my options. Do I tell her I've been back for nearly two weeks? Do I tell her I'm still in New Orleans? How do I explain not seeing her? How would she react if she knew the truth?

There I was with a bunch of questions and no answers. There was only one way to get them—answer the damn phone.

Just as I reached for the phone, it stopped ringing. The

silence returned back to the room and I waited a brief moment for one of two things to happen. I waited for a voicemail notification to pop up on my screen, or for Coco to call back. But neither happened.

I placed the phone back on the table and leaned back in the chair. I was conflicted about the relief I felt.

It was at that moment I gave myself permission to hop off of the tightrope I had been walking. Looking at Junior, I finally spoke up. "Tell me about this plan."

Jack nodded his head, giving his son permission to share.

"The robbery is the easy part," Junior said. "But it will require some aggressive action to set it up."

"Well, I'm all ears now," I said.

"Glad to hear it," Jack said. "Because the very first thing we need to do is get Grem."

"Who the hell is Grem?" I asked.

"Short for Gremlin," Jack said. "He's known as the Gremlin."

"Wait, what?" I said. "Why do we need a Gremlin? And what the hell is a Gremlin?"

Junior laughed before answering my question. "A Gremlin is an imaginary or mischievous sprite regarded as responsible for an unexpected problem or fault. Especially a mechanical or electrical one."

Remo interjected. "As in... *The Gremlin in my computer deleted my homework assignments*."

"Ok... cute nickname. Where is our Gremlin? Let's pick him up and get this over with."

"That's the thing," Junior said. "He's in jail and we kinda need to bust him out."

Chapter 75

Johnnie

Nick Nick had Johnnie's full and undivided attention. The idea of retrieving the stolen money from the Broken Brotherhood sobered him up.

Johnnie's crew had already gone toe-to-toe with the motorcycle club and lost. He was motivated to settle the score. His gambling houses had been robbed. The money he stole was stolen from him. And the Broken Brotherhood invaded his base of operations.

Johnnie didn't know if he could trust Nick Nick, but he wanted the money. It was worth the risk. But first, he had to make sure his guys didn't kill him. They still had their guns pointed at Nick Nick.

"Drop your guns," Johnnie said.

Johnnie's guys looked at each other and slowly complied. Beaux and Squid did the same. The tension in the room was broken.

Nick Nick leaned on his cane and stepped away from Marina. He walked closer to Johnnie. "You always were the smart one. I spent far too much time grooming Anthony. You are a true Ribisi. You should have been the one I groomed all along."

"Tell me about the biker gang," Johnnie said. "Where are they? Where's my money?"

"It's not that easy, Johnnie."

Johnnie rolled his eyes and groaned aloud.

"They're a whole gang and what do you have here? Four or five guys? You can't engage them with so few men," Nick Nick said. "Besides, the Brotherhood is out of town right now. And I'm certain they didn't leave the money piled up on a folding table, like some people."

"Are you playing with me?" Johnnie said. He had quickly grown impatient and snatched a gun out of his waistband. He was now the only one holding a firearm. Its barrel was jammed into the side of Nick Nick's neck. "Don't play with me!" Johnnie shouted. "I swear to God, I'll shoot you dead right here."

Nick Nick froze. He was careful not to make any sudden movements.

"I know you will, Johnnie. All I'm saying is that we need a plan to get your money back. A diversion. And I have the perfect one."

"Too late, Nick Nick. I don't trust you anymore. You and my father never thought I was smart enough. Strong enough. Or ruthless enough to be Anthony. You all saw me as a joke! But not this time. You won't cut me out of what's mine." Johnnie pressed down on the safety lever on his gun. Nick Nick flinched at the sound it made.

CLICK

"That's not true!" Nick Nick blurred out. "I have a plan and it'll work. But we all have to work together. Only you can pull it off."

"What if I decide to pull this trigger instead?"

Nick Nick glanced at Marina. She looked calm and

appeared unbothered. Nick Nick had wiggled his way out of tighter situations before. He always had a plan. And this moment was no different.

"You can pull the trigger," Nick Nick said. "And you'd be no closer to getting what you want. No Broken Brotherhood. No money.

"Kill me for killing your father. It seems like a fair exchange. But what's really fair in this world? I'd be dead and you'd still be broke and living with the pain of being fatherless. Does that seem fair to you?

"You said I didn't see you as smart, strong, or ruthless enough. If you want to be those things, then you have to *be* those things. Be smart enough to see the right move, strong enough to commit to it, and ruthless enough to carry it out. Killing me isn't any of those things."

Johnnie tightened his grip on the gun. His eyes narrowed. He took a deep breath and reassessed his situation. "I think you're right," he finally said. "I want my money and killing you won't bring it to me. And you wouldn't feel the pain I've felt since you killed my father."

Johnnie then whipped his gun toward Marina.

"But your lady," Johnnie said, "killing her might do the trick. For now. And that leaves you alive long enough to help me get the money back."

The barrel of the gun was aimed at Marina's torso. Her eyes bulged. The calm expression on her face was replaced with worry.

"Nick?" Marina said.

It sounded as if she was pleading for her man to do something. But he didn't move. He just watched.

When it was clear that Nick Nick wouldn't intervene, she called out for someone else. "Beaux! Please. Help me."

But Beaux didn't move either.

"Killing her won't make us even," Johnnie said. "You do know that."

"I know," Nick Nick said.

"But I bet it's smart, strong, and ruthless enough for us to move forward," Johnnie said.

Nick Nick took a final look at a shellshocked Marina.

"Yes, it is," Nick Nick said. "And it's the needed sacrifice on my part to show you the lengths I'm willing to go to make amends."

"Amends? Maybe," Johnnie said. "But we are not even. Not yet."

And then Johnnie pulled the trigger.

Chapter 76

Anthony

"You guys are crazy," I said. "This thing has gone from being the easiest horrible idea I ever heard of to just plain horrible. What do you mean we have to bust this guy out of jail?"

"Hear him out," Remo said.

"It's the Eighteenth Amendment," Junior said. "You ever read it?"

"What the hell is this, civics class? No, I haven't read the damn Eighteenth Amendment."

"It's simple. Within it, there's a clause that makes cruel and unusual punishment of the incarcerated unconstitutional."

"And how does this help us? Is Grem being tortured?"

Junior rolled his eyes. He was becoming impatient with me again.

"It also means that if an inmate has a rare or complicated medical condition that can't be treated at the prison, the state is obligated to transport him to a specialist who can provide the treatment.

"Prisoners get essential health care and dental care. They

also get basic mental health services. But if they had something like—"

"Testicular cancer," Remo said.

"Right. Well, then that's something the prison isn't equipped to treat. And leaving the prisoner to suffer and die from a treatable disease would be considered cruel and unusual punishment.

"The jail has to take him to an oncologist who can treat him."

"And let me guess, the plan is to break him out during the transport?"

Jack, Remo, and Junior all nodded their heads up and down and spoke at the same time.

"Yeah."

Junior added, "He was convicted of a non-violent crime. Couple that with his age and the nature of the disease, he isn't considered a high risk. The security accompanying him would be minimal."

"How big will our team need to be to get the job done?" I asked.

Junior rubbed the stubble on his chin. "The two of us certainly couldn't do it alone. We probably need a total of four or five men. We might get away with four to keep it light, so we need two extra people."

I immediately thought of Brandon, the man raising my son with Jena. "That's funny. Someone just asked me for a job not too long ago."

"Do you trust him, Anthony?"

"Not really. But he's the only one that's coming to mind."

"He's not enough," Jack said.

"Jack's right," Remo added.

"What about Smitty?" I asked.

"He's got other jobs he's working. He doesn't have the capacity for this as well," Jack said.

Then it hit me. I overlooked the obvious. I picked my cell phone up from the table and tapped away with my thumbs.

It only took a few seconds before the reply lit up my screen.

"There you have it. I have a fourth. We're good. And this one, I do trust. But I'll need to get him a plane ticket from New Orleans."

"Done," Jack said. "Can he and the other guy be here tomorrow?"

"I'm sure he can," I said. "But what's the rush? Doesn't the groundwork need to be laid down? The whole Eighteenth Amendment thing sounds complicated."

"It is complicated and the plan does take time," Remo said.

"That's why Grem has been meeting with one of our doctors for the last seven months," Jack said. "He's been receiving transportation to his 'treatment' for at least six.

"And his next appointment... it's in two days."

Chapter 77

Johnnie

Beaux and Blake cleaned up the mess Johnnie left behind from Marina's murder. Her body was wrapped in multiple layers of black plastic from a few contractor bags. Black electrical tape spiraled around the packaged body from head to toe.

Just as they carried the body out the back, Nick Nick called out to everybody. "Listen! I think we've had enough excitement for tonight. Everyone go home. I need some alone time with Johnnie."

A look of exhaustion and relief flashed across the face of all the guys.

"Thank God," Blake said. "I need some rest."

"Call later with the plans," Axel added.

Beaux and Blake left out the back with the body. Axel and Squid walked out the front door.

Once the room was empty with the exception on Johnnie and Nick Nick, the old man hobbled to the table and pulled out a chair. Before he sat down, he removed a white handkerchief from the inside pocket of his blazer to wipe the seat of the chair.

Maroon streaks slashed across the white cloth. It was left over blood splatter. Marina's blood.

Nick Nick reached into that same pocket and retrieved a cigarette case and lighter. The fluorescent light bulbs beamed off the silver. He pulled out a cigarette, placed it between his lips, and lit the stick. Then he closed his eyes and sucked in the smoke and nicotine. Almost half of the cigarette disappeared with one pull.

Johnnie wrinkled his face.

"I don't think I've ever seen you smoke," Johnnie said.

"Yeah, well... a bunch of things change when you almost die."

"Next time you might not be so lucky."

"You're mad," Nick Nick said. "I get it. Put that aside, if you can, and think about this... if you had to choose between being wealthy or feared, which would you pick?"

"I don't have time for games and dumb ass questions. I'm leaving." Johnnie stomped past the seated Nick Nick, heading toward the door.

Nick Nick reached out and grabbed Johnnie by the arm before he could get too far away. "Make time," he said. "Wealthy? Or feared?"

Johnnie huffed but then considered the question. "Feared."

"Why?" Nick Nick asked.

"Wealth leaves space for disrespect. But fear, not so much." Johnnie said.

"Good. And?"

"And what?"

"And if you're feared, the people who fear you will make you wealthy." Nick Nick stood up from the table and looked at Johnnie, eye-to-eye.

"You've always wanted more. Your problem is that you've also never thought big enough.

"Gambling houses? That's good, but it's too small. There's so much more. In the recent past, each organization controlled a piece of a larger pie. I'm suggesting you control it all."

"How?" Johnnie asked.

"Through fear. Inescapable, unmitigated fear. The city is fractured. Now is the time to strike and break it into a million little pieces.

"Make shop owners pay you to protect them. Then violate them. Nobody should rob, steal, or sell drugs or sex without your say so.

"If someone revolts against you, crush them. Hammer them repeatedly."

"You're talking extortion. And racketeering."

"It's something Anthony never understood."

Johnnie groaned and rolled his eyes at the mention of his name.

"Look," Nick Nick continued, "you can still have your gambling houses. But who's to say you can't have the rest of the city? Just know that sooner or later, factions in the city will have to choose who they will align themselves with. It's going to come down to him or you."

"Is this why you've come out of your hole?" Johnnie asked.

"Yes. But not for me. For you. Johnnie, my dear boy... stick with me and I'll make you feared and wealthy. Not Anthony.

"He'll be dead. And you... you'll never have to choose between fear and wealth again."

Chapter 78

Anthony

Friday, September 20th

The next day, I pulled up to a waiting and familiar face at Dulles International Airport. Gabe stood next to a Southwest Airlines decal that was stenciled on a large window behind him.

"Need a ride?" I called through the open car window.

Laughing, Gabe grabbed the door handle of the back passenger side and swung it open. He tossed his black roller-board suitcase into the back seat.

After closing the door, he hopped in the front and stared beyond the windshield. There wasn't a response.

I shifted the car from park to drive and sat for a second before putting it back into park.

"Gabe. You good?"

"I don't know. Are you?" he said.

"What do you mean?"

Gabe turned and looked at me for the first time.

"The only reason why I'm here is because you asked me. The only reason I hopped a plane at the last minute and got stuck in a middle seat between two big Berthas is because you asked me. The only reason I'm ready to break laws in a jurisdiction outside of the one I've grown accustomed to is because you asked me!

"No hesitation. Drop of a dime. I'm here. But what about you? Is there any hesitation on your part? Because last I remember, you didn't want to have anything to do with this life.

"And yet, here I am."

Gabe stared out of the front windshield again. "Just let me know, man. Are you ready for this? If you aren't, it's not too late for me to get a returning flight back home."

"I thought it through. Makes no sense to go back and forth," I said. "One day I want to be out of the life and the next day I'm dressed like Santa Claus, robbing armored trucks."

Gabe wrinkled his face. "Huh?"

"Long story," I said. "But the point is that I've got to grab my nuts and make a decision. The only thing worse than a bad decision is indecision. I want a legitimate life, but chances are, that's not really an option for me right now. For now, I need to accept who I am and govern myself accordingly. No more sitting on the fence."

"Are you down?" Gabe asked.

"Without question," I said. "I'm down."

That wasn't enough for Gabe. "Nah man. Are you down down?"

I jabbed my middle finger toward the floorboard and said, "Like four flat tires."

Chapter 79

Johnnie

A bell dangled from the top corner of the door. It clanked against the frame as Johnnie, Axel, and Blake walked in.

"Welcome to Southeast Sandwich Shop!" a short rotund man with a large smile yelled from behind the counter.

No response was given, so he began wiping down a display case of wheat and whole grain loaves of bread. His pudgy sausage-like fingers swallowed the gray cloth. He wore baggy white pants, a white, short sleeve T-shirt, and white sneakers. His curly blond hair was covered by a white hair net. The only drop of color was the name "Southeast Sandwich Shop," which was embroidered in red on his white apron.

"You sure this the place?" Blake asked. "A deli?"

Johnnie had just placed his phone in his pocket. "This is the address he gave us."

The three men looked at each other. Axel stepped away to glare out the large front window to the shop. "Hey!" he said. "Here he comes."

The men watched as Nick Nick approached the sandwich shop with Beaux and Squid.

The lone worker rolled himself and his large smile to the counter once again. "Welcome to Southeast—"

Nick Nick held his hand up before he could finish. "They're with me, Wallace."

"Sure thing, Mr. Nick," Wallace said. "Are you eating today, sir?"

Nick Nick patted Johnnie on the arm as he brushed past him, walking to the counter. "We'll all have a sandwich."

"I'm not hungry," Johnnie said.

Without acknowledging what Johnnie had just said, Wallace asked, "The usual, sir?"

"Yes. The spicy Italian with provolone. For everyone."

"I'm not hungry," Johnnie insisted again.

Blake pushed by Johnnie, approached the counter and looked up at the menu. "Shoot, I am. But I don't even see a spicy Italian on the menu. Nah... lemme get a roast beef and cheese."

"I'm not hungry!" Johnnie yelled.

The outburst caused everyone to freeze. Everyone except Nick Nick and Wallace, that is.

"Six spicy Italians, coming right up."

Wallace reached under the sandwich counter and fiddled with lever and then pressed a button. Everyone heard a loud series of clicks, gears grinding, and a sliding of metal on metal.

"Gentlemen," Nick Nick said, "you see those two doors?" He pointed to the two doors. One in each corner, behind Wallace and the counter. "Door number one, to your right, is a storage room. The door to your left is not. But to find out what's behind door number two, you'll need to order a spicy Italian sandwich.

"The thing is, it's not on the menu. If you don't know to ask for it," Nick Nick said, shrugging his shoulders, "then you don't get access."

"I guess that's clever," Axel said.

"It's clever enough," Beaux replied.

Wallace jumped in to make an announcement. "Guys. Your spicy Italian sandwiches are that way." He pointed to door number two.

Nick Nick approached, grabbed the knob, and twisted.

After Nick Nick slung the door wide open, Johnnie looked beyond it. His eyes grew wide in astonishment. His mouth hung open.

"Hell yeah," Johnnie said. "I'll take a spicy Italian too."

* * *

The guys ran around and explored the room like children at an amusement park. Everything was brand new—the tables, the chairs, the signage, and the chips. The sandwich shop was a front for an illegal casino.

Nick Nick smiled at the flurry of activity by the young men.

"As you can see," he said, pointing to the ceiling corners. "There are cameras all over the place. Security is paramount."

Johnnie stopped running around long enough to ask a question. "What's up with the games?"

"The old gambling houses had too much going on," Nick Nick said. "But this one is streamlined. Research shows the top four games are poker, blackjack, craps, and roulette. So that's what we have. Five of each."

"This space is certainly big enough for all of the players it'll bring," Axel said.

"And there's more," Nick Nick said. He cleared his throat and pointed. "Blake. Go peek over there."

Blake tentatively walked to an alcove, segregated by a red velvet curtain. He stuck his head between the curtains and then snatched it back out. "Holy shit! We've got slot machines!" he shouted.

The commotion caught everyone's attention just as Blake drew back the curtain. "It's gotta be twenty-five of them back there!"

Johnnie took in the entire space. He nodded his head in a sign of approval. He then walked over to the slot machine alcove and ran his hand against the velvet curtain. "Nice," he said. "I like this a lot." Johnnie turned to face Nick Nick. "But you promised me DC and this is still just a gambling house."

"I did. And you will have it," Nick Nick said. "But this is home base. You have space to plan, as well as a way to rake in extra cash."

"Sounds good. But what about Anthony?"

"We'll deal with him in time. For now, enjoy this," Nick Nick said.

Johnnie pondered those few words for a second. His bottom lip poked out slightly. His eyes grew narrow.

Nick Nick's perceptible gaze knew what was happening. Johnnie was pouting. So the impatient Nick Nick called out to everyone. "Guys! Can you give us the room?"

The men looked at each other, trying to figure out when the shift in demeanor happened. Then they shrugged and walked out in single file.

Once everyone had exited the space, Johnnie was the first of the remaining two to speak.

"How?" Johnnie asked.

"You tell me," Nick Nick replied.

Johnnie had nothing to say.

Trying to mask his frustration at Johnnie's inability to see the big picture, Nick Nick finally offered his plan. "We use the

Brotherhood. They've been a pawn of mine. So we get them to do it."

"A pawn of yours, you say." Johnnie said.

"I told you... they working for me. They wouldn't even be in this town if it wasn't for me. But they think I'm a hidden hand, setting them up to control the scene. The truth is, I'm just setting them up."

"What you're saying is that we need to get Anthony and the gang together, and let the gang take him out?"

"Exactly," Nick Nick said.

"But how do we make that happen? And how do we smoke out Anthony?"

"Must I think of everything?" Nick Nick said. "How about I get the bikers by presenting Anthony as the only obstacle to their dominance. And you..."

Sixty seconds passed and the only sound that could be heard was the buzz of the fluorescent lights above.

Johnnie looked toward the floor until it hit him. He lifted his head and snapped his fingers. "The girl!"

"The girl," Nick Nick repeated. "From what I understand, you found her once. Find her again."

"And then what?" Johnnie said.

"Jesus Christ," Nick Nick mumbled to himself. Then he addressed Johnnie. "We make Anthony come to us. And the Broken Brotherhood will handle the rest."

Chapter 80

Anthony

Saturday, September 21st

We met in a heavily wooded area on the side of I-95, outside of Fredericksburg, Virginia. It was moments before the sun was to rise. Junior was the last to arrive.

His jet-black Kawasaki Ninja ZX-14R rolled to a stop next to the two black sprinter vans, already parked on the side of the road. Junior's jeans, motorcycle jacket, helmet and tinted visor perfectly matched his motorcycle. The sight prompted Brandon to say to me with a chuckle, "All black everything, huh?"

"Yeah," was the only response I could muster.

Junior hopped off his bike and went straight to the van on the left. He opened the door and dragged a duffel bag closer to us. Junior loved his duffel bags.

"Over here," he said.

Brandon, Gabe, and I walked over to the van.

"Just to make sure we're all clear." Junior unzipped the bag. "Nothing in this bag can be tied, traced, or tracked back to us."

The bag contained no less than twenty-five ghost guns with five times as many high-capacity magazines.

Junior continued, "To reiterate the plan: When the magazine is empty, drop the mag, leave it where it is and reload.

"Don't worry about shells or anything else left behind. If you don't feel like reloading, toss the gun and grab a new one. I don't suggest doing that, but hey, it's your prerogative. When the job is over, toss all of the guns."

"All of them?" Brandon asked.

"We don't need them," I said. "We have a damn near endless supply. And who wants to run the risk of holding on to a gat from this job? Drop the guns where you stand."

Junior reached in the bag and pulled out a gray rectangular brick, made of what looked to be putty, wrapped in plastic. He handed to it me. "You know what to do with that?" Junior said.

"Absolutely," I said. And then I passed it to Gabe.

Junior reached back in the van and pulled out a carrying case for an extremely long rifle.

"This one's mine," he said. "We need to disable the bus and retrieve Grem before they get to Richmond."

We all nodded our heads.

"Ok then," Junior said. "Any questions?"

He looked at each of us to confirm that we understood the plan as laid out. "Great. You each know what you're supposed to do. It's important that you play your positions, gentlemen."

"Wait," Brandon said. "I do have a question."

"Yes," Junior replied.

"The bus. Where is it? What's the ETA?"

Junior pulled back the sleeve of his motorcycle jacket. "If it's on time, it passed us about two minutes ago. Load up and let's get the party started. We have a bus to catch."

We all reached into the duffel bag and strapped on four

pistols each. We also grabbed as many high-capacity magazines as we could carry.

Junior hopped back on his bike. And the rest of us jumped into a van. Gabe was with me. And Brandon was in the other van by himself.

"Brandon? You good?"

"Yeah... yeah. I'm good."

I took his word for it. Everyone started up their vehicle. One by one, we drove away.

Because as Junior said, we had a bus to catch.

Chapter 81

Anthony

Riding south on I-95, I watched the all-white prisoner transport bus bounce on the road in the distance. It reminded me of a kid's yellow school bus. The bus was less than a half a mile in front of us on the empty interstate.

Junior rode the middle of the three lanes. From what I could tell, the bus shared the same lane.

Brandon took the far-left lane. Gabe and I... the right. We all increased our speed to catch the bus.

"This is it, guys. Time to go to work," Junior said through the two way earpiece stuck to the side of our heads.

Glancing out the window at Junior, I saw him give me a hand signal to indicate he was continuing without us. He shifted gears, hit the throttle of his motorcycle, and sped away in the blink of an eye. Going at top speed, it only took less than a minute for him to reach the bus and zoom pass it.

Brandon and I both pushed the pedal to floor and gained ground on the prisoner transport bus. Before long, we flanked the bus with a van on each side.

"Ride their driver's side," I said to Brandon. "Keep pace and—"

"I know," Brandon shouted though the two-way. "I know! Don't let them switch lanes!"

I yelled back toward Gabe, "You strapped in yet?!"

"Hold tight!" Gabe shouted back. Between checking the rear-view mirror and sneaking looks over my shoulder, I watched Gabe struggle with the harness.

The black nylon utility harness was strapped over his shoulders, across his chest, and between his legs. It looked like he was about to parachute out of a plane.

There was a black belt, made of the same material, that anchor the entire harness to his waist. Stainless steel metal rings were woven into the material.

Once the harness was properly secured around Gabe, he tugged on it from all angles to ensure that it wasn't loose and wouldn't slip off.

Gabe snatched a pair of loose black straps from the seat. Metal clips dangled from each end. First, Gabe clasped the clips to the metal rings on the belt. He carefully threaded the straps through rings on the shoulder straps. He did it twice and pulled tight. Then Gabe's last step was to attach the free end of the straps to metal rings, bolted into the ceiling of the vehicle. At that point, he was locked in. Gabe had become one with the van.

Brandon rode alongside the bus on its other side. And I pulled our van as close to the front door of the transport bus as I could.

We couldn't see past the tinted windows. I remembered that non-violent inmates received lighter security details, but there was no way of knowing for sure. There could have been two guards on the bus. It could have been twenty.

None of that mattered now. I was driving seventy-five miles

an hour, inches away from another moving vehicle, and the most dangerous part of the plan had not been executed yet.

"Let's go!" I shouted at Gabe.

Gabe took a deep breath and with the deliberateness of a surgeon, he placed his hand in the sack attached to his belt. It wasn't long before he pulled out the rectangular putty brick. It was the gift from Junior— Composition C-4, which is more commonly just referred to as C-4.

With the deadly item in hand, Gabe looked at me through the rearview mirror. "Only for you, brother! Only for you!"

He grabbed the handle of the driver's side door, unlatched it, and slung it back.

And then, holding an explosive device on a van moving at high speed, he stepped out.

Chapter 82

Junior

Junior pushed his motorcycle to the limit at one hundred and seventy miles an hour. He left the bus and vans in his dust. He needed to get twenty miles ahead to have enough time to get set up on an overpass. He had already canvassed the area and knew exactly where he was going.

The exit ramp to his preferred overpass was a mile away. Gabe slowed down, took the exit and made a sharp left turn. No cars traveled east or west on the road. It was deserted. Perfect.

The overpass was perfect as well. Many of them along I-95 had walls of mesh fencing, which would have made his job more difficult.

But this one only had a metal railing. Just like the road and just like overpass, the railing was also perfect.

Junior laid the canvas rifle case on the ground, unzipped it, and removed the long gun. He stabilized the rifle using his six-inch rifle bi-pod and peeked through the scope.

"Ok. Where are y'all?" he said to himself. He was expecting the vehicles to come into his sight within a few seconds.

For the moment, he slowed down his breathing and visualized hitting his target. He mentally could see where his target would need to be and when he would need to pull the trigger. He was ready.

Junior was an expert marksman at long distances. But that was when he was shooting at stationary targets. This time, he'd be shooting at a high speed target, possibly driving erratically and swerving across the road. It wasn't the best circumstances and he only had one shot.

In the next second, Junior saw the bus and the vans. His heart raced.

"No! No! No!" Junior shouted into his mic. "Brandon! What the hell are you doing?!"

Chapter 83

Anthony

"What's taking you so long?" I shouted back at Gabe.

"This ain't so easy," he snapped back. Gabe held onto the straps tethered to the van with his right hand. With his outstretched left arm, he tried to attach the explosive to the front door of the moving bus.

"Get me closer!" Gabe yelled at me.

I carefully pulled the van a foot closer to the bus. That's when the transport driver caught on.

I needed to get the van a couple of feet closer to the bus, giving Gabe a better chance to attach the C-4.

"Slowly!" Gabe shouted into the van. "A little closer, but slowly!"

With a steady pair of hands at two and twelve on the steering wheel, I followed his directive.

"Pull back! Pull back! Pull back!" Gabe yelled at me.

Out of the sideview mirror, I watched as the bus violently encroached closer to my lane. They made us. And honestly, how could they not?

I jerked the van away from the bus. The movement was

harsh and Gabe was whipped back and forth. His footing came loose.

To stop himself from falling out of the open van, he used both hands to hold on between his straps and the van's door. And in doing so, he inadvertently tossed the explosive to the back of the van.

We were quickly approaching Junior's bridge. And without the C-4 in place, our window of opportunity was closing.

Chapter 84

Junior

"No! No! No!" Junior shouted into his mic. "Brandon! What the hell are you doing?!" From his position on the bridge, he watched the madness unfold through the scope of his rifle.

"Something's wrong!" Brandon shouted back. "The bus is all over the road!"

"I can see that!" Junior said. "Gabe?! Y'all are about to pass me! Forget it! Plan B! Blow the door off that bitch right now!"

"I can't!" Gabe was out of breath, but his voice still came through Junior's earpiece, loud and clear.

"I lost the brick! I lost the brick!" Gabe said.

"What do you mean by 'lost'? It's not like it's a cellphone! If you don't do it now, you're going to pass me!"

Junior watched as Brandon accelerated in his van. He sped up and passed the swerving bus, being ever so careful not to collide with it in the process.

"This isn't the plan, Brandon! What are you doing?"

"This isn't which plan? A or B? Gabe needs more time, so I'm giving it to him."

Brandon switched from the far-left lane to the center lane so he was directly in front of the bus. Not knowing if he was going to be rammed from behind, Brandon muttered to himself, "Oh dear sweet Jesus," and began to decelerate.

Junior watched as the bus swerved to its left. Anticipating the move, Brandon did the same. He remained in front of the bus. Junior watched the other van do the same thing. By moving to the front and forcing the bus over a lane, Brandon had given them a chance to pin the bus between the vans and the left shoulder.

Brandon slowed down. The bus slowed down too. Junior watched and held his breath. He braced himself in anticipation of a collision. But it never came.

Instead, Junior watched the bus and vans pass beneath him under the bridge.

"I got it!" Gabe grunted into Junior's earpiece. "I got the C-4."

After a few seconds of silence, Gabe came through again, "There! It's done."

"That's all well and good," Junior said. "But y'all already passed me!"

"So what?!" Gabe said. "Why don't you just jump back on the interstate and find another bridge? Why have a bike that tops out at over one hundred and seventy miles an hour if you're never going to push it over one hundred and seventy miles an hour?!"

Junior ran to the other side at the bridge and watched the bus pull away. He glanced back at his bike.

"You're right," he said, running back to the Kawasaki. Junior threw on his helmet as he hopped on. "I don't know what hell I was thinking."

Chapter 85

Anthony

Gabe nearly kicked me in my head as he climbed back into the front seat. He was soaked with sweat. His fingers fumbled throughout the metal clasps of the harness he still wore. "Get this shit off of me," Gabe said to himself.

"So glad you didn't slip off the side of this van," I said.

"Me too, man... me too."

"Do you think Junior is going to find another bridge before getting too close to Richmond?" I asked.

"I'm not sure. We're cutting it..."

Before Gabe could finish his thought, he was cut short by the growling rumble of a motorcycle's exhaust. It was deep and bounced off the pavement. It felt like the sound whipped pass us faster than a jet.

When we looked in front of us, we saw Junior and his Kawasaki flying at the speed of sound.

If there was another suitable bridge, Junior was most certainly about to find it.

Chapter 86

Junior

Junior's eye darted from highway signs to exit signs. He didn't want to miss his exit. And at the speed he was going, it would've been easy to do.

Junior had already blown by what appeared to be a perfectly good bridge at exit 104. But there wasn't a direct path from the off ramp to where he would need to position himself. The bridge also had a huge chainlink fence which stood over ten feet high. It would've surely made taking the shot harder than Junior wanted it to be.

There was another problem. His timetable was shot. He didn't know where the bus was and how long it would take to reach him.

Then off in the distance, he saw it. *Exit 110*. No fence. No railing. Just a concrete edge to set his rifle on.

The bridge was thirty-four miles to Richmond. Junior knew they needed wrap it up before getting any closer to the city limits. Since Richmond was the closest major city, there was a bit of a problem. The city would probably have more resources to investigate a jail break that moved into its jurisdiction. And that was something Junior didn't want to risk.

"Junior... Junior," blasted in his earpiece. It was Gabe.

Junior didn't respond. Instead, he focused on navigating his Kawasaki at breakneck speed.

Gabe's voice continued, loud and clear. "If you can hear me, the explosive is in place. The bus is about forty miles to Richmond."

Perfect, Junior thought to himself. Approximately six minutes away.

Time moved forward at warp speed as he approached the exit ramp. He had two options before him. The conventional route would be exiting on the paved road, but the risky move would be launching himself up the grassy hill between the highway and the exit ramp.

The hill was dangerously pitched at a steep angle, but it was the most direct way to the bridge. Junior decided to take the hill.

He squeezed the brake to begin decelerating, but he was still approaching the hill at a breakneck speed. He veered to his right, rolled over the rumble strips, and found his way to the grass.

He still had time to cut over to the paved exit ramp, but his adrenaline got the best of him.

"Let's do this," he said.

Junior shifted gears and hit the throttle. Instead of slowing to a stop, he did just the opposite. Both the angle of the hill and his speed caused the bike to be catapulted into the air.

Junior was airborne for three seconds.

His bike landed on the street, back wheel first. In one motion, Junior was able to lean the bike to one side, whip his leg around to the other side, and take a coordinated hop off the motorcycle.

It slid across the asphalt. The sound of metal and plastic scraping against the street was accompanied by the visual of sparks flying up from the ground.

Junior's body slammed against the edge of the bridge. He wrestled his shotgun from his back. Within seconds, he was set and in position.

Looking through the scope, he watched the bus speed closer. Junior took a few deep breaths, trying to steady his body and hands, and focusing on the moving object.

His finger was wrapped around the trigger. The bus pulled into his imaginary strike area. Junior took another deep breath and pulled the trigger.

The bullet left the gun, traveled through the air, and collided with the front of the bus.

Bullseye!

It struck the engine. The bus began to slow. Junior watched as steam erupted out of the front. Without a functional engine to power the vehicle, the bus ultimately slowed to a complete stop.

Tracking the bus, the van slowed down as well.

Through the scope, Junior watched the guys empty out of the vans. They wore masks for anonymity, but Junior knew who was who. Anthony was Michael Myers. Gabe was Freddie Krueger. Brandon was the Joker.

Junior moved the scope to Freddy Krueger. He pulled a remote trigger out of his pocket, held it high above his head, and depressed the button with his thumb.

That was the sign for the guys to duck for cover. They did so, but nothing happened.

After five seconds, the masked men looked back and forth between each other. Junior watched as Gabe stepped from his covered position.

He took three steps toward the stalled bus and without

warning, a deafening explosion took the bus's door off. It flew twenty feet away from the vehicle.

The explosion threw Gabe back as well. But he recomposed himself quickly.

Junior watched the men draw their untraceable firearms. Brandon, the first to fire his weapon, emptied a full magazine between the buses' two passenger side tires.

Junior didn't understand. It's not like the bus was going anywhere without an engine. Anthony did say he wasn't the brightest.

Now fully back on his feet and poised to engage, Gabe rushed into the bus. It was smoking from the engine and the space where the door once was.

After Gabe, one by one, they each ran in.

Chapter 87

Anthony

"I can't believe it," Gabe said.

We all stood outside of the vehicles in a heavily wooded area east of the interstate. Junior hadn't caught up to us yet.

"Yeah. I'm a little stumped, myself," I replied. "Those guards, if that's what you wanna call them, gave up without a fight. All of our work and planning, and they just let us take him."

"Think about it, they probably make just above minimum wage. I emptied half of my magazine to get their attention. After that, no one's risking their lives for a few coins," Brandon said, pointing to their newly acquired passenger, "...let alone risk their lives for him?"

"That's the other thing puzzling me," I said.

We heard Junior's motorcycle approaching. Everyone stopped talking and waited the few minutes it took for Junior to roll to a stop, dismount, and join the group.

"Junior," I said. "I thought we was breaking out a monster or beast. It was supposed to be someone who was going to get us in and out of banks! But it can't be this guy. He looks like ol' dude from those Ghost Buster movies."

And for the first time, our guest spoke. "Rick Moranis."

"What?" Brandon said.

"Rick Moranis," the guest said again. "People say I look like Rick Moranis."

"Yeah... well, whatever," I said. "This can't be the guy. There's no way."

"No one said he was a beast or monster. We said Gremlin. And that's exactly what we have."

Junior walked past his crew and embraced Grem. "Grem... It's been a while, " Junior said.

"All the more reason not to waste any more time," Grem said. "Let's go."

Chapter 88

Anthony

Grem sat in an armchair near the fireplace. The smell of charred oak wood filled the room. A maroon fleece blanket draped his shoulders and body. He stared into the flames as if the fire sung to him. "The state police have certainly teamed up with the FBI by now. They're looking for me. We don't have a lot of time. We need to do this tomorrow," he said.

"It took a little bit of time getting the pieces together to spring you from jail," I said. "And now you expect us to rob a bank tomorrow?"

Grem looked at Remo. "I don't think your nephew likes me very much. Not yet, at least." He turned to me and the group. "Here's the deal... I don't want to go back to the slammer and you, you don't want your plan to fail. The wonderful thing is that for your plan to succeed, you need my plan to succeed.

"This is something I have been working on long before you all thought up a jail break. Even if you were a pack of fools, and there's always at least one fool in a crew, this robbery is fool proof. It will work no matter what."

"Fool proof, you say," Gabe said. "With a night's worth of planning?"

"Jack. Where did you find these idiots? Is no one listening to me? It's already been planned out!" Grem stood and shook the blanket off his body in one motion. He approached me as if he wanted to fight. There was aggression in every step he took. But he didn't know I was ready to wipe the floor with all five foot six inches of him.

"Look guys, I don't want to be here any longer than I need to be. There's a piña colada on an undisclosed tropical island with my name on it. And the longer I sit here arguing with you imbeciles, the longer it'll take me to get there. This job is ready to go. Are you? Because lord knows, I am."

"Ok," I said. I rolled my eyes and let out a deep and audible sigh. It sounded like a growl. My patience was gone. "Let's hear it."

Grem cracked a crooked smile. "Get me a laptop," he said, "and I'll show you."

I looked at Brandon. "Grab the machine in the living room."

Brandon ran out of the room. It only took a minute. Grem didn't move from his spot in front of me as we waited.

When Brandon walked in, he handed me the laptop, and I handed it to Grem. He turned around and walked back to his chair.

Jack reached forward and held out his hand, giving Grem what looked to be a USB device. Grem sat down and inserted it in the side of the laptop. It was indeed a memory stick.

"With all the time your generation spends on your smartphones, what do you know about cybersecurity?"

We looked at each other and shrugged our shoulders.

"That's what I thought," Grem said.

He clicked away on the keyboard, stopping a minute to read the computer screen before he began typing again.

"We live in an era where people can steal identities, pretend to be others, and bring businesses to a halt. The good hackers can even topple governments. But the really good ones..." he said as he stopped typing, gave the screen one final look, yanked the USB drive out and held it up, pinched between his fingers. "The really good ones," he said again, "can rob banks without stepping one foot inside."

At this point, I had to admit I was intrigued.

"Jack," Grem sang out before tossing it to him.

"Gentlemen," Jack said. "Our dear friend had been working on a computer program for nearly a year. It's the perfect program, I might add. Of course, he was unexpectedly arrested before finishing the job."

"It was a setup," Grem rumbled. "They arrested me for a ransomware attack against the Google headquarters in Fairfax, but I had nothing to do with it. If I had, there's no way they would've caught me."

"Because you're really good..." I couldn't resist.

"Precisely," he said. "I was tired and put off finishing the program to the next morning. But I was arrested that night and never got a chance to finish. I just needed a few more keystrokes to complete my masterpiece.

"And now, il et finie."

"What does this masterpiece do?" I said.

Grem beamed with pride. "This particular code does its damage via WiFi access points. So I'd go to a coffee shop or Starbucks.

"Once you connect to their WiFi, whether free or password protected, it will automatically download a virus to every other device connected to that same network. Laptops, tablets, and smartphones, you name it.

"At that point, it becomes a nasty little bloodhound, sniffing around in the device's history for all online financial interactions, both banking and credit. Then it goes to work.

"This code will imitate the keystrokes used to gain access to the banking platforms. It'll find checking, savings, and credit card accounts. For accounts with liquid money, it'll bleed them down to the last thousand dollars. If the account has less than a thousand, it'll suck out half.

"For the credit accounts, it'll run up a bunch of dummy charges and all of the funds will be funneled to an untraceable off-shore account. And, it'll only take a hundred and twenty seconds to begin mimicking fund transfers."

"Hold your horses," Jack said to the guys. "This is when it gets fun."

Grem continued with wide eyes, "Yes, the fun part. This is more than a code that hits the accounts of the device owners. It's a virus, in every sense of the word. Once this bitch gets in the system, it spreads throughout the whole banking institution.

"It plunders every account it comes into contact with. And it replicates its action for a full hour. At the one-hour mark, it commits digital suicide and destroys itself. It will leave no evidence of its existence, but the funds will be safe and secure with us."

Jack added, "Unless someone literally lives in their accounts, they won't notice the drain of funds while it's happening. The banks might. But once in the system, it'll be too late for them to do anything about it."

"My code will have robbed countless accounts, making us the beneficiaries of all the riches."

"So let me get this straight," I said. "Go into a coffee shop, connect to the WiFi, open the program, and let the code do the rest?

"That's right," said Grem.

"I'm a little uneasy about posting up in a coffee shop long enough to be caught on camera," I object.

"Well," Grem said. "This code doesn't require you to open it or click on anything for it to work."

"How does it get uploaded to the WiFi then?" Gabe asked.

"All my precious baby needs is for the flashdrive to be inserted into a computer, any computer. Then it'll run its operation in the background. The owner of the device won't even know. I suggest you walk into a cafe, sit down to some tea, and carelessly leave a few flash drives behind."

"People are nosey," Jack said. "Someone will pick it up and pop it into their computer to see what's on it. Maybe they'll even try to see if it has space on it, so they can use it for themselves. Leave three or four behind, one of them is bound to get open. That's all we need."

"What happens when someone finds one of the others lying around?" Gabe said. "Can't this come back to you, and then us?"

"No," Grem said. "The code is already scheduled to auto-delete from the USB at four o'clock tomorrow afternoon. You just need to get this out to the lunch crowd. By dinner, they'll be no trace of the code on the flash drive. And we'll be rich. Any more questions?"

I looked at Gabe in amazement. It was in that moment that I remembered Junior's definition of a Gremlin.

An imaginary or mischievous sprite regarded as responsible for an unexpected problem or fault. Especially a mechanical or electrical one.

Whether I called him Rick Moranis or Gremlin, one thing was apparent to me. He most certainly was also a beast.

I nodded my head to the guys. "Fellas, I guess we have some work to do tomorrow."

Everyone nodded in agreement. Then we retreated to separate rooms to rest. On my way out the den, I pulled my phone out and disconnected from the WiFi network at the house.

Then I thought to myself, *I'll never do online banking again.*

Chapter 89

Brandon

Brandon was quiet throughout the night. After everyone left, he took Grem's place in front of the fire.

He took his phone out, scrolled through his text messages and found a thread he had been keeping with Jena.

Hey babe. Just giving you a heads up. I had to run because I picked up a side gig. It's good money too. We'll talk more about it later. For now, just know that I got you and little Marco. I'm about to go to sleep. But everything's gonna be alright.

Brandon hit *SEND*. He put the phone back in his pocket. Then he reached his hand to the small of his back. He spun his head around to make sure no one was about to walk in, before pulling a gun out of his waistband.

It was one of the ghost guns from the jailbreak. Brandon removed the magazine to inspect it. Full of ammo.

After jamming the magazine back into the gun, he stood and put it back from where it was retrieved.

Staring into the fire, Brandon thought about the text he just sent to Jena. "Yeah," he said. "everything's going to be alright."

Chapter 90

Agent Hicks

Sunday, September 22nd

The next day there was a traffic jam sprawled up and down I-95 in Virginia. Cars in the southbound lane were stopped. And the northbound travelers slowed their traffic to a crawl, just to be nosey.

No fewer than a hundred law enforcement professionals scoured the area in search of clues. Local police, state police, ATF, and the FBI.

One representative from each investigative unit was huddled around the hood of a state police car. They had unfolded a map of the area and spread it out in front of them.

A tall, freckled, redheaded mountain of a man with ATF on the back of his jacket spoke first. His name was Becks. "They headed south. That's where we need to focus our attention."

The uniformed officers, from local and state police, both nodded in agreement. Coincidentally, both were also white. The lone person of color looked around and shook his head in disagreement. "I'm not sure about that. Just because the action took place on the southbound side doesn't mean they headed south. They could've just as easily turned around and gone north," he said.

Becks looked at the others and then incredulously shook his head. "What is it, Josiah?" he said.

"Hicks. You can call me Agent Hicks." Agent Hicks' caramel coated babyface betrayed a youthfulness. But what he lacked in years on the job, he made up for with a healthy dose of intelligence and common sense. The men of his present company lacked those qualities.

Beck stood taller. "Well, Agent Hicks... I grew up around these parts. These men live and work here too—probably longer than you've been alive.

"It makes much more sense for the assailant to have headed thirty miles to Richmond. It's the quickest route to a big city with a bunch of places to hide. We need to head that way and find them before this gets any more out of control than it already is."

"Yeah!" sounded from his chorus of countrymen.

Becks continued, "This little egg-headed convict is keeping us from our homes and families. We head south. To the city."

"Richmond? You call that a city?" The raspy woman's voice came from behind them. It had a hint of a Spanish accent. More specifically, she was of Dominican descent. Her frame was slender. Her hair was pulled back in a ponytail and her olive tinted skin was unblemished. She wore a navy-blue pantsuit, a yellow blouse, and an FBI jacket over her shirt.

"Guys," Agent Hicks said. "This is the S.A.C. Dally Perez."

One of the local police officers leaned over and whispered into Becks' ear.

Becks attempted to whisper back but everyone heard him say, "Special Agent-in-Charge." Then he addressed the newcomer. "Yes. Richmond *is* a city."

"I guess 'city' can be a subjective word."

"Look here, Miss Perez. I don't know who you think you are," Becks said. "But you can't come here insulting people's home."

Unmoved by the mini tirade, Perez responded to Agent Hicks, "I just think the word 'city' is being used loosely."

"Ok. That's it!" Becks exploded. "We're not listening to whoever this woman is. Get your stuff," he said, pointing to the men. "You're coming with me."

Perez waited patiently as the men grabbed their belongings. As they exited the staging area, she called out to get their attention. "How many guns did you recover?"

The question stopped the men in their tracks.

"I'll ask again," Perez said. "How many guns?"

Becks spun around. "Ok. I'll bite. Eleven."

"And according to witnesses, they just threw them away," Perez said with a hint of sarcasm.

"Have you even looked at their pistols? They had high-capacity magazines and untraceable parts. No serial numbers. These guns are homemade. Do you know any place in Richmond that can produce this quality of gun? I don't."

"What's your point?"

"I bet it's far easier to make these weapons up north. Like, let's say... in the DC area. I'd bet my left tit that's where they went."

"Well, I don't give a damn about your left or your right tit. They went south. That's where we're going," Becks said.

"Agent Becks," Perez said. "I'm sorry if you thought it was a suggestion. But the FBI has rank here. Not the ATF. You don't have to like it, but I'm going north. And so are all these wonderful investigative resources."

The weight of reality hit Becks and his men. Perez was right. She was going to take the investigation north. No matter what Becks had to say about it.

"Fine," he said. "It's your show. But it's also yours if you mess this up."

Becks and his men unloaded the items they grabbed earlier by dropping them on the ground.

"One last thing," Perez said. "You said you recovered eleven guns."

"Yeah. And..." Becks said.

"According to various witnesses, we have three gunmen. All throwing their guns away.

"Four guns a piece is what's been reported. Do you need a multiplication table to do the math? There was probably twelve guns in total. Not eleven. And in that case..."

Becks finished Perez's thought. "There's a twelfth gun out there, and probably still with one of the gunmen."

"Exactly," Perez said. "We find the gun, give ballistics a chance to get a match, and we find our guys."

Becks pursed his lips and furrowed his brow. Agent Perez read that as a sign of agreement or mild interest. At least he didn't rebut her hypothesis.

"So..." Perez said, "you coming north with us or what?"

Chapter 91

Anthony

Busboys and Poets was a trendy restaurant, bar, bookstore, and co-working coffee shop. I rarely spent time in Hyattsville, MD, but I thought it would be as good a place as any to rob a bank.

The restaurant was one in a chain of establishments throughout the DC area. Starting first, within DC proper, it quickly became a popular place to meet friends, conduct meetings over a meal, work on projects, or listen to poetry. It was named in honor of the poet, Langston Hughes, who once worked as a busboy in a prominent DC hotel.

I walked through the door and took in the overtly liberal, racially diverse, sexually fluid community of diners, drinkers, and workers. I was greeted by a short Asian man. He had pink hair, blue eye liner, and black fingernail polish. "Hey sweetie. You looking for a table or want a sofa?"

I pointed to the sofas in the lounge area.

"Ok sweetie. Sit wherever you want."

I sat down and placed my backpack on my lap. After unzipping the sack, I pulled out a laptop, opened, and turned it on.

The machine hummed to life. A purple glow came from the screen.

Trying to be as inconspicuous as possible, I retrieved a flash drive from my pocket. I held it with a white handkerchief to avoid leaving fingerprints. I would've used plastic gloves but thought that would have drawn unwanted attention.

When no one was looking, I slid the flash drive between two sofa cushions. I didn't push it all the way down. I wanted it exposed just enough, so the next person who sat in the area would discover it.

One down. I figured two more to go. I quickly gathered my things, stood, and walked toward the sign pointing to the bathrooms.

I passed the bar, walked through the bookstore, and entered the men's bathroom.

Once inside, I peeked under the toilet stall door to ensure I was alone. Then I grabbed the second flash drive and laid it on the sink, right under the paper towel dispenser that was centered between two mirrors. I turned around and flushed a urinal. Then I went back to the sink, washed my hands, dried them with a paper towel, and left.

I walked back through the bookstore, passed the bar again, but this time I stopped. I rested both hands on the bar and leaned into it to get the bartenders' attention. "Hey man," I said. The bartender had just finished pouring beer from the tap. "Do you all have bottomless mimosas as a part of brunch?"

The bartender didn't even stop to look at me. He served the beer he had just poured for a customer on his right and began pouring another for the customer's friend. Yet he had enough environmental awareness to talk in my direction. "Nope," he said. "Mimosas are five bucks."

"Thank for the info," I said in return. I pushed away from the bar with both hands. The bartender still hadn't looked at me, so he didn't notice me leave my last flash drive in the same place where my left hand was.

I started making my way to the door and I could see the spot where I initially sat out of the corner of my eye.

A different guy had taken my place and there was activity between him and the host who had let me sit there.

Out of my peripheral view, I saw the host start to wave his hands frantically at me. Then he raced after me. Stopping me from exited the building.

The guy who had taken my seat moved slowly but joined a few seconds later.

"Hey sweetie," he said, out of breath. "This USB drive, is it yours?"

"I found it in the sofa when I sat down," the other guy said.

For a quick moment, anxiety built up in me. Butterflies in my stomach and a few beads of sweat on my forehead. But I kept it together.

"Nope. That's not mine. Looks like someone's got themselves a free flash drive."

"Yes!" The other guy said. He snatched the drive out of the host's pinch. "I love freebies!"

Keeping an eye on the man, I watched him walk back to the sofa, grab his laptop, and insert the flash drive.

That was it. We only needed one USB plugged to a device, with the device connected to the WiFi. Having this one connection made the other drives I left behind irrelevant.

Anxiety gave way to excitement. *This might work,* I thought to myself. Were we just a few key strokes away from raising enough funds to set us up for life?

For the first time that day, a smile broke across my face. *Gotta love technology,* I thought. Technology was about to make us rich.

Chapter 92

Johnnie

A crew of men worked throughout the new backroom gambling space. Most of the construction had been completed. Now it was just the finishing touches, like the gold trim on the edge of the bars. The ceilings had recessed lighting and crown molding. Red velvet couches sat along the walls. Clear plastic protected them against dirt, dust, and debris. The space had taken shape but wasn't quite finished.

Johnnie reviewed the sketches and other blueprints with Beaux at the bar. The other guys engaged in testosterone driven horse play near the front door, until the front door flew open with a force that almost took it off the hinges. The guys scattered.

Nick Nick rushed in as fast as his hobbling would allow. The bottom of his cane clicked against the hardwood floor with every step into the room.

Nick Nick's eyes bulged as he screamed into the phone attached to his ear. "You need to find him! As soon as possible!"

he yelled. "I don't care how you do it!" He threw his phone against the wall. It shattered into unrecognizable pieces.

Johnnie jumped to his feet, nearly knocking his chair over. "Nick?" he said with a pause immediately after.

He gave him a few seconds to respond but Nick Nick didn't say anything. Instead, he walked behind the bar and retrieved a black leather-bound ledger. He slammed it on the bar top and feverishly turned page after page.

"What's going on?" Axel asked from across the room.

"I'll let you know as soon as I know," Johnnie said. "Nick, you wanna tell us what's going on?"

Nick Nick stopped fingering the pages of the ledger. He clasped his eyelids shut.

"Ok... calm down. Think," Nick Nick said to himself. He drew in a few deep breaths. By the time he opened his eyes, he had made a complete turnaround.

His jaw was unclenched. His brow was no longer furrowed. A much more relaxed Nick Nick had returned to the group. "Gentlemen," Nick Nick waved his arms and beckoned everyone to toward him. "Time for a history lesson."

Everyone took a seat with Nick Nick on the other side of the bar. He grabbed shot glasses and a bottle of tequila.

"Before any of you were a thought in your father's testicles, DC was a much different place.

"The town you know was shaped by what I call two phases of criminality. The most recent is the one you're familiar with." Nick Nick pointed toward Johnnie. "You remember there was a council, a committee of sorts. Everyone was responsible for their own lane. It kept a dividing line between families and organizations, allowing everyone to work and get paid without encroachment from others. And no one person, family, or organization jumped tracks. Ever."

"Yeah. And then Anthony and I set fire to that system," Johnnie said.

"Yes, he did," Nick Nick replied. "Quite literally if I recall. But before there was crime by committee, it was done a little differently. Your father, your uncle, me, and two of our closest friends ran the criminal underworld.

"A band of brothers, if you will. Crime didn't happen if it wasn't run through us first. It was like this for decades."

"What happened?" Johnnie asked.

"The simple answer? We made it look easy. Others thought they could do it better. Up and coming nobodies got greedy and tried to take us down. So, war broke out. The fighting started off bad and only grew worse. There were gunfights every single night. And even some in the broad daylight. Everyone lost people they cared about.

"That's when Marco thought of the idea of the council. We carved up the town. Gave every crew an industry to work. The violence stopped and a newfound Golden Age had begun.

"Again, of course, until you and Anthony burned everything down."

Squid raised his hand. "Uh, this is nice and all. But what's with the walk down memory lane?"

"If you don't know your history..." Nick Nick said.

"You're doomed to repeat it," Axel replied.

"Precisely," Nick Nick said. "Gentlemen, we are at the doorstep of a renaissance. We can form a new brotherhood to run DC. And then Maryland. And then Virginia. Then up and down the east coast and beyond."

"But..." Johnnie said.

"History is about to repeat itself," Nick Nick said. "In so many ways. I spoke about two of our closest friends. One of whom you may know. Jack Lowinger. He's responsible for building half of the city. His money is going to back Remo and

Anthony. I know for a fact that his resources are limited right now.

"But then there's also Mark Sauer, aka the Grem. Short for the Gremlin."

Squid chuckled aloud after hearing the nickname.

"You shouldn't laugh. He's brilliant. And he's devised a plan that could provide them with resources we would never see in a hundred years. It would make them unstoppable and us... impotent. It's a plan he created and shared with us years ago, before going into the penitentiary."

"Good," Squid said. "He's locked up. Let's find out where and get someone on the inside to knock him off. Problem solved."

"Well, that's the problem," Nick Nick said. "I just got word he was broken out of jail. Yesterday. I'll give you one guess as to who has him and what they're doing. It's just a matter of time before they have enough money to run us out of town."

"What do you suggest we do?" Johnnie asked.

"There's only one thing to do," Nick Nick looked at Beaux and nodded his head.

"On it," Beaux said. He pulled out his phone, dialed a few numbers and walked into the private alcove in the corner of the room. "Let me speak to Priest," Beaux said before disappearing behind the velvet curtain.

"We're left with only one option gentlemen, which needs to be executed as of yesterday." Nick Nick cleared his throat. We need to kill them. All of them. Remo, Jack, Grem, Anthony. All of them."

Axel spoke up. "So how do you expect us to do that? Do we even know how to find them?"

"We may not," Nick Nick said. "But we don't have to. We just need to know how to make them find us. It's a storyline as old as time." Nick Nick looked at Johnnie. "It's time you reach out to the girl."

The wheel's of Johnnie's brain turned. It was visible. He patted down each of his pockets in search of something. And then he found it. He snatched out his phone.

"She called the other day, probably looking for Anthony. I checked the message," he said as he navigated to his voicemail messages. "But I never called her back."

Nick Nick rolled his eyes. "Well, call her back," he said. "Tell her you and Anthony are going to be at the warehouse off Bladensburg. Tell her Anthony can't wait to see her."

"I don't know," Johnnie said. "Been there, done that. She's not going to fall for being used as bait... again."

"Coming from me, of course not. I'm dead, remember? But she trusts you. Make the call."

"Then we'll get word to Anthony. And I bet you he'll show, along with everyone else. The ambush will be set.

"We'll be waiting along with the Broken. They'll be nothing they can do... other than die."

Chapter 93

Anthony

I sat in a quiet room. It was down the hall from all the commotion. Boisterous voices and jovial laughter invaded my solitude. I needed a little time to myself.

We were at the end of one road and at the same time, the beginning of another. Once the money from the cyber heist came in and was divided, we would each have enough to decide our next steps.

Gabe would probably go back to New Orleans. Jack and Junior would probably build on their plans of expansion. Remo might head back to New York. And Brandon... he'd return to his life of being a father to my son.

But what about me? What would be my next steps? Do I head back to New Orleans too? Could me and Coco start over there?

Am I thinking too small? I will have millions at my disposal. We could go anywhere and start over. Or was I ignoring the obvious? I could stay in DC.

Money meant independence. It was freedom. The pressure

of living up to the reputation of being the Black Ribisi was gone.

Then it dawned on me. My next moves could be made without fear or anxiety. I could finally be Jelani Jones. Maybe that was a foolish thought, considering I had been Anthony Ribisi longer than I could remember.

Discovery. That's where I was. The money from this heist would allow me the space to uncover who Jelani Jones was and who he could become.

It would allow me the space to also explore what a relationship would be like with Coco. I could finally unchain myself from living in survival mode. I could learn how to thrive in a brand-new life. I no longer had to hide. I no longer had to live on the run. I no longer had to work in the shadows. And I could put a life of crime behind me.

No matter what the world threw at me, I could live life on my terms... with the woman I loved. I could build a relationship with the child I fathered.

The death of an old world was happening and there was the gravitational pull of a new world coming into being. For the first time in a long time, I was happy. I was scared shitless by all of my unanswered questions, but happy, nevertheless.

I turned my head to the door as soon as I heard its creaking hinges disrupt the silence. The sound was louder than my own thoughts.

"Anthony," a soft woman's voice came from around the door before her face and body did. It was Metty. She walked in a few feet and leaned against the wall. "They don't want to get the party started without you."

"That's not what it sounds like to me," I said with a laugh.

"You're right." She laughed back. "But at least they think they're trying to wait. And it's the thought that matters, right?"

We both shared another laugh. Metty walked over and sat in the chair next me, just on the other side of the coffee table.

She didn't say a word. She just sat in her chair and decided to let the silence speak to me again. But what she did do was watch. She watched me intensely.

I felt connected to her and wondered if she was reading my thoughts. Did she peep them as they passed through my mind? If she did, then she knew how intimidated I was by the opportunity in front of me.

After a few minutes, she reached across the coffee table and took my hand within hers. She rubbed the back of my hand, lightly massaging me with her thumbs. It was soothing. "I ever tell you about the night I met Remo?"

I shook my head.

"To say it was eventful, would be an understatement," Metty said.

"Did it involve bloodshed?" I asked.

"Oh yeah," Metty replied. "A lot. And some very dangerous people came after me... to get to him. And I was scared out of my mind. But I knew once I found Remo, he would take care of me. Everything would be okay."

"Was it? Do you consider this 'okay?'" I asked.

Metty considered the question and then shook her head, side to side. "No," she whispered. Her eyes watered, but tears didn't fall. Metty willed herself to composure. "I used to be a waitress, splitting tips and living a stable life. I thrived in predictability and here I am, not knowing what I am anymore.

"There is one thing I know, though," she said. "Remo kept his promise. I'm alive. Soon to be a little richer. He did take care of me."

"Why are you sharing this with me?" I asked.

"Anthony... we won. And everyone's in the other room

having a great time. But you're in here by yourself. You shouldn't be by yourself."

"You didn't answer my question."

Metty got up and walked to the door to head back down the hall.

"You're not going to answer my question? That's how you're going to do me?" I chuckled.

Metty turned around and said, "My father used to say, 'Metty...don't be the girl who dances with everyone except the guy who brought you to the party. He got you there. He'll be the one to take care of you and he'll be the one to make sure you get home.'

"Anthony... I don't know what you're going through. But I do know that you are scared. You're probably even thinking about leaving. My two cents is that you should stick around. Remo brought us to this party. He'll take care of us."

Chapter 94

Anthony

"There he is!" Junior yelled after I walked in the den.

It was exactly as I had imagined. The room looked like volcanic eruption of champaign bottles, beer cans, and shoot glasses.

The staff prepared a feast and had it spread over two six foot long rectangular tables.

Remo rushed over, put his arm around my shoulder and pulled me toward him.

"Congratulations nephew. You're about to be a very rich man."

It was music to my ears. "What's the timeline?" I asked.

"Grem said it shouldn't take longer than few hours before we started to see an increase in the offshore account. Once there's a final tally, we take care of the expenses first, and then it's an even split for the rest. They'll be more than enough money to go around."

"Sounds good to me," I said. I smiled and looked around the room. I noticed a couple of people had disappeared. "Where is Grem? And Brandon?"

"Grem stepped out. Said he'd be back in a little bit," Jack answered. "But I don't know about Brandon. He was just here."

Out of the corner of my eye, I saw Junior leave the room. Here I was, thinking that this was a party. And now another person has gone.

"Remo," I said. "Did you see Brandon leave?"

Remo shrugged his shoulders. "Maybe he's in the bathroom. I don't know."

That's when Junior came running back into the den. "Brandon's gone! I don't see his car out front."

Chapter 95

Brandon

Brandon drove east on Interstate 66, headed back toward the city. His phone rang and connected to the car's Bluetooth. He looked at the six-inch screen, above the radio, and it read 'Junior.'

After going back and forth in his mind, he answered the call before it went to voicemail.

"Hey," Brandon said.

"What's up Brandon? Umm... where are you buddy?" Junior asked.

"Everything looked like it was going well. The job is done and I had to get out of there. I'm going to check on the family. I didn't think it would be a problem."

"I get it. But couldn't you have waited? Or at the very least, told someone you left? We are in a very vulnerable spot right now, you know?"

"It's all good," Brandon said. "I'll be careful."

Junior was silent for a few seconds and then followed with what could've been perceived as a warning. Maybe even a threat. "Okay...you better."

Chapter 96

Coco

Coco turned the corner and drove down the street of the warehouse. She pulled out her phone and double checked the address that Johnnie texted her.

"This must be it," she said to herself.

After driving past the door, she looked for an available parking space. It was three car lengths beyond the door.

Coco parked, exited her car, and walked back to the warehouse. Before walking in, she stopped and tried to investigate by peering through the window. It was impossible to see through the opaque film that lined the glass.

She pulled out her phone again. This time, instead of looking at the text message between her and Johnnie, she did what she should've done from the start.

"What the hell was I thinking?"

Coco opened her phone log of recently called numbers. She scrolled to Jelani's name and tapped it.

The phone rang on the other end of the line. She turned around and started walking back to her car. "Come on Jelani. Pick up."

But he didn't answer. It went to voicemail. Again.

Coco let out a sigh and started walking even faster.

"Hey! Coco!" she heard the shout coming from behind.

Turning back around, she saw Johnnie walking from the opposite direction.

"Where you going?" he said. "Anthony—I mean Jelani, is waiting for you inside."

Johnnie rummaged in his pants pocket until he found the keys. He approached the door and unlocked it.

"I... I... just called him. He didn't answer."

"Oh! He's probably just cleaning and organizing in the back room. We've been busy trying to get this place straightened up."

Coco slowly began walking towards Johnnie and the opened door.

"Straightened up?" Coco said. "Why?"

"Well... Jelani and I decided to go into business together. Again. But this time, it's legitimate. We're starting a t-shirt line. That's why he's straightening up. We're getting ready to get our first shipments."

Coco's slightly twisted face betrayed her thoughts. *A t-shirt line?* She didn't believe that at all. Especially since the last time she was with Jelani, they agreed on her moving to New Orleans. None of what Johnnie said made sense to her.

"You know what, Johnnie, I don't think this is a good idea." Coco started backing up as she was talking.

"Coco..." Johnnie said. He knew he messed up. "Come on!" he yelled. His voice grew louder and firmer. "Where you going?!"

The tone left Coco frozen for a split second. Then Johnnie bolted after Coco to get her before she turned to run for her car.

It frightened Coco. She let out a scream and turned around to run away. But then she ran right into a pack of bikers. They crept up behind her. Some bikers blocked her path. Others sat on the hood of her car.

The terror and shock caused Coco to hesitate long enough for Johnnie to catch her. She kicked and screamed as she was dragged back to the open door of the warehouse.

Johnnie pulled her inside. The biker gang followed behind them. Coco's screams slipped out of the open portal.

The last of the bikers walked in and shut the door behind him. That's when the screaming stopped.

Chapter 97

Brandon

With just seven miles before Interstate 66 merged into Constitution Avenue in DC, Brandon decided to give Jena a call. He wanted to update her with his ETA.

Brandon could've used the screen in his car to dial Jena directly, but muscle memory had him reaching for his phone. It sat in the cup holder between the seats.

Keeping one eye on the road and the other on his phone, he balanced the device in his right hand as he scrolled for Jena's name. The distraction caused him to slow down to approximately forty-five miles an hour. It wasn't terribly slow, but it was far too slow for the speed demons who drove in the Washington, DC area.

Before he knew it, an SUV pulled up behind him and the driver wildly honked his horn. He knew it was an SUV, because the lights felt like high beams being flashed in his eyes. The vehicle startled him and caused him to accidentally eject the phone out of his hand. It bounced around the cabin of the car and then settled on the floorboard between the gas pedal and the break.

To allow some space between him and the angry driver, Brandon sped up a little bit. The SUV did the same. It ultimately switched to the passing lane and gunned past Brandon. Honking as he passed, Brandon looked to his left at the profile of a geriatric white man.

Brandon was annoyed, but still shook his head in amusement. He let the man pass by and get a decent distance ahead of him.

"Oh shit!" he said. "Lemme call my girl." Brandon looked down and saw the phone on the floorboard. He carefully reached down with his right hand, keeping his left hand on the steering wheel and his head high enough to see over it.

He had a long wingspan, but his arm wasn't long enough to reach the phone. To make it easier to retrieve it, Brandon lifted his foot off the gas pedal and used his heal to knock the phone closer. It worked.

Now that the phone was closer, Brandon tried to grab it again. He slowly extended his arm between his legs and locked onto the phone with his hand.

But something went wrong. Even though the phone was closer, there was an unexpected strain on his shoulder muscle. Maybe it was from overextending his arm moments ago. This time, there was pain. And a lot of it. Brandon jerked up to ease the discomfort he felt. In the moment, it caused him to jerk his vehicle to the left.

Brandon swerved into the passing lane. He was lucky no other cars were around. But in somewhat of a knee-jerk reaction, Brandon yanked the wheel to get back in his lane. Unfortunately, he overcorrected.

Brandon yanked too hard. The car swerved further into the right lane. He rolled over the rumble strips on the side of the road and slammed into the guardrail. The force of the impact caused the vehicle to flip and tumble down a small embankment. The vehicle rolled twice before coming to a stop.

After about sixty seconds of no movements or sounds, another car came to a screeching halt at the site of the crash.

* * *

Flashing blue lights at the crash site lit up the night sky. Virginia State Police officers blocked off Interstate 66 so they could safely clear and investigate the crash scene.

"How's the guy doing?" an officer asked. He pointed to the ambulance and the EMTs as they loaded Brandon in the medical vehicle.

"Bruised. Scrapes. A few broken bones. He'll probably have a concussion. But nothing too serious. He's a lucky guy," his partner responded.

One of the EMTs walked back to officers who talked about Brandon. "Hey guys," he said. "I didn't know how to bring this up. But when we pulled the guy out of the vehicle, we also found this."

The EMT pulled a 9mm pistol from out of his medical bag.

"I figured I'd hold on to it until you guys arrived. I didn't know what to do with it."

The first officer took the gun and examined it. "Hmm. Why doesn't it have a serial number?"

"That's never a good thing," his partner responded. "I guess he's not that lucky of a guy after all. Call it in."

Chapter 98

Anthony

"I'm telling you guys, Brandon is a Class A screw up. This will come back to bite us. He shouldn't have left," I said. "I've got a bad feeling about this."

"Calm down," Jack said. "We had a fool proof plan. And there's no evidence to lead back to us. He came through for us on the highway, didn't he? Maybe give him a little more credit."

"I think he's right," Junior said to his father. "We've got to get him back. At least until we have the money."

"Brandon is a grown man. If he wants to leave, then he'll leave," Jack said.

"Forget it. I'm not debating this, I'm calling him," I said.

"And how exactly will you get him to return?" Jack said.

"By telling him the truth about something he's not going to like." I was being cryptic and vague at the same time. And no one challenged me to go deeper. "What did I do with my phone?" I said out loud. Scanning the room, I saw it on the edge of one of the banquet tables. I walked over and picked it up.

Looking at the phone, I noticed three missed calls. All from

Coco. Each call was approximately five minutes apart, leading up to the most recent, made five minutes earlier.

Brandon can wait, I thought. It was no time better than the present to talk with Coco. I owed her an explanation... and probably a lot more.

Just as I was about to dial her number, my phone rang. The screen flashed her name and my favorite picture of her. I ducked into the corner of the room and answered it.

"Hello... hi—" I said.

But before I could get another word out, a frantic Coco yelled into the phone. "Jelani! Help!" she said before I could hear her voice being muffled.

"Hey Anthony. It's me," the male voice said. I knew who it was immediately.

"Johnnie? Is Coco with you? What the hell is going on?"

"I didn't want it to come to this. You should've stayed in the south."

"Is this a joke? I'm only back because *you* asked *me* to come back. What the hell is going on?" I said.

"Does this feel a little like deja vu?" Johnnie said. "As long as you have one foot in and one foot out, Coco will never be safe."

Beads of sweat swelled on my forehead. My stomach was uneasy. I felt as if I could vomit in any minute.

"Deja vu?" I said. "Johnnie... this isn't funny, man." I felt a rage bubbling inside of me. "Put Coco on the phone!" I finally exploded.

It drew everyone's attention to me. Remo's instinct was to grab my phone and put it on speaker. And that's what he did.

"You want to see her again? How much is she worth to you? You see... a little birdie told me that you just came into a lot of money."

"I don't know what you're talking about."

"Don't lie!" Johnnie yelled. "I know all about it! The jailbreak! Some guy named Grem and his high-tech plan for bank robbery! I know you have money!"

I noticed Jack and Remo look at each other.

"I'm going to ask again... how much is she worth to you?"

I was at a loss for words. I didn't know what was going on. The last time I saw Johnnie, everything was good. Or so I thought.

"Whatever you want," I sputtered out. "Just tell me what you want. Let Coco leave and it's yours."

"That's not how this is going to play out," Johnnie said.

"Johnnie... I don't even have the money yet." I pleaded. "We're still waiting on the wire transfer to the offshore account. That won't happen for at least another hour or so."

"Well then, that's perfect. I'll see you at the warehouse in two hours. Come alone and be prepared to initiate an electronic transfer from your account to mine.

"If you call the cops, she dies. If you bring guests, she dies. If you don't have access to the money, she dies. And then you die shortly after. I need to hear you say you understand me."

I looked up at Remo. He closed his eyes and nodded his head.

"Yeah. Yeah, I understand you," I said.

"Great. Oh... one last thing." As if this wasn't enough. "When you get here, I have a surprise for you."

* * *

Junior and Gabe wrapped their torsos around me, strapping me down to the armchair. It's all they could do to keep me from running out and hopping in my car.

Struggling against their body weight, I said, "Get off!"

"Not yet," Jack said. "You'd be running into a trap. No sense in getting you killed."

"He's right," Remo said. "When have you ever acted without thinking it through?"

I stopped fighting but my breathing was labored and deep. "I have a plan," I said. "I plan to kill him. And whoever's with him."

"Think about it. Kill him?" Remo said. "You've called each other brothers since childhood. There's no coming back from that."

"So what! The moment Johnnie thought this was a good idea is the moment he stopped being my brother."

"I get all of that, but you still need a plan. The best way to get your lady out alive is to ensure that you don't get killed. He's asking you to come alone, but he won't be alone."

"How do you know he's not alone?" I asked.

"Oh, that's simple," Jack said. "Only five of us who knew Grem's plan for the digital robbery. Grem, naturally. Then Marco, me, Remo, and Nick Nick.

"That's his surprise for you, Anthony. Nick Nick didn't die. He's alive. And he's with him. That's the only way Johnnie would know."

Whatever energy I had left in my body was knocked out, along with my wind. The idea that Nick Nick survived our battle at the restaurant was unfathomable. But then again, so was this whole damn scenario.

Remo motioned to Gabe and Junior to let up off of me. "So..." he said. "Johnnie has Coco. He's with Nick Nick, and probably a small crew. You can't just walk in there solo. What's... your... plan?"

Remo was partially right. I needed a plan. But he was also partially wrong. Who says I can't walk in that warehouse solo?

"Actually... I think I will walk in by myself. But I won't be alone. Remo, give Smitty a call. Let him know what's going on."

I looked at Junior. "We need to pack a bag. Get your rifle ready and bring the C4. I never wanted to go back to this life. I'm constantly being pulled into a war of someone else's doing. But if a war is what they want... it's exactly what they'll get."

Chapter 99

Priest

Priest knocked on the door of the warehouse and awaited entry. He was accompanied by Maddox, his Enforcer, and six members of the motorcycle club.

The door slowly opened. Johnnie was on the other side. Before Priest noticed Nick Nick and the rest of Johnnie's crew, he saw a woman tied to a chair in the center of the room. He rolled his eyes.

"A little notice would've been great," Priest said.

"This it?!" Nick Nick used his cane to motion at the limited number of men.

"What can I say... everybody deserves a weekend off. Besides, weren't we just here? You wanted disruption. You wanted them to lose their money. You called and we came." Priest pointed at the Enforcer. "Besides, he's worth ten men alone."

Nick Nick shook his head and said, "I also wanted you to kill Anthony and that didn't happen."

Priest looked at his brother Maddox. "What? You don't say?" Careful not to air their dirty laundry in front of Nick

Nick, Priest just pointed to woman he noticed earlier. Changing the discussion. "Who's that?" he said.

Coco was sitting in a chair with her hands and legs tied.

"Insurance," Nick Nick answered.

"For what?"

"Anthony is on his way. Probably not alone. We need the upper hand."

Priest looked at Maddox again and said, "Good. Maybe we'll do it right this time."

Maddox shifted his weight and looked away.

"There isn't much time," Nick Nick said. "Get your men ready." He turned to Johnnie, saying, "Put some tape over her mouth and take her to the back."

Johnnie retrieved a roll of electrical tape. With the tape in one hand and Coco in the other, he led the shellshocked woman out the room by the arm.

Priest walked over to his Enforcer and Maddox to have a private conversation. They talked just above a whisper. "What the hell, Maddy? If you had done your job, this girl's life—"

Maddox interrupted his brother, shaking his head. "No. Don't put this on me. You wanted DC and this is where it's gotten you. If this girl dies, it's on you.

"If?" Priest said. "The girl will die tonight."

Maddox was horrified at the certainty in Priest's tone. "Well, I don't want anything to do with it. I'm done," he said.

Priest laughed at the sound of Maddox's resignation. While he thought it was funny, he was also insulted at the idea. "I've had enough of you. Brother or not, you can't choose to walk away. Not here, not now."

Without warning, the Enforcer wrapped his bulky arms around Maddox and squeezed him in a vice grip. The scuffle caught Nick Nick off guard. Johnnie had returned, just in time to witness the Brotherhood's inner turmoil.

Maddox was now off his feet as Priest searched his pockets, looking for weapons. He removed two handguns and a switchblade.

At that moment, self-preservation kicked in. Maddox launched his head backwards and the back of his skull crashed against the bridge of the Enforcer's nose.

Force of the blow startled the giant. He let go of Maddox as blood gushed. The Enforcer stumbled back and fell to one knee.

Priest was frozen in shock at the sight of his Goliath being taken down. He had but a few seconds to gather himself before his brother rushed at him.

When the bodies collided, the weapons ejected out of Priest's hands and slid across the floor, coming to rest in the corner of the room.

Fists were thrown by both men. The younger Maddox managed to get on top of his older brother and get the best of him. That's when the other bikers interceded. They overwhelmed Maddox and dragged him off Priest.

Three men pinned Maddox to the ground. Priest pulled himself off the floor, first attending to the Enforcer.

"I'm good," the giant said.

Then Priest approached the struggling Maddox, who was still restrained against the floor. Priest unleashed a furious flurry of kicks. His boot caught Maddox on the side of his head, multiple times.

"Get the gun!" Priest commanded, pointing to the corner of the room.

All the while, Nick Nick, Johnnie, and the rest of the guys looked on with no intention of getting involved.

One of the gang members walked over to the guns and picked both of them up. He handed the guns to Priest. Out of breath, Priest knelt on one knee. He placed one gun under Maddox's chin and the other to the temple of his head.

"You're right, Maddy. All of this is my fault. Not killing Anthony when we had the chance. The fact that this innocent girl will die. Allowing you to be a pretender to the Brotherhood. All of it is my fault.

"But tonight... I fix all my mistakes." Priest pulled himself up from the floor. "And if that means Anthony, the girl, and *you* die, then so be it.

"Take those colors off of him," Priest commanded. He also motioned for his men to grab and carry his brother off.

They snatched up Maddox. He was stripped of his biker jacket and the men left it on the floor.

"Tie him up. Put him in the stockroom with the girl. I'll take care of him later."

The men dragged Maddox away. Beaux followed closely behind them.

Nick Nick called out to Beaux. "If he gives you any trouble, shoot him."

Chapter 100

Anthony

Across the street from the warehouse stood a three-story abandoned building that was as wide as the entire block. The third-floor window made it the perfect location for us. Far enough away from the action but close enough to become a part of the action when the time came.

"So, you're really going over there by yourself?" Junior asked.

"Mmm hmm. I will," I responded. "As long as you're ready, Junior."

"Always," Junior patted the side of his rifle.

"I've seen this man in action," Gabe said. "I have no doubts that he'll be alright."

Remo stood by the window and eyed as much of the action as he could. He knew that Nick Nick and Johnnie were inside the building with his crew. "Interesting," he said.

I joined him at the window, and we watched more bikers walk in.

"That fucker is huge," Remo said, pointing to the man with the mohawk.

"I already had a run-in with those guys. The younger brother had a chance to put a bullet in me but didn't. It was right before you came and got me," I said.

"Very interesting," Remo said. Then he turned his attention to me. "Ok. It's go time."

"Yes it is." I pulled out my handgun and handed to Remo.

"Keep it," he said. "Let them find it."

I returned the gun to my holster and then walked toward the stairs.

"Hold on," Remo said. "That's actually a nice gun." Remo lifted his pants leg and pulled a .22-caliber revolver. "Let them find this piece of shit instead. We can risk losing this one."

I laughed as I exchanged guns. I placed the tiny gun in my waistband, at the small of my back. Then I headed down the stairs.

Chapter 101

Remo

Remo, Junior, and Gabe watched as Anthony walked across the street to the warehouse. He was like a calf walking toward the slaughterhouse.

"You think this is going to work?" Gabe asked Junior.

"I hope so. Let's get in place."

Remo listened to the exchange but didn't offer his thoughts. His phone vibrated in his pocket. A call came in.

He looked and saw it was Jack. Remo walked away as he answered it.

"You've got to be kidding me," was the first thing Jack shouted through the phone. "The dirty little weasel screwed us!"

"Whoa... calm down," Remo said. "What are you talking about?"

"I've been checking our accounts for the last three hours and there's nothing! The money should've been transferred by now and we don't have a dime."

"Banks are closed. Maybe it's still processing."

"Our offshore account is in Beijing. That's almost twelve hours ahead."

"So the bank's actually open. Oh. Well, maybe—"

"'Well, maybe' nothing. I called the bank. No transfers have been initiated."

"What does Grem have to say about this?" Remo asked.

"Nothing. His phone is disconnected."

"Damn. I probably would've led with that," Remo said. He lowered his voice. "We have nothing?"

"Not a penny."

Remo burned with rage. "Tonight, we focus on the warehouse," he said. "If we make it through the night, then tomorrow we find Grem."

Chapter 102

Anthony

I scanned the front of the warehouse before walking up to the door. Glancing back at the building across the street, I prayed that the guys wouldn't let me die tonight.

I inhaled a deep breath and banged on the door. A biker opened the door and jammed a gun in my face. I slowly lifted my hands up to show I was unarmed. Well, not really.

He did what we expected. He grabbed me by the collar, spun me around, and searched me. It took him longer than it should have, but he finally found the peashooter I had stashed on me.

"What's this, huh?" He asked. The question was rhetorical.

After dragging me inside, the first face I saw was Nick Nick's. The biker passed my gun to him. "I pulled this off of him," the man said.

Here I was, face to face with a man who was my mentor and my enemy. A man who had, up to this point, been dead. And death had not been kind to him.

His face had continued to age. Hair had silvered. And he limped toward me, holding his frame upright with the aid of a black cane. I thought I was mentally prepared to confront him, but I wasn't.

Blinded by rage, I charged at the Machiavellian man. But before I could get there, I was tackled by three bikers. I struggled against the men who held me back.

Nick Nick approached me. "It's been a long time," he said.

"You smug son of a bitch," I said. "Hey Nick Nick. I promise... Hurt Coco and I promise to be the one to kill you. And it'll stick this time."

"Really? I guess we should get this started then."

Nick Nick retreated to the back of the room. And Johnnie walked up to me. Rage turned into hurt and disappointment.

"Johnnie," I said. "Where's Coco?"

"You probably should be more concerned for your own safety."

"Come on... How could you?"

"Me? How about you?" Johnnie said, "You're the one who disappeared? Why did I have to track you down and beg you to come back to help your own family? But you never came back. Maybe physically, but I could tell you weren't in it anymore. You haven't been the same since my father died."

"You mean since he was murdered? By him," I said, looking at Nick Nick. I looked back at Johnnie. "Your father? That's not what this is about, is it? Why are we really here?"

Johnnie contemplated the question. He shook his head at me and then walked away. He was intent on not giving me an answer. But the idea that I would be sent to my death and not know why must have eaten at him. He turned around approached me with rage burning in his eyes. "If you must know, there's no way I'm going to live in your shadow anymore. And that's the truth."

There it was. Johnnie's problem with me was front and

center. It was as clear as glass. Johnnie felt as if he had been living in my shadow. His words, not mine.

He was prepared to piss away his father's legacy, aligning himself with his father's killer, just to be on top.

The moment shared both tragedy and irony. I was restrained by a motorcycle club called the Broken Brotherhood. Fighting for my life against a man who I once called my own brother. But now we were broken. And it was a repeated cycle.

Nick Nick and Marco, once brothers too. But like Cain and Abel, one brother killed the other. And it all boils down to one thing. The only thing that causes brotherly bonds to break.

Envy.

Chapter 103

Coco

Coco was secured to a chair. Tape was over her mouth. She had a fighter's spirit and defiantly bounced around, but her arms and legs remained tied.

Maddox was at her feet, sprawled out on the floor. He was hogtied and fighting against his ropes too. It was futile for both of them.

Beaux watched the two of them struggling from the corner of the stockroom. "I suggest you save your energy. What you're doing won't help."

Maddox ultimately stopped moving. He looked up at Coco and saw the fear in her eyes. Now they locked onto each other, tears started to well at the bottom of her eyes. Before long, tears trickled forcefully down Coco's face.

"Hey... hey!" Maddox called out to her. "It's going to be okay. Don't worry. It'll be okay."

Coco started shaking uncontrollably. His attempt at reassuring her wasn't working.

"Please!" Maddox begged. "I'm telling you. It'll be alright.

Just breathe. In and out. In and out." Maddox modeled the breathing pattern. "In. And out."

Coco began to mimic Maddox.

"That's it," he said. "Just like that."

While the two were having their mini meditation session, Beaux calmly stood and crept to the door. As quietly as possible, he slid the lock and cracked the door open to covertly peek out. Beaux kept his position and was content to watch.

Coco was still following Maddox's meditational instruction. She breathed in and out. She inhaled and exhaled. Her shaking and tears slowed.

"Good," Maddox said. "By the way, I'm Maddy."

Without notice and in hurried movement, Beaux locked the door and bolted back to his chair in the corner. Both Coco and Maddox whipped their heads toward the door at the sound of the clunky metal lock being undone.

All of the work Maddox put into calming Coco was quickly undone. Three bikers rushed in the room. Two of them untied Coco. They held her by each arm. Dragging her toward the door.

She kicked and screamed the entire time. The third man, holding a black pillowcase, followed his brothers, pulling the chair out of the room with him.

After waiting a couple minutes, Beaux inched his way back to the door. He was back to observing the mayhem.

Chapter 104

Anthony

"Do you remember me?" he asked before his fist slammed against my jaw like a steel sledgehammer colliding with granite. I remembered him. Priest packed a hell of a punch.

Pain coursed through my jaw. The force of the punch should have knocked me out.

But it didn't. My vision was blurred. A mixture of light and dark images floated in front of me. Then I heard the echo of a crisp baritone voice. "Anthony," it said.

The metallic taste of blood was in my mouth. It felt like a roll of pennies had been opened on my tastebuds. I tried to focus on what was going on around me, but it was difficult to concentrate.

He said my name again. "Anthony." Then the echoed voice became one singular sound. "Nick Nick tells me you've come into more money. Is this what our relationship has become?" he asked. "You get money and I take it?"

I was tied to the chair. My torso was tethered to its wooden back and my wrists were wrapped with rope in front of me. For the first time, I was able to clearly see the brawny baritone man.

"I don't have it yet." I managed to slur out.

The biker motioned to the mohawked biker I also met before. He walked out of the room.

When he returned, he was followed by a man who was carrying a chair. The chair was dragged to the center of the room.

My heart sank at the sight of what came next. Two additional bikers carried Coco out. She had a black pillowcase over her head. Her body was slammed into the chair that sat across from me.

Coco's shrilled response was muffled. She was either gagged, her mouth was taped shut, or both. The pillowcase was removed, showing black electrical tape covering her mouth.

Across from me sat the woman I loved my entire life. There were tears and a look of horrific bewilderment on her face. I almost cried at the sight of her.

"Jelani!" she tried to shout through the mouth covering.

She was helpless and I burned with hate. I hated these men for what they were doing. I hated that Coco was in this situation. I hated Johnnie. I hated Nick Nick. And I hated myself for letting this happen.

With a wild-eyed look, Priest mocked her muffled scream. "Jelani!" he mimicked, as if his mouth was full of marbles.

"To be honest, I don't care about money. And I don't care about them," he motioned to Nick Nick and Johnnie. "I don't care about you or her. I care about legacy.

"And you all have been obstacles, in great or small part, to the Broken establishing a legacy in this town. So, if I must kill every single one of you to establish the Brotherhood in DC, I will, starting with her."

Without warning, he drew a pistol from his holster. He aimed the gun at Coco.

"But since this is about money for them," Priest said, referring to Nick Nick and Johnnie. "The sooner you give it up," Priest said, "the sooner we can get this over with. Where's... the... money?"

This time, Priest didn't give me a chance to answer his question. He paused just long enough to roll his eyes and say, "This is going to hurt." Then he pulled the trigger.

Coco howled in pain as the bullet tore through her thigh. I screamed and bucked against the ropes and chair. I managed to get to my feet, and everyone piled on to restrain me. First, it was three of the bikers and then Axel and Blake climbed on top.

In the commotion, I could hear Blake ask Axel, "What the hell did we sign up for, man?!"

Priest snapped his fingers to draw my attention. "Hey! Hey!" he said. "The next one goes in her head. And I'm only asking one more time. Where's the money?"

Chapter 105

Remo

Remo fixed his gaze on the front of the warehouse, across the street from their location. He hadn't moved from the third-floor window. Junior was to his right and fiddled with the scope on his rifle.

"I can't see through those windows," Junior said.

"Don't worry. We've got that covered." Remo pulled out his phone and made a call.

When the call picked up, he said, "Smitty. What's your ETA?" Remo leaned out the window and looked to the middle of the block.

He saw Smitty with a backpack over his shoulder. Using the shadows as much as possible, the big man was still hard to miss, bustling toward the front of the warehouse. "Great. I see you."

As Remo tracked Smitty, the sound of gunfire snapped his attention back to the warehouse. "Was that gunfire?!" Remo yelled into the phone. "Shit. Hurry up, we need to move quickly."

Gabe walked up from behind and patted Junior on the shoulder. "Okay, sharpshooter. We're counting on you."

"Then you're in good hands," Junior said.

Remo nodded his head at the two men. And with that, Gabe and Remo dashed down the stairs.

Chapter 106

Anthony

It took five grown men to subdue me. And that almost wasn't enough.

The more Coco cried in agony, the more it fueled my anger. First, I wanted to rip Priest apart. Then I wanted to follow through on my promise to Nick Nick. To kill him.

It was Nick Nick who unleashed the Broken Brotherhood on our city. Nick Nick who had gotten into Johnnie's head. He was the one who was responsible for Coco's harrowing torment.

Amid the scuffle, I ended up on the floor again. But this time, the force of the fall and extra bodies on top of me caused the chair to splinter into pieces.

The only thing holding me back now were the ropes. My wrists were bound, but my legs were free. I kicked violently, hoping to hit whomever was closest.

My foot connected with the jaw of one biker. Bone shifted from the force of the blow. He spun around and hit the ground. Luckily, he was knocked unconscious.

Axel and Blake jumped back to avoid being kicked in the face as well.

"What are you doing?!" Johnnie yelled at them. "Get back in there!"

Axel and Blake stood back and looked at each other. It was clear that Blake had reached his tipping point. "That's it. This is ridiculous and I'm not going to jail for this," Blake said. He started moving to the front door.

Squid jumped from behind Nick Nick's shadow and stood between Blake and the door. "Where do you think you're going?"

Squid put Blake in a chokehold and dragged him back. "You don't leave until the job is done."

By this time, the other bikers were joined by the giant with the mohawk. It was game over. The giant lifted me from the ground. I tried to headbutt him, but he jerked his own head out of the way to avoid impact.

In a countermove, the giant brought his knee up and my head down at the same time. I adjusted my body as it was happening. He aimed for the bridge of my nose, but caught the side of my head instead. If he had connected with his target, he likely would've killed me.

The hit stunned me but not enough to disorientate me. I noticed in all the fighting, the ropes that bound me began loosening. After a couple more goes at this guy, I was sure I'd be able to slip them off.

It was pandemonium. I was locked in battle with a biker giant. Squid and Blake fought each other. Nick Nick watched everything play out. And Priest... his patience must have whittled away to nothing. He approached me and the giant and stuck a gun in my chest.

"Yes... That's it," I heard Nick Nick yell from the corner of the room. The raising of his voice prompted Squid and Blake to put a pause on their tussle.

"That's it!" Nick Nick shouted again, rushing closer to Priest. "Finish him! Kill him off!"

Nick Nick's eyes burned with the intensity of fire. His tone was patriarchal with an air of supremacy to it. In that moment, Priest paused.

Priest's eyes narrowed as he looked at the seething Nick Nick. He scanned the room and took in the expression on the faces of his men, the giant, and Nick Nick's crew. I could only imagine that for the first time, Priest felt like the tool that he was. Nick Nick's tone had made it clear. He was the player, and the Broken Brotherhood was just another pawn on the chess board to be maneuvered... and played.

In a flash, what I suspected was confirmed. Priest whipped out another gun, hidden in the small of his back, and held it up to Nick Nick. He swore at the Italian and yelled, "You do not give me orders!"

Priest picked one hell of a time to exert authority and control. "Take another step," Priest dared Nick Nick.

"We have a deal," Nick Nick said.

Priest shook his head from side to side and then looked at Nick Nick and said, "We *had* a deal."

"But—" Nick Nick began in protest.

Priest cut him off. "This entire time I thought you had tipped me off so we could come in and take over. Just knock off Anthony, and the city would be ours. Isn't that what you said? But that wasn't your angle. You wanted Anthony gone so you could take over. You used us to do the work you and your team couldn't. And for that, we want the whole thing. The money, the city, and every last one of you dead. We hunt, we catch, and we kill."

As if on cue, all the members of the gang pulled guns, aiming them at Nick Nick's unsuspecting men. His people were outnumbered. Nick Nick had been exposed as a manipulator. And the motorcycle gang was ready to make him pay.

For the moment, everything was calm and quiet. For just a fleeting slither of time. And then stupidity disrupted the stillness. His name... Squid.

To protect Nick Nick, Squid tossed Blake to the side and went for his firearm. He jumped in front of Nick Nick, knocking him to the ground. He pushed Priest back a few yards at the same time. Squid also fired two shots from his pistol toward members of the motorcycle gang. Striking no one.

But in turn, the gang members returned fire. Everyone scrambled, looking for protection from the onslaught of bullets.

Instinctively, I curled up in a fetal position. I covering my head with my arms. As if that would protect me from a bullet. I looked up when the shooting paused to see everyone had found sufficient cover, leaving me and Coco exposed.

Crawling on my belly toward her, I shook the ropes from my wrists. And while I moved in her direction, something caught my eye. I saw Blake being ushered out of the room by the arm. But I didn't get a look at who escorted him. It looked like there was an escape route through the stockroom.

"We don't have to do this," Nick Nick yelled from his hidden position.

"Like hell we don't," Priest replied.

"I'm serious!" Nick Nick yelled back. "And to show you that I mean you no ill will, I'm going to step out! We all are! Don't shoot and let's work this out. This town is big enough for both of us!"

Nick Nick yelled out instructions to his team. Complying with his commands, those who were left in the room stepped back into the center of the space. Nick Nick, Squid, Johnnie, and Axel.

After a few seconds, Priest, the Enforcer and his six other men abandoned their hiding spaces as well.

"Good," Nick Nick said. "Now let us talk like—"

But before he could finish his sentence, there was a loud boom. The building quaked from an explosion. The windows in the front shattered into thousands of tiny glass shards. All the men were thrown to the ground. All... except the giant.

As the men started to recover to their feet, I heard the crack of rifle fire come from across the street. One shot whizzed through the gaping hole in the building, where windows had been. The force of a bullet spun one of the bikers around. He hit the floor. Another shot came through and put Axel on the ground, just as he stood up. Both Axel and the biker were certainly dead.

I looked out the hole to the street, and was relieved to see Smitty standing there. Behind him, Remo and Gabe ran toward the building with their guns drawn.

Smitty tossed a bag into the room. Flying through the air, the bag landed near me. I fumbled with the zippers until I was finally able to open it, and it had what I needed for this precise moment—two fully loaded pistols.

Three more rounds of rifle fire made its way into the building. Junior was the epitome of precision with his shots. He struck one more biker before putting a bullet in the giant's leg.

The giant shook it off and used a side exit to hobble out of the room. The rest of men did the same. They ran deeper in the warehouse, trying to escape. Meanwhile, Gabe exchanged gunfire with Squid. He and Johnnie guided Nick Nick out of the warehouse.

While all of this was going on, I was deathly afraid of what was happening with Coco. She had been shot in the thigh and wasn't moving. Was she dead?

Remo's attention was drawn to Coco as she was on the floor and bleeding. He ran to her, removing his belt as he got closer.

"Anthony! Go after them!" he said.

At this time, Junior had rushed into the building.

The first thing Remo did was check Coco's pulse. "She's alive," he said. He wrapped and twisted his belt around Coco's leg, making a tourniquet. He tightened it as much as possible. "This will slow the bleeding," Remo said. "I'll stay with her. Now go and get 'em."

Junior and Gabe turned around and left the warehouse the same way they came in. And I ran out the side exit, trying to decide who I would kill first.

Chapter 107

Beaux

Beaux let go of Blake as soon as they made it into the stockroom. He shut the door behind them before they both noticed Maddy tied up on the ground.

"Oh, just great," Beaux said. He rolled his eyes and pulled out a straight razor, approaching Maddox.

"What are you going to do? Kill him?" Blake asked. There was a smear of disgust across his face.

The sound of gunfire in the adjacent room and the sight of Beaux's blade had Maddox frozen in fear. Beaux rolled him on to his stomach and grabbed the man by the back of his shirt.

"Don't move," Beaux said. He slashed down Maddox's back. He severed the ropes that restrained him. Maddox was a free man. Confused, but free.

Blake was confused as well. "I thought you worked with the nutjobs in there."

"Oh... and you don't?" Beaux said with sarcasm. "But when is anything what it seems? Let's just say I'm working for my own self interest."

Maddox was on his feet and rubbing his wrists. "Thanks man."

"You wanna thank me, I have the perfect way," Beaux said. "But now isn't the time. With all those explosions and shit... it sounds like a war zone out there and I'm not trying to stick around."

"Me neither," Maddox said. "How do we get out of here without walking into fire?"

Blake pointed to a door at the back of the storeroom. "That'll take us to a back alley and a side road. We'll be on New York Avenue in a couple minutes."

Another shot rang out.

"Sounds good to me," Beaux said. "Lead the way."

Chapter 108

Anthony

Surrounded by the nighttime sounds, only traffic could be heard from blocks away. Cars honked, distant laughs and screams faded in and out of hearing, and the night was faintly active.

But there was one thing I didn't hear—police sirens. The cops weren't on their way. At least not yet. That was good news to me, because I wanted to catch these guys. And that required more time. I chased the sounds of footsteps running through the alley.

"This way!" I heard someone yell. He was coming from around a trash bin at an intersection.

Without thinking, I took the adjacent alley as quickly as possible. I should've taken my time because I almost got my face blown off.

As soon as I made the turn, two bullets crashed into the building's concrete structure, just above my head.

I caught a glimpse of the giant and Priest. They had run themselves into a dead end. The other bikers must have taken a different turn. And what made it worse was that Priest was the only one with a gun. The giant lost his weapon back in the warehouse.

I peeked into the dead-end alley again. As I thought would happen, Priest fired three more shots. He had a six-shot revolver. One more shot and his gun would be empty. We both knew it.

In the distance, but quickly approaching, I heard the shuffle of another set of footsteps. Was someone searching for me? I camouflaged myself in the darkness of the shadows.

Just then Squid came running around the corner. He must've been separated from Johnnie and Nick Nick. Squid walked past without noticing me. Heading straight towards Priest.

He turned the corner, leading to the dead end. Probably looking for a way out.

But before he found it... before he could react, he came across Priest and the big man. They may have been surprised by Squid or they could have been lying in wait for me. Either way, Priest squeezed the his trigger of his revolver three times.

The first sent a bullet into Squid's head. His skull exploded and his body slumped to the ground. The other two trigger pulls were met with the sound of loud clicks. Priest's gun was empty, but mine was not.

I stepped out of the shadow and walked around the corner. I faced both the giant and Priest, who had their backs against a brick wall.

The giant saw me and ran as ferociously as he could in my direction. He made it to within five feet. But I stopped him in his tracks with two shots to his torso. He looked at his chest and then back at me in amazement. I walked closer to the giant as he fell to his knees. Then I put a third slug in his head.

By this time, Priest retreated backwards as far as he could.

His back was against the wall, literally and figuratively. With nowhere to go, he resigned himself to his fate.

"I'm not begging you for my life," he said.

I raised my gun and aimed for his head. "That's fine," I said with a shoulder shrug. "It's not the begging that brings me satisfaction." I lowered the gun slightly so he would see the seriousness in my eyes. "It's the dying."

With my gunsights realigned, I pulled the trigger one time.

The forty-five-caliber slug hit Priest just below his right eye. It caused the back of his head to erupt, leaving a hole the size of a golf ball.

Chapter 109

Anthony

I ran back to the warehouse at breakneck speed. Along the route, I bumped into Junior and Gabe. We walked back together.

"What took y'all so long? What's the update?" I asked.

"We got the other two bikers," Gabe said.

"Johnnie and Squid got away," Junior added.

I shook my head. "You mean *Johnnie* got away. Squid is back there in the alley." Then it hit me. "What about Nick Nick?"

"You wanted to know what took us so long. We have a surprise for you in the trunk of the car," Junior said.

"Christmas come early, huh?" I said. "Let's finish this tonight."

That's when Junior and Gabe stopped walking. The both of them. "Anthony..." Junior said. "When you say, 'finish...' what does that look like to you?"

I also stopped walking as soon as I heard the question. I didn't quite understand what he was getting at. "I mean, let's take care of Nick Nick, once and for all."

"And then what? Do you head back to New Orleans? Are you taking Gabe with you?" Junior asked. "I only ask because we just survived something that should've killed us. We've also eliminated the only real competition we had. And if you think about it, there's no reason for you not to stay. We can rebuild everything that Marco and my father had, and more. Especially once we get the money from the last job."

"I hear you," I said. "But I'm not in the mindset to think about that right now. I need to get back to Coco and make sure she's well. Nothing else matters. " I looked at Gabe. "Besides... Gabe, tell this man how phenomenal it is in New Orleans. I'd be stupid not to go back."

Gabe cleared his throat. "I don't know man. I'm starting to like it up here. Especially if we can get our own thing going. I mean... what was all the fighting and killing for, if all we're going to do is give it to someone else so they can benefit from it? I'm with Junior on this. You should stay. And if you stay, I'm sticking around. You're not having all the fun without me."

Chapter 110

Remo

It was quiet back in the warehouse. Everyone had left the building, except Remo and Coco. Remo sat on the ground with Coco's head in his lap. Remo's tourniquet had stopped the bleeding, but Coco was nearly unconscious. She occasionally fluttered her eyelids and mumbled out what was probably Jelani's name.

After attempting to correct her a third time, Remo repeated, "Jelani? No, my dear. His name is Anthony."

Coco had no idea what Remo was saying to her because delirium had set in. But Remo kept talking. "Anthony," he said. "I want you to say his name."

Coco's eyes began to roll to the back of her head. And it gave Remo a terrible thought.

With Coco in Anthony's life, calling him back to be Jelani, there would always be a fight between two opposing worlds. One legitimate leaning world with a regular job, taxes, and a boring family. The life of a well-trained tool.

The other life, however, was one he had a genetic predisposition to excel in. Anthony could be the monster that terrified all other monsters. And Anthony didn't need Coco clouding his judgement.

He had been straddling the fence between the criminal and legitimate worlds since Marco's death. And Remo knew that after tonight, it would the perfect time for Anthony to make his decision once and for all.

But Anthony needed a little motivation. Remo knew that Jelani had to die for Anthony to live in his true purpose.

It finally made sense. The only way Jelani would die, was if Coco did the same.

Remo gently moved Coco's head from his lap. He stood and walked around the warehouse. He peeked in the storage room, checked the exit to the alley, and looked out of the hole at the front of the warehouse. No one was around.

Remo made his way back to Coco. He bent over Coco's sprawled body and kissed her on the forehead. "This is for the best," he whispered in her ear.

With that, Remo placed a hand on Coco's chest and covered her mouth and nose with the other. Then he shifted his weight down and pressed as hard as he could.

After a minute, Coco gasped for air. Even in her state, her hands moved up to Remo's wrist and she fought him. But it was an exercise in futility.

After another couple minutes, her lungs sent signals to her brain. She wasn't receiving oxygen. In response, her brain short-circuited and shut her body down.

It was the body's way of forcing her to breathe. It didn't work because Remo was smothering her. She couldn't breathe.

Another few minutes more and Coco's body stopped. It stopped breathing. It stopped convulsing. It stopped trying to will itself to life.

With tears in his eyes, Remo watched as Coco's body stopped everything.

Chapter 111

Anthony

We barreled back into the warehouse as the sounds of police sirens finally began to make their way across the precinct. It was time for us to load up and get everyone out of there.

I ran up to Remo and Coco. Both still on the floor.

"Ok uncle. Help me get Coco in the back seat."

He didn't move.

"Come on," I said. "Cops will be here soon."

Again... he didn't move. He was looking down at Coco and stroking her hair. I didn't understand why he had tears in his eyes. And he wasn't moving.

And then I realized that he wasn't the only one. Coco wasn't moving either. I dropped to ground and pulled her up within my arms and put my ear to her chest. "I... I... I don't hear anything! What happened?!"

Remo shifted to make room for me.

"She was fine when I left. What happened?!" I yelled.

"I think the wound was too high," Remo said just above a

whisper. "The femoral artery. The tourniquet wasn't enough to stop the bleeding."

"No," I cried out. "That can't be."

Smitty and Gabe came to the front of the warehouse, looked in and stopped. They saw a lifeless Coco in my arms. They didn't walk in any further.

The sound of sirens grew louder. Closer.

"We have to go," Remo said.

But I barely heard him. I couldn't string together thoughts that weren't about Coco. Words failed me. I was supposed to keep her safe. This wasn't how everything was supposed to end. All I did was feel the torment of losing her and the guilt of knowing it was my fault. I thought I could protect her and I was wrong.

To call the sensation in my chest pain wouldn't do it justice. It wasn't the worst pain I ever felt. In fact, it was the worst anything I ever felt. I sat on the ground, rocking Coco in my arms. Tears uncontrollably streamed down my face with my mouth agape. The muscles in my body convulsed. Air couldn't move beyond the immense lump in my throat. I couldn't breathe.

I gasped for air and inaudibly cried out at the same time. My heart, my love, my Coco... was gone.

Epilogue

Agent Hicks

Monday, September 23rd

Virginia Hospital Center was the closest hospital to the accident site. So that's where the ambulance brought Brandon.

He woke up in the hospital bed. His folded clothes sat neatly in the chair next to his bed. He was ass naked apart from the blue and white hospital gown, a white hospital wristband on his left wrist, and a set a steel handcuffs on his right wrist. He was chained to the bed frame.

When it hit him that he was cuffed, he unsuccessfully pulled against them and realized two things. First, he wasn't going anywhere. And second, his legs had shackles on them too.

"Hey!" he called out. "What's going on here?!

No one immediately came to his call as he continued to

struggle against his restraints. Then the door to his room slowly opened.

In walked two unrecognizable people. One was male and the other female. Neither of them was dressed like doctors.

"Good morning, Brandon. Welcome back. You gave us quite a scare," the man said.

"Who are you?" Brandon asked tentatively. "And why am I chained up?"

"We'll get to that," the man said. "Because we're dying to get more information about this."

He placed the ghost gun that had been recovered at the scene of Brandon's car accident on the bed.

"I'm Special Agent Josiah Hicks. And that's my boss, Special Agent Dally Perez." Hicks slid a chair closer to the bed and sat down. Perez stayed by the door and leaned against the wall.

"Help us out here, Brandon," Agent Hicks continued. "Well, actually I want you to help yourself. Where'd you get this gun? And tell us everything about the people who made it."

Anthony

Wednesday, September 25th

The night air was unseasonably mild for the time of year. The sky was obsidian, littered with countless specks of light. Even the stench of manure from the compost heap was like perfume for the night's air.

Brandon and Jack were the last to join the group. Brandon and I greeted each other. This was my first time seeing him since he left us at Jack's house.

"You missed out on all of the fun," I said to Brandon.

"I know. Gabe filled me in. I was just trying to get back to Jena and little Marco. You understand, right?"

"I get it," I said.

My attention turned back to the business at hand. I was still astounded that none of us died. It was a miracle everyone survived the bedlam at the warehouse. Jack kept Nick Nick in his cellar for a few days. I needed time to process the loss of Coco.

I notice Jack tap Remo's shoulder and lead him away from the group. But they weren't so far away that I couldn't hear them talk.

"It didn't take long," Jack said to Remo. "I think I've found him."

"Grem?" Remo said.

"Mmm hmm."

I closed the distance between us and walked over.

"Please don't tell me he's living the life on some remote island... and with our money," Remo asked.

"Yes and no," Jack said. "He's definitely living the life. But the island isn't remote. It's very accessible. But don't we have more immediate fish to fry?"

"Yes, we do," I interjected. Then I called out to my partner, "Gabe!"

Gabe and Brandon snatched Nick Nick off the ground and dragged him closer to me and the older men. Nick Nick was a mess. He smelled of urine and feces. His left eye was swollen shut. He had cuts all over his face.

"Congratulations boy," Nick Nick laughed through a series of gravelly coughs. "You win. Just make sure you actually kill me this time. Is your aim better than Johnnie's?"

I don't know if I had zoned out or if I was just tired. It felt like only a second had passed. But in that time, Jack and Remo backed away. I was face to face with Nick Nick, staring in his defiant eyes. Holding the collar of his dirt soiled shirt in my left hand, I dug the barrel of my gun into his forehead with my right.

Nick Nick stopped laughing. "Is this it," he said. "Wait! I think we can–"

Before Nick Nick finished his sentence, I pulled the trigger. Still holding him by his shirt, I felt his head snap back and his body go limp.

Unmoved by the warm droplets of blood, splattered across my face, I watched his arms flail. He lost the ability to support his weight with his legs. In that moment, everything about his existence flickered away.

I held Nick Nick's lifeless body for a moment, before letting it drop to the ground.

The end...

Made in the USA
Middletown, DE
07 October 2022